A Bedside Book of

EARLY SHERLOCKIAN

PARODIES AND

PASTICHES

Charles Press, Editor

Paperback ISBN 9781780926308
ePub ISBN 9781780926315
PDF ISBN 9781780926322

Published in the UK by MX Publishing
335 Princess Park Manor, Royal Drive, London, N11 3GX
www.mxpublishing.com

Cover design by www.staunch.com

The Table of Contents

2

SHERLOCK TRIUMPHS

MIXED RESULTS

IN AND AROUND BAKER STREET

3

CHARACTERS FROM LITERATURE AND LIFE

SHERLOCKIAN PARODY ELSEWHERE

A CLOSING COMMENT

AN INTRODUCTION

Sherlock Holmes has been the target of parodists and writers of pastiches since November 28, 1891, just four months after the first short story about him appeared in **The Strand** *magazine. And lampoons of Sherlock Holmes have continued up to the present day. During Arthur Conan Doyle's life, close to four hundred Sherlockian parodies and pastiches were published with many, many more since. (The latest count at Philip K. Jones' data-base available at Christopher and Barbara Roden's web-site* www.ash-tree.bc.ca/Sherlock.htm *is more than 10,000).*

As a retirement hobby, I collected the early parodies and pastiches---those published while Sir Arthur Conan Doyle was alive and able to appreciate them---if he wished to. A few years ago, I summarized my thoughts about them. **1**

But I have also long thought that some of the best of the less well known parodies and pastiches of that early period deserve to be brought together in one place so the audience of modern Holmesians and Sherlockians may enjoy them. My selections tilt heavily to pre-World War I items, with only a few from the post war period that ends in 1930, the year of Sir Arthur Conan Doyle's death.

You will find some of the better known, but other favorites, readily available elsewhere, are not included so we can admit more of the lesser-knowns. Even so there are still enough interesting ones among those unpublished lesser knowns for another full collection.

Vincent Starrett, the revered Sherlockian, argued that every pastiche should also contain bits of parody and such was indeed the case with the pastiches published during Conan Doyle's life.

---

1   Charles Press, ***Parodies and Pastiches, Buzzing 'Round Sir Arthur Conan Doyle,*** Shelburne, Ontario, Canada, The Battered Silicon Dispatch Box, 2006.

We Sherlockians and Holmesians have a confession to make right off. We have adopted a very broad and many would say an outrageously loose way of defining what we call a pastiche. By the standard definition, a pastiche should be an agonizingly tedious attempt to reproduce precisely the style as well as the content of an author's work. If we followed that formulation, we could count the number of true Sherlockian pastiches on our thumbs, maybe on only one thumb.

What we Sherlockians and Holmesians have come to call a pastiche is often a kind of long parody. The piece need not include Baker Street atmosphere or the turn-of-the-century prose style of Conan Doyle, or even include Dr. Watson. All that is required is some semblance of a plot and Sherlock Holmes. He may be present by name, have a funny made-up name, or be unidentified, but recognizable. Or the piece may just have someone trying to imitatethe Great Detective. The author may be Watson, someone else, or the pastiche may be written in the third person. As Cole Porter could have observed---in Sherlockian pastiche---Anything Goes!

So even if what emerges is not really, strictly speaking, a pastiche, we Sherlockians still identify it as such and go on enjoying.

While Conan Doyle was publishing new stories of Sherlock Holmes, writers of pastiches were few in number and understandably were more hesitant about infringing on the Conan Doyle territory. By including a bit of parody, they signaled their efforts were not the work of A. Conan Doyle.These early writers also looked for other ways to distinguish their work from Conan Doyle's. Some wrote in the third person and at least one didn't even identify his detective as Sherlock Holmes, except through broad hints. Some of these pastiches were published anonymously and some were only circulated among a close circle of friends. Scholars have even discovered a few that were written but never published.

Sherlockian Parodies differ from pastiches in that they are much more numerous. The authors had the advantage creating something obviously distinct from the Conan Doyle stories and also of having the first crack at the Great Detective. And sometimes along the way they took a few swings at Conan Doyle as well. They were the first to devise all those gimmicks and clever turns of plot. Indeed the first three or four, published in 1891 and 1892, contain a good many of the tricks and treats elaborated on by later parodists.

In making my selections, I'd like to think I chose pieces having the two qualities which many regard as indispensable to good parody and pastiche---humor or light-heartedness, and brevity, or if the piece be long, crispness. But alas! It isn't true. Others somehow crept in for reasons I can hardly explain.

But I did make sure the items I selected varied from the broad slapstick, through gentle spoofing, to biting humor, with gentle humor predominating.

Some of these parodies and pastiches stay close to the Conan Doyle stories. They lampoon the many idiosyncrasies that flourish there, from Holmes shooting holes in the wall to Watson mentioning unrecorded cases with intriguing names and tantalizing details.

But others mention only a few of what have become the standard Sherlockian traits---the cocaine, the fiddle, and the arrogance of the Great Detective.

Finally, others take little note at all of Conan Doyle or his stories and only borrow Conan Doyle's central figure for their own singularpurposes.

But all contain that single trait that may in time cause your eyes to tire and start skipping, as you read along---those ever present Sherlockian deductions. This is the defining characteristic of the Great Detective. It is why Sherlock Holmes has been such a tempting target for both parody and pastiche---more by far than any other fictional character or living individual.

Parody, like many jokes, is aimed at human frailty, especially at the shortcomings of the high and mighty. And who is more high and mighty in that quality we Homo Sapiens so take pride in, the trait that allows us to lord it over the whole of God's creation---that quality we like to think of as our special uniqueness---our superior intelligence?

It is Sherlock Holmes who was seen as a thinking machine, who bragged he applied unbiased reasoning to problems. He could tell at a glance what you did for a living and who knows what other secrets he could discern with his keen glance, and his great intellect meanwhile unraveled the most mysterious and complicated mysteries.

A little skepticism, now and then, about this prodigious intelligence is a major theme of Sherlockian parody and pastiche. But, especially in pastiche, a bit of admiration also occasionally seeps in.

One note of warning. Reading parodies and pastiches is a little like eating chocolate nut candy, so tasty, but perhaps it's best not to gulp down too many all at once. But then it depends on your stomach and your taste.

Diamond Jim Brady took his seat at the table and ate until his stomach touched the tablecloth. His evening meal included several boxes of candy along with his vast helpings meat, fish, and other delicacies. But then he ended his life consulting doctors of urology and internal medicine and left his fortune to establish a facility specializing in this discipline at Johns Hopkins Medical Center, so it's perhaps best to be a little careful about over indulging.

Remember that the original audiences for these parodies only read them one at a time, with gaps of days, weeks, or months or more, in-between. They would not as you will, be as aware of old formulas or repetitions. Meanwhile, you may be trying to gulp them down one after another. So take care.

Rather than having you face the daunting prospect of a collection of many parodies or pastiches to be swallowed all in one gulp, I have separated them by easily understood categories---Sherlock Stumbles, Sherlock Triumphs, etc. It should be easy to skip about according to your taste.

Or, you might regard this as a bedside book and take the parodies in small gulps, say one or two just before sleep.

An interesting fact emerges. In making my selections, I included as many Sherlockian triumphs as stumbles. Still even when triumphant, the detective and his deductions are often made to look slightly ridiculous.

Special thanks are owed to many anonymous discoverers of a single parody or pastiche, but more is owed to a very few persons who can be credited with stimulating the search for and unearthing many of these early parodies and pastiches. And much is owed to Ronald Burt De Waal whose three Sherlockian bibliographies guided researchers to original sources of the parodies and pastiches; parodies which I later found in the Sherlockian library collections.

*Foremost among the pioneer discoverers was Ellery Queen, the pen name for the mystery writers Frederic Dannay and Manfred Lee. In 1944 they published a collection of twenty-seven parodies and pastiches as **The Misadventures of Sherlock Holmes.** But the Queens had inadvertently published elsewhere pieces that they were unaware were still under Conan Doyle copyright. The Conan Doyle sons, who disapproved mightily of Sherlock Holmes parody or unauthorized pastiche, refused a financial settlement and insisted instead that **The Misadventures** be suppressed. It was and has remained so.*

But the Doyle brothers were not immortal and the search for parodies and pastiches and even their publication after a time resumed.

*George Locke's Ferret Fantasy press published two short but quality collections in 1973 and 1975 in **The Affair of the Lost***

10

Compression and Other Stories, *and* ***At the Mountains of Murkiness and Other Parodies.*** *Ferret Fantasy was also publisher of the next item.*

In 1981, John Gibson and Richard Lancelyn Green issued a collection of eighteen pieces in ***My Evening With Sherlock Holmes.*** *They came across them as they were preparing their monumental bibliography of the published writings of Arthur Conan Doyle. Green also subsequently found and published a number of additional parodies and pastiches on his own.*

During this same period John Bennett Shaw collected unnumbered parodies and pastiches, unearthed by himself or other early Sherlockians. Sometimes, perhaps in the elation of the moment, he neglected to identify who discovered what, though he no doubt discovered many himself. Some appeared in ***The Baker Street Journal*** *as "Inculabrum" and in edited works of its first editor, Edgar Smith. Shaw's gatherings are housed at the Sherlock Holmes Collections at the University of Minnesota and many in what follows came from the collection of the indefatigable John Bennett Shaw, with the able help of Julie McKuras who dug them out for me.*

In 1973, Jon Lellenberg collected and edited, John Kendrick Bangs, ***Shylock Homes, His Posthumous Memoirs,*** *(ten cases) that he discovered in the files of* ***The New York Herald*** *of 1903. In 1974 and 1975, he also published in two sections, an annotated bibliography of 59 Sherlockian parodies that he and fellow Sherlockians had thus far unearthed. His citations were limited to parodies published during Victorian and Edwardian times up to the beginning of World War I.*

During the same period the Aspen Press of Tom and Enid Schantz published several collections of parody/pastiche.

Ronald Burt De Waal, a librarian with Sherlockian interests, edited three extensive bibliographies of writings about Sherlock Holmes, the first volume appearing in 1974. All included a section on parodies and pastiches. His third update appears in a five volume set and is also available on the University of Minnesota Sherlock Holmes Collection website and was published by George Vanderburgh at The Battered Silicon Dispatch Box. Other publishers of parodies and pastiches are Otto Penzler at The Mysterious Bookshop Press, Christopher and Barbara Roden at The Calabash Press, and of course Steve Emecz of MX Publishing.

*In 1981, Bill Blackbeard,in **Sherlock Holmes in America,** re-published some of the classic parodies and a number of fugitive parodies and comic strips, published in newspapers, especially by the Hearst newspaper syndicate.*

*Robert C. S. Adey, in **As It Might Have Been** edited thirty-eight parodies published between 1893-1950, made available for the first time in this 1998 publication.*

Several librarians and one volunteer gave cheerful and always efficient assistance: Julie McKuras and Curator Tim Johnson at the Sherlock Holmes Collections at the University of Minnesota, Catherine Cooke at the Westminster Library in London, and Victoria Gill and Peggy Perdue at the Arthur Conan Doyle Collection at the Metropolitan Toronto Reference Library

And I owe much to Peter Blau, the late Richard Lancelyn Green, and Robert Adey for guidance and practical help.

If you are interested in further exploration, you will some day, when I can part with them, find my collection housed in the Sherlock Holmes Collections at the University of Minnesota.

While assembling these copies, I found I had to make notes to keep things straight. This included plot summaries, information about the authors, when available, an excerpt to give the parody flavor or non flavor, and sometimes my own reaction. For what it is worth, when I get around to it, CD copies will be sent to the three libraries mentioned and the Richard Lancelyn Green collection at Portsmouth, England.

Also I should be neglectful if I did not thank the three people who helped me make this book possible: my wife Nance, our adolescent granddaughter, Halley, who it seems, like all the young these days, has effortlessly mastered computers and such, and my publisher, Steve Emecz, who patiently waited as we solved the mystery of how to transfer a manuscript from Wordperfect to Word.

In some cases, I have changed the titles of items to show more clearly their content. The original titles are found in the introductions.

But before we begin to savor and enjoy, we should pause for a moment and tip our cloth hats, the one with the ear flaps, to The Founder of this Feast of Sherlockian parody and pastiche---

Sir Arthur Conan Doyle (1859-1930)

It is he, without seeming to appreciate fully his achievement, was truly---

THE MASTER

THE FIRST PARODIES ANDPASTICHES

An Evening With Sherlock Holmes

Anonymous (James M. Barrie)

*This anonymous parody popped up on November 28, 1891, only four months after **The Strand** magazine had published the first short story of Sherlock Holmes, "A Scandal in Bohemia."This makes it the earliest parody we know of. A discovery of**Gibson and Greene.***

*A little over a month later, on January 6, 1892, in a letter to his mother, Conan Doyle wrote that at an **Idler's** magazine dinner he had met James M. Barrie. He adds, "It was Barrie who wrote the skit on Holmes in **The Speaker.** A mystery of authorship is solved thanks to the editorial efforts of Jon Lellenberg, Daniel Stashower, and Charles Foley, who prepared, **Arthur Conan Doyle A Life in Letters.***

*James M. Barrie, (1860-1937) made his initial reputation with a number of sentimental novels with Scottish themes. He is better known today for his plays, **Peter Pan** and **The Admirable Crichton**. And we now accord him another honor, though perhaps a more dubious one, the writer who started the fad of Sherlockian parody.*

Perhaps of interest to some Sherlockians: we note that from the beginning of satirical comment, Sherlock Holmes is treated as a living person consorting with other living persons such as Arthur Conan Doyle and the anonymous interviewer.

****

I am the sort of man whose amusement is to do everything better than any other body. Hence my evening with Sherlock Holmes.

Sherlock Holmes is the private detective whose adventures Mr. Conan Doyle is now editing in the **Strand** magazine. To my annoyance (for I hate to hear anyone praised except myself) Holmes's cleverness in, for instance, knowing by glancing at you what you had for dinner last Thursday, has delighted press and public, and so I felt it was time to take him down a peg. I therefore introduced myself to Mr. Conan Doyle and persuaded him to ask me to his house to meet Sherlock Holmes.

For poor Mr. Holmes it proved to be an eventful evening. I had determined to overthrow him with his own weapons, and accordingly when he began, with well-affected carefulness, "I perceive, Mr. Anon, from the condition of your cigar-cutter, that you are not fond of music," I replied blandly, "Yes, that is obvious."

Mr. Holmes, who had been in his favourite attitude in an easy chair (curled up in it), started violently and looked with indignation at our host, who was also much put out.

"How on earth can you tell from looking at his cigar-cutter that Mr. Anon is not fond of music?" asked Mr. Conan Doyle, with well-simulated astonishment.

"It is very simple," said Mr. Holmes, still eyeing me sharply.

"The easiest thing in the world," I agreed.

"Then I need not explain?" said Mr. Holmes haughtily.

"Quite unnecessary,"said I.

I filled my pipe afresh to give the detective and hisbiographer; an opportunity of exchanging glances unobserved, and then pointing to Mr. Holmes's silk hat (which stood on the table) I said blandly, "So you have been in the country recently, Mr. Holmes?"

He bit his cigar, so that the lighted end was jerked against his brow.

"You saw me there?" he replied almost fiercely.

"No," I said, "but a glance at your hat told me you had been out of town."

"Ha!" said he triumphantly, "then yours was but a guess, for as a matter offact I---"

"Did not have that hat in the country with you," I interposed.

"Quite true," he said smiling.

"But how –" began Mr. Conan Doyle.

"Pooh," said I coolly, "this may seem remarkable to you two who are not accustomed to drawing deductions from circumstances trivial in themselves (Holmes winced), but it is nothing to one who keeps his eyes open. Now as soon as I saw that Mr. Holmes's hat was dented in the front, as if it had received a sharp blow, I knew he had been in the country lately."

"For a long or short time?" Holmes snarled, (His cool manner had quite deserted him.)

"For at least a week," I said.

"True," he said dejectedly.

"Your hat also tells me," I continued, "That you came to this house in a four-wheeler --- no, in a hansom."

"---" said Sherlock Holmes. "Would you mind explaining?" asked our host.

"Not at all," I said. "When I saw the dent in Mr. Holmes's hat, I knew at once that it had come unexpectedly against some hard object? Probably the roof of a conveyance, which he struck against while stepping in. These accidents often happen at such a time to hats. Then though this conveyance might have been a four-wheeler, it was more probable that Mr. Holmes would travel in a hansom."

"How did you know I had been in the country?"

"I am coming to that. Your practice is, of course, to wear a silk hat always in London, but those who are in the habit of doing so acquire, without knowing it, a habit of guarding their hats. I, therefore, saw that you had recently been wearing a pot-hat and had forgotten to allow for the extra height of the silk hat. But you are not the sort of man who would wear a little hat in London. Obviously, then, you had been in the country, where pot-hats are the rule rather than the exception."

Mr. Holmes, who was evidently losing ground every moment with our host, tried to change the subject.

"I was lunching in an Italian restaurant to-day," he said, addressing Mr. Conan Doyle, "and the waiter's manner of adding up my bill convinced me that his father had once ---"

"Speaking of that, I interposed, do you remember that as you were leaving the restaurant you and another person nearly had a quarrel at the door?"

"Was it you?" he asked.

18

"If you think that possible," I said blandly, "you have a poor memory for faces."

He growled to himself.

"It is this way, Mr. Doyle," I said. "The door of this restaurant is in two halves, the one of which is marked 'Push' and the other 'Pull.' Now Mr. Holmes and the stranger were on different sides of the door, and both pulled. As a consequence the door would not open, until one of them gave way, then they glared at each other and parted."

"You must have been a spectator," said our host.

"No," I replied, "but I knew this as soon as I heard that Mr. Holmes had been lunching in one of those small restaurants. They all have double doors which are mark 'Push' and 'Pull' respectively. Now, nineteen times in twenty, mankind pushes when it ought to pull, and pulls when it should push. Again, when you are leaving a restaurant there is usually someone entering it. Hence the scene at the door. And, in conclusion, the very fact of having made such a silly mistake rouses ill-temper, which we vent on the other man, to imply that the fault was all his."

"Hum!"said Holmes savagely. "Mr. Doyle, the leaf on this cigar is unwinding."

"Try anoth---"our host was beginning, when I interposed with –

"I observe from your remark, Mr. Holmes, that you came straight here from the hairdressers."

This time he gaped.

"You let him wax your mustache," I continued (For of late Mr.

19

Holmes has been growing a mustache).

"He did and before I knew what he was about," Mr. Holmes replied.

"Exactly," I said, "and in your hansom you tried to undo his handiwork with your fingers."

"To which," our host said with sudden enlightenment, "some of the wax stuck, and is now tearing the leaf of the cigar!"

"Precisely," I said, "I knew he had come from a hairdresser's the moment I shook hands with him."

"Good-night," said Mr. Holmes, seizing his hat, (he is not as tall as I thought him at first) "I have an appointment at ten with a banker, who---"

"So I have been observing," I said. "I knew it from the way you---"

But he was gone.

Sherwood Hoakes Rescues Sherlockian Parody

C. C. Rothwell

*Little is known about C. C. Rothwell whose initial contribution to Sherlockian parody was to keep the kettle boiling, the top spinning, the parodies coming. He wrote the second and third parody/pastiches thus far discovered. They appeared in April and May of 1892, in a penny magazine called **The Ludgate Weekly**.*

But he made an even bigger contribution to Sherlockian parody. He saw the possibilities of satirizing the idiosyncrasies of Sherlock Holmes as found in the Conan Doyle stories, as well as lambasting right off his deductive prowess.

We have Chasemore, a Watson-type narrator. Rothwell uses comical names for his detective and other characters, as well as for the detective's cases including the unrecorded ones. His detective's name is a pun---Sherwood Hoakes. And of course his detective's many confidently stated deductions all go haywire. Even when he gets a case similar to one of Sherlock Holmes, a groom disappearing on his wedding day, things work out differently and badly.

But these pieces, despite all their fine qualities, lack one essential feature of first rate pastiches---brevity or perhaps one should say conciseness.

Each contains a long section showing Sherwood Hoakes

21

floundering, which I omit, and instead concentrate on the parody parts that Rothwell provides us in both sketches. The first large chunk of parody is from "An Interrupted Honeymoon, and the second from the one with the more interesting title "The Yellow Cockroach."

****

from: An InterruptedHoneymoon

My first introduction to Mr. Sherwood Hoakes, that eminent specialist in crime, took place under circumstances of the following singular nature. I was walking home inoffensively enough one evening in a late autumn, when about half-way down Butcher-Avenue, in the City, an open house door attracted my attention. It was a very ordinary door, in a very ordinary row of flat-faced houses, but on a panel below the knocker there was the following inscription in chalk:

PUT IT DOWN WITHOUT KNOCKING

I smiled, and wondered, and would have passed on, but at that instant, as my eye traveled down the short lobby and into a room behind, I perceived to my astonishment and alarm that the fringe of the carpet adjoining the grate was on fire, and that the flame was eating its way toward the window curtains. Without a moment's hesitation I entered the house, hurried into the room, and crushed out the fire under my boot.

Contrary to my expectation, the room was occupied by a gentleman, who slowly rose from a basket chair, showing neither annoyance nor surprise at my intrusion. I was about to offer explanations but he intercepted me by speaking first.

"Good evening, sir. No apologies, I beg. You are welcome. I perceive you are a cheesemonger by trade and a widower. Also I regret to observe that you lost your eldest son two years ago---from the

22

measles, I think. Your daughter is married to a jeweler, who, I am afraid, is not quite so steady as he might be. Won't you take a seat? Ah! I perceive you were at Margate last month with your grandchildren."

I stood looking in amazement at this man, who I had never seen before in my life, who as his eyes traveled over me, read out the biographical details I have given above.

"Now, how on earth--?"

"Do I know all these things?"

He smiled a pleasant, if rather superior smile.

"There's no magic in it. A trained eye and a logical brain. For instance, how do I discover you are a cheesefactor? My nose tells me so, and my eyes corroborate it by observing the peculiar glossy yellowness of your right hand, which, of course, must handle many thousand cheeses a year. That you are lately a widower, that locket containing brownish-grey hair at your watch-chain leads me to presume."

"And about my son---my poor dead son? How can you tell---?"

"By your collar, sir. It was one of his. That is evident by the fact that not only is it half a size too small for you, and therefore not your own purchasing, but the collar is one which came into fashion two years ago, and was much in vogue among young men, which leads one to conclude that he bought it then, and probably died soon after of the measles, which you will remember, caused great mortality that year."

"Well, well! And the jeweler, my drunken son-in-law---and Margate, I gasped."

"Nothing could be simpler. A glance at the bridge of your nose assures me that you rarely use those gold eye-glasses dangling before you, and the fact that you wear plain bone studs in your shirt affords a strong presumption that you wouldn't be the man to buy a pair of useless gold pince-nez. They have therefore been presented to you, but presumably by someone not thoroughly acquainted with your habits, and yet sufficiently intimate to make you a handsome personal gift, this being so the additional fact that the eyeglasses are an old pattern, evidently furbished up and refitted with new cork nose-clips, points strongly to their having been presented by someone in the trade, no doubt a son-in-law anxious to make a handsome gift and get rid of an unsalable article. The burin-scratches on one of the glasses seem to indicate the unsteady hand of a drinker."

"Oh, you wizard!" I said in gay reproach. "You scandalous old sorcerer!"

"As regards your trip to Margate, those three long stiff donkey's hairs---"

"Never mind about Margate and the donkey's hairs. What's under that hat on the table?"

He lifted the silk hat in some confusion and betrayed the flat bottle underneath.

"Won't you sit down and take some?"

I sat down, and while my host moved about the room, I took note of his appearance and surroundings. He looked a man of about forty, who time and fortune had conspired to ill-use. His face was long and blanched, his eye large and boiled, his red hair was cropped so short that it might have been under a lawnmower, his general expression was

24

badgered and harassed, and that of a man constantly striving to accomplish something against adverse conditions. He wore a frock coat with inked seams, and his vest, which was unbuttoned askew, showed that he was one of those few remaining individuals who take snuff.

Having equipped me with a cigar and a glass, he resumed his chair.

"By the way," I said, "I can tell you something interesting about those vanilla cheroots. I was asked to analyze one the other day, in the ordinary course of my business---"

"Analyze? But, my good sir, you---a cheesefactor?"

"Not for the world! I am a chemist and druggist, sir, from my youth up."

Mr. Hoakes fixed a puzzled jaded eye on me.

"Dear me! That's odd now. But how comes it---your yellow hand---the odour of cheese---I can smell it this moment, distinctly!"

"No wonder," sir, said I, "with half a pound of Gorgonzola on your own sideboard there. And as for my hand, it was mixing iodoform ointment all morning, which may well account for the colour."

The badgered look on the poor man's face deepened perceptibly.

"At any rate you are a widower," he urged.

"Quite the contrary. Nor am I wearing up my poor dead son's linen. The collar is all my own buying and the hair in his locket is said to be Queen Charlotte's; I bought it at a sale."

"But at least your daughter is married to a jeweler,"

"Never had either son or daughter. Bought the eyeglasses myself. Haven't been to the seaside for years, these donkey's hairs must have come out of the clothes-brush this morning."

Mr. Hoakes sighed, and gazed dejectedly into the fire.

"I don't know how it is, but try as I will, I never seem to get the knack of it. It's most disheartening and yet I do my best. I strain every nerve. Induction, deduction ratiocination---I apply 'em all but I'm almost always wrong. By every rule of evidence, you ought to have been a cheesemonger, and your daughter married to a tipsy jeweler."

"Well, I said, "I'm sorry to disoblige you. Have you been at this business long?"

"About three years."

"I suppose you would call yourself a private detective?"

"'Criminal pathologist' would be more suitable, sir. I have always had a strong leaning toward crime - mean, of course, the detection of crime - and having been unfortunate in business, I took up my present profession some three years ago."

"Indeed! I am myself a student of humanity, but without any special leanings toward crime, and your case interests me greatly. Have you had many successes?"

"Well - yes - perhaps one or two - partial successes. There was the Notorious Backgammon Case, which I am confident I should have unraveled if the police had only left me alone. There was that remarkable case known as the 'Four and Twenty Jailbirds,' and the other, the great Hoxton Blue Pearl Robbery."

"Ah, yes, I remember that well."

"So do I," said Mr. Hoakes, gloomily, "for I served a light sentence at Millbank in connection with it. How was I to know that those plausible ruffians were only using me as a cats paw?"

He groaned bitterly.

from: The Yellow Cockroach

Next to the Great Crumpet Mystery, which, as you no doubt you remember, stirred London to its inmost heart, and went very near bringing my poor friend to the gallows, all innocent as he was, but too easily confiding, the case which most thrilled the popular imagination at the time, filling the newspapers with sensational columns under the heading of "What's Become of the Bishop?" is the one I am about to lay before you.

I had seen nothing of Hoakes for several weeks, though I never failed to glance at his succinct little 'ad' every morning in the second column of the *Daily Catterwaul.*

On my last visit at Butcher-Avenue, I had found him much ruffled in his temper and rather out of spirits. It transpired that some officious old clergyman of the neighborhood had called on him, and in the kindliest way had invited him to attend their annual thieves' supper, and give the company a short account of his personal experiences before reformation and after.

"It's Scotland Yard has done this," he said bitterly.

The Coleslaw Jewel Robbery

Roy L. McCardell

*An American humorist finally gets around to writing a Sherlockian parody, almost three years after that first one by James M. Barrie. It was published in the leading humor magazine **Puck** on October 24, 1894 as "The Sign of the '400." It also appeared in **Current Literature** in April 1895 under the title "Sherlock Holmes Americanized."*

*By the time Conan Doyle died, the Americans had almost caught up to the English in the production of Sherlockian parody (if we Americans are allowed to set to one side, for the moment, the hundred or so that appeared in a boy's paper, **The Magnet,** on the grounds that this seems a little like unfair competition.) Still that wouldn't be quite cricket, would it?*

*For many years this parody was credited to R. K. Munkittrick. However, assiduous Sherlockians dug up a listing of authors in the **Puck** files and found the credit for it should go to Roy L. McCardell (1870-?)*

*McCardell is thought to be the first salaried writer of the silent movies. He is credited with 43 silents and one sound movie. His most popular screenplay was that Theda Bara morality tale, **A Fool There Was**. (She vamps him from wifey and the kids and then discards him, a broken husk, and just when wifey gets him put back together again, Theda once more slithers onto the scene, to vamp him again, this time to his final destruction! R. I. P!)*

But McCardell's parody, reprinted here, is tamer stuff.

****

For the nonce, Holmes was slighting his cocaine, and was joyously jabbing himself with morphine---his favorite seventy-per-cent solution---when a knock came at the door; it was our landlady with the telegram. Holmes opened it and read it carefully.

"H'm," he said, "What do you think of this, Watson?"

I picked it up. "Come at once, we need you. 72 Chinchbugge Place, S, W.,"I read.

"Why, it's from Athelney Jones," I remarked.

"Just so," said Holmes. "Call a cab."

We were soon at the address given, 72 Chinchbugge Place, being the town-house of the dowager Countess of Coldslaw. It was an old-fashioned mansion, somewhat weather-beaten. The old hat stuffed in the broken pane in the drawing room gave the place an air of unstudied artistic negligence, which we both remarked at the time.

Athelney Jones met us at the door. He wore a troubled expression. "Here's a pretty go, gentlemen," was his greeting. "A forcible entrance has been made to Lady Coleslaw's boudoir, and the famous Coleslaw diamonds are stolen."

Without a word, Holmes drew out his pocket-lens and examined the atmosphere. "The whole thing wears an air of mystery," he said quietly.

We then entered the house. Lady Coleslaw was completely prostrated and could not be seen. We went at once to the scene of the robbery; there was no sign of anything unusual in the boudoir, except that the windows and furniture had been smashed and the pictures had been removed from the walls. An attempt had been made by the thief to steal the wall-paper also. However, he had not succeeded. It had rained the night before and muddy footprints led up to the escritoire from which the jewels had been taken. A heavy smell of stale cigar smoke hung over the room. Aside from these hardly noticeable details, the despoiler had left no trace of his presence.

In an instant, Sherlock Holmes was down on his knees, examining the footprints with a stethoscope. "H'm," he said, "so you can make nothing out of this, Jones?"

"No sir," answered the detective; "but I hope to; there's a big reward."

"It's all very simple," my good fellow, said Holmes. "The robbery was committed at 3 o'clock this morning by a short, middle-aged, henpecked man, with a cast in his eye. His name is Smythe, and he lives at 139 Toff Terrace."

Jones fairly gasped. "What! Major Smythe, one of the highest thought-of, richest men in the city?"

"The same."

In half an hour we were at Smythe's bedside. Despite his protestations, he was pinioned and driven to prison.

"For Heaven's sake, Holmes," said I, when we returned to our rooms, "how did you solve the problem so quickly?"

"Oh, it was easy, dead easy!" said he. "As soon as we entered the room I noticed the cigar smoke. It was cigar smoke from a cigar that had been given a husband by his wife. I could tell that, for I have made a study of cigar smoke. Any other but a henpecked man throws such cigars away. Then I could tell by the footprints that the man had had appendicitis. Now, no one but members of the '400' have that. Who then, was henpecked in the '400,' and had had appendicitis recently? Why, Major Smythe, of course! He is middle-aged, stout, and has a cast in his eye."

I could not help but admiring my companion's reasoning, and told him so. "Well," he said, "it's very simple if you know how."

Thus ended the Coleslaw robbery, so far as we were concerned.

It may be as well to add, however, that Jones' arrant jealousy caused him to resort to the lowest trickery to throw discredit upon the discovery of my gifted friend. He allowed Major Smythe to prove a most conclusive alibi, and then meanly arrested a notorious burglar as the thief, on the flimsiest proof, and convicted him. The burglar had been caught while trying to pawn some diamonds that seemed to be a portion of the plunder taken from 72 Chinchbugge Place.

Of course, Jones got all the credit. I showed the newspaper accounts to Holmes. He only laughed and said: "You see how it is, Watson; Scotland Yard, as usual, gets the glory."

As I perceived he was going to play Sweet Marie on his violin, I reached for the morphine myself.

The Best Laid Plans, Etc.

Peter Pericarp

*This pastiche was published some time in 1894 about three years after the first short story of Sherlock Holmes in **The Strand.** As another pastiche also appeared that year, it is either the first or second, or if we call Rothwell's efforts pastiches, the third or fourth of its kind. Anyhow, it's old.*

*It was chapter seven, "Modern Miranda" in a book called **The Sapling,** edited by John R. Yates. The initials attached to this chapter's art nouveau drawings were those of the book's editor and may indicate he wrote this pastiche as well. No other chapter had Sherlockian content.*

The collection seems to have been part of a private publication among friends, each writing a part. All were possibly part of the arts and crafts movement of the day, given the decorative illustrations. The writing is cursive and by hand, with only one correction throughout. Sherlockian Jon Lellenberg reports that only forty copies of the book were ever made---possibly reproduced by an offset lithograph process.

*The pastiche is an example of an enthusiast, clearly an amateur in the art of writing fiction, who comes up with a neat plot twist suggested by an event in the stories. The copy gives evidence of his being university educated, (Miranda is the innocent girl in Shakespeare's **The Tempest**). But as written, it is a meandering tale that tells you more than you need to know. But when you finish it you will be able to say* *you have finally read a story in which the word "forsooth" was used, and not as some Fawlty Towers joke.*

And don't miss the part about nurse, Sister Helen. She is memorable.

You may need a little help with the plot. One or more thugs have invaded a garden-party, and for some reason or other seriously injured a man named Harding with of all exotic things, a gilt arrow. Someone then kidnapped a woman named Iris. Her boy friend Lawrence Hathaway calls in Sherlock Holmes.

****

On leaving Iris at the flat in Chelsea, Hathaway had at once returned to Mrs. Moreton-Plunkett's to seek for Mr. Grey. Re-entering the garden by the side-gate and finding that everyone had disappeared, he felt impelled toward the precise scene of the tragic incident. What is that? An arrow! The arrow!! Snatching it, he snapped it into a dozen pieces, then on the very site where Harding fell, ground it to splinters under his heel.

On enquiring at the house he learned that Harding had been at once attended by Dr. Delaney, Mrs. Moreton-Plunkett's brother who was fortunately present and that the patient (whose injury was less severe than at first stated) had shortly afterwards been removed to a surgical home.

Finding that Mr. Grey had started homeward half-an-hour ago, he at once drove to Cheyne Mansions. Horror upon horrors! Iris had disappeared. Her father, unnerved by the events of the afternoon, seemed unable to realize this further disaster. Lawrence did so only too keenly. Seldom had his usually cool head undergone so severe a trial. For a few moments he paced the room in agitation. Suddenly he stopped as if struck by an idea.

"Mrs. Goodman," he cried to their excellent housekeeper, "Take care of Mr. Grey!" and without waiting for an answer dashed downstairs and leapt into the hansom he had retained and at once gave the driver his directions.

It must have been quite half past six, though still perfectly light, when, after a three mile drive, the cab turned out of Oxford Street into a well-known thoroughfare leading towards the Marylebone Road. "221B, ain't it Sir?" said the cabman, speaking through the trap door in the cab top, and the next moment, after the manner of his kind, pulled up the horse on to his haunches.

Two minutes later Lawrence Hathaway entered upon an experience which in after years he always regarded as one of the most intensely interesting in his somewhat eventful life. The room in which, and the man before whom, he stood seemed perfectly familiar to him although neither of them had he ever actually seen before. His agitation was at once checked by the consciousness of being in the presence, and therefore under the influence of the most remarkable genius in his own sphere of thought and action that the world had ever known; the man who had snatched at least one Imperial Dynasty from impending annihilation; who had sought, discovered, and removed that which would probably have plunged Great Powers into a sanguinary war; who in a thousand less famous cases, had rescued the weak from the toils and machinations of the unscrupulous; who first checked and now had well nigh strangled that higher intellectual criminal life which spread like a web over European Society---a life far above the sordid class of clumsy crime with which Scotland Yard and its Continental counterparts are more or less able to grapple.

Sherlock Holmes, for he was none other, was seated at a table covered with chemical appliances. On these his mind, his entire being, seemed concentrated. Of a stranger's presence, he seemed completely unconscious. "Solved!" he at last cried triumphantly, as a phial of amber-colored fluid rapidly assumed the hue of emerald.

"Oh! pardon me," said he, picking up Hathaway's card which the servant had placed on the table five minutes before. "To what do I owe the pleasure of this visit?"

"First of all," said Hathaway, "I must insist that Dr. Watson shall have no finger in this case."

"I have yet to learn what the case is," said Holmes, comprehensively scanning his visitor from crown to sole.

"A young lady has disappeared."

"And you wish to find her. Well, that ought not to present any insuperable difficulty," he interrupted, "as I see she was with you this afternoon."

"Few things are more important than trifles," continued he, detaching at the same time from the seam of Hathaway's right sleeve a small spring hook of the kind now often used instead of button's on ladies' gloves.

"H'm, the fifth hook of a row of eight," he remarked after carefully examining with a lens the soft vicuna coat sleeve. "Her arm appears to have pressed somewhat heavily on yours, I observe, and ultimately was withdrawn with a jerk. This afternoon too---for the jacket you wore during the morning, as the slight mark on your collar tells me, was a dark blue, cut a third of an inch higher in the neck than the frock coat you now wear."

Hathaway, as a reader of current literature, was fairly familiar with

Holmes' methods and was determined to evince no surprise at his extraordinary acuteness of perception.

"Pray take that seat," said Holmes, pointing with a cigarette he had just lighted and which, apparently by accident, slipped from his fingers on to the floor. In stooping for it, as Hathaway turned to sit down, the latter half fancied he felt a hand brush past the side of his boot. Being now seated, he saw Holmes standing by the window gazing intently into the palm of his own hand. Presently he threw himself back into a chair facing his visitor and, with a look akin to satisfaction, proceeded with his cigarette.

"Now," said Hathaway, "let me state to you the whole story."

"Pray spare yourself the trouble," replied Holmes, "but tell me what is the last report as to poor Mr. Harding."

"What!"cried Hathaway springing to his feet. "Great Heavens Sir! are you man or fiend? How do you know anything of Harding?"

"Be calm, be calm; I claim no supernatural power. The cause of your call is as clear as day. Read that!" said he, tossing across the six o'clock edition of the *Evening Magnet*.

Hathaway resuming his seat, read an account of the 'Terrible Termination to a Garden-party' with names and full details even to the 'gilt feathers on the arrows' and of course the 'blood on the grey cinder path.'

"Gilt feathers on the arrows," repeated Holmes significantly, "a most remarkable colour for the purpose. Must have been specially ordered."

"It is all very well," said Hathaway, rising in angry impatience, "for

36

you to make these guesses because you happen to have seen the evening paper."

"I never guess,"came the quiet, frigid interruption, "I observe and I deduce. Please carefully examine this small shred of feather," handing it on a sheet of note paper. "You will note that it is cut obviously for an arrow feather; that it is glued at the inner edge; and lastly that it is gilt. Look closely through the lens and you will discover several particles of cinder---grey cinder---which exhibit clear traces of blood. Within the last three minutes," continued Holmes, deliberately lighting a second cigarette, "I detached the shred of gilt feather from the edge of your right boot-heel in which there still sticks a small splinter of the arrow itself. Well," after a pause, "perhaps it was not an unnatural impulse which urged you to crush the arrow under foot on the spot where Harding fell."

Hathaway subsided.

During a brief further conversation Holmes explained the necessity of his crossing by that night's boat to the Continent on other business and that it was quite uncertain how soon he could give complete personal attention to this case. "But," said he, "write on the back of this card the name and address of an intimate friend. And I may implicitly rely on his discretion?" inquired Holmes, glancing at the endorsement.

An abrupt conclusion of the interview was at that moment brought about by the sudden opening of the door, when a tall man of foreign appearance with a soft hat drawn down over his eyes, strode into the room.

****

Picture a moderate-sized brightly furnished clean looking apartment half bedroom, half sitting room. On a couch slanting across the front of the fireplace lies a man clad in a loose dressing gown, his head raised on a pillow immaculately white. The door opens and a woman with nurse's cap, apron and surgical chatelaine, enters the room.

"How do you feel now?" she inquired.

"Much better, thanks to your nursing!" replied the patient, over whose face passed a flush of pleasure.

"I have brought some illustrated papers," said Sister Helen pushing before him a small table and placing upon it *The Sketch* and *The Graphic.*"Look at these, and do not think of your illness. The wound is far slighter than was believed when the accident occurred a month ago. The fever which supervened was our most serious danger and that I am happy to say we have now overcome."

Harding had indeed been in a most critical condition. Nothing but the most skillful nursing could have saved him, and that he certainly had experienced at the hands of Sister Helen, the Lady Superintendent at the Paget Nursing Home. She was a bright, cheery, dauntless woman whose spirits no amount of work or worry could check. Though barely thirty her experience was wide and full of interest and included field hospital work in one or two Indian hill campaigns.

In congenial employment she had escaped the ceaseless unrest of those misguided maidens who merely look on life as a lottery with husbands (forsooth) as prizes. Nor had she worried herself or others about the imaginary rights or visionary wrongs of her sex. A single life of good work well done sufficed for her---was in fact her ideal, and she declined to change it. Assiduous in her attention to her patients, she possessed the happy knack of appearing so to interest herself in each one of them as to make him or her to think that he or she was of all others *the* one of her particular predilection. So thought Tom Harding.

"Sister Helen," said he one day several weeks later, the day in fact before his intended departure from the Home, "How can I ever sufficiently thank you? You to whom I owe my life. How?" he was continuing with evident warmth as he rose from his seat.

At this moment the door opened and Edith Deschamps, formerly Cohen, nee Hamilton, the future Mrs. Harding, entered. As with a slight cry she ran forward to Tom's arms, Sister Helen left the room. So will we.

"Just in time!" said Sister Helen to herself, as she walked along the corridor, "I believe the foolish fellow was getting fond of me and fancied the feeling mutual."

Edith, after the nearly tragic incident of the Garden-party had been seriously ill and for a time it was feared that her brain might be permanently affected. No communication had been allowed between herself and Harding and today was their first, and to him, unexpected meeting.

An hour later they strolled down into the Hall and telephoned for Miss Deschamps brougham which had been sent to the stables a few minutes distant.

"Edith," said Tom sentimentally as they rested on the settee "do you remember the old days at Southsea?"

"How slow they are with that carriage!" said she with some impatience. "Yes, of course, I do remember them, but after all, Tom, we were very young. I have thought of them during my illness," she continued after a pause, "of your boyhood and seafaring life, after, you dear clever old thing."

"Clever!"

"Yes, of course you are clever! Show me another who has written so brilliant a play as **Tempest-tossed.** But do tell me, dear, where you acquired your literary faculty and knowledge of stagecraft."

"My darling," said he, rising hurriedly, "the brougham is at the door."

"But you have not answered my question, Tom dear."

"That, my sweet Edith," said he uneasily, "involves a little secret. You remember at the rehearsals the man with a dull drabbish---well---I will tell you the pedigree of that play after we are married."

"Now remember," said Edith as she stepped into the brougham, "you are to be sure to get the license tomorrow," adding with a twinkle in her eye "you may be considered convalescent but I shall not feel you are quite out of danger till you, I mean we, are married."

****

It has been averred that the fine range of building, which from the rear of old Whitehall, overlooks the Victoria Embankment and the Thames, has a site unequaled in the world.

This no one will dare to deny, who, by day or night, has looked out from an upper balcony of Whitehall Court; whose eye has swept the grand River-bend and garden from St Stephens to St Pauls and thence on to the grim outline of the Tower; who has felt throbbing beneath and around him, the pulse of the Great City who has turned again to watch the flow, calm but eternal, of the mighty artery which is London's life-blood.

It was in the drawing room of a flat in Whitehall Court that Mr. and Mrs. Lawrence Hathaway one evening in May awaited the arrival of their guests for dinner. Well as Hathaway himself had worked, Fortune, that fickle Goddess, had been unusually kind to him. Owner and Editor of the leading weekly **Review** he now occupied a lofty position in the literary and political world. But the most valued of his successes was his election, by his old 'Varsity' to be her representative in Parliament, where he was steadily advancing in estimation as a thoughtful and forcible speaker. Lastly, in that most fateful of all experiments, marriage, he felt himself fortunate beyond his brightest hopes.

The little dinner party to be given that evening by Iris---for she was now his wife---and himself was of a specially interesting character. It marked renewal of their friendship with Mr. and Mrs. Tom Harding, now, not only happily married, but also the proprietors of a twelvemonth old curly headed cherub whose like (of course) the World had never previously seen.

Sister Helen, through whose good offices the reconciliation had been affected, and old Mr. Grey were also to be among the select dozen of guests. But the chief interest centred in the fact that the story of the finding of Iris, at present a secret even to herself, and to Lawrence was to be told tonight by none other than Sherlock Holmes, himself who had formed something approaching a friendship for the Hathaways.

"However you could have been induced," said Lawrence to his wife, "to bury yourself for all those months in that Batterseas back-alley passes my comprehension."

"Not half so incomprehensible as that I, Iris, should have allowed that horrid, untidy, slum-hunting fellow with that awful beard to propose to me without my hitting him over the head. What I said to him I have not the slightest idea. I had to talk to stop his flood of nonsense. Need I add details?"

"Of course you know he was supposed to be keeping a look-out for you on behalf of Holmes during his absence abroad. But for his opportune elopement with the Baroness Bleithauer, Heaven only knows what would have become of you or whether you would have been found at all. Robinson, poor chap, after proving a failure at the Bar, gradually changed his principles for the customary cant about 'freedom' for everybody and everything---free breakfast---tables---education, speech, thought, and apparently, love!"

A quarter of an hour later all the guests had arrived but one. The conversation turned almost entirely on the anticipated appearance of Sherlock Holmes who was not what is known as a 'diner-out' and who evaded the wiles of the genus lion-hunter, charmed the never so wisely.

Mrs. Moreton-Plunkett who had been the earliest arrival was in a state of excitement even greater than usual. She did not believe he would turn up. Others mentioned the rumour that he was at present grappling with a gigantic conspiracy which had already undermined the foundations of the Throne itself. Hathaway remarked that if alive Sherlock Holmes would be present, while Harding referred to a report current during the afternoon that Holmes had at length met in the ranks of crime, his own intellectual equal, a former mathematics professor at one of the Universities, a man of iron nerve, of endless resource and steeped in the life of infamy.

"How very terrible," ejaculated the irrepressible Mrs. Moreton-Plunkett who found it necessary to fly to her smelling salts.

At that instant, above the hum of distant traffic, and through the half-open windows, came the stentorian tones of two newspaper men who on impressive occasions invariably hunt in couples.

"Orrible! Orrible! Murder! Death o' Sherlockomes!"

A few moments later Lawrence Hathaway read to his guests the following telegram in the *Evening Magnet.*

Zermatt Switzerland, Wednesday.

"This morning the Englishman Sherlock Holmes and a certain Professor Moriarty fell from a precipice more than a thousand feet in depth. Near the verge of the abyss the ground affords evidence of a severe struggle."

Dead! And with him died the secret of the finding of Iris.

The End

The Missing Box

Anonymous

This is first advertising parody we know of that features Sherlock Holmes and Dr. Watson. It seems fitting that we find it discloses a pharmaceutical firm touting its wares, television not being available at the time.

And Sherlock tries to make a joke, of sorts. An Adey discovery.

It appeared November 18, 1893 in **The Family Doctor**.

****

Yes, it had gone! Where and how no one could fathom. Evidently the only thing to be done was to call in my good friend, Sherlock Holmes, whose marvelous detective feats and miraculous deductions in tracing the perpetrator of mysterious crimes had startled the entire civilized world and set them wonderingly twiddling their thumbs while discussing his extraordinary ingenuity.

The box itself was not of much intrinsic value but its contents were absolutely priceless. I had carelessly neglected to secure it in the safe, and left it lying on my dressing table---I was confident of this. The servants were closely questioned---I did not care to search their boxes at this stage. They all indignantly protested absolute ignorance of its whereabouts; my wife repudiated all knowledge of it. In my dilemma, I wired as follows:

To Holmes, Baker Street W.

COME IMMEDIATELY, IN GREAT DISTRESS

BOX AND VALUABLE CONTENTS MISSING

NO CLUE.

WATSON

Within a short period I recognized his characteristic ring at the door.

"Ah, Watson," he said as he rushed into the sitting room, "you were at a banquet last night and stayed till very late, failed to obtain a cab, and walked home in the rain along the Strand without an umbrella, smoking a possener clay, which you had the misfortune to break. How do I know? Nothing so simple; I saw your silk hat in the hall as I came in, bearing unmistakable signs of a recent wetting, if you had taken a cab or had an umbrella it would have been in its usual glossy condition; your boots are covered with tar and cement---the Strand is being relaid---I recognized fragments of your pipe and favorite mixture, Latalia and navy cut, lying on the step.

"I know you had a dozen 'poseners' specially made for you of a peculiar shape and I see on the table a menu card of last night's Masonic banquet; a man with half an eye can see you have a severe bilious attack in consequence of the rich food you partook of---Now about the box."

"Well," said I laughingly, "you have unwittingly mentioned the very reason that makes me so anxious to find it. I only paid 12 for its sad contents---the latter are certainly worth a guinea; to me at the present moment they are simply invaluable and indispensable; the chemist is closed and if I don't find this box of Beecham's Pills tonight, I shall---with this beastly bilious attack on me---be quite incapable for work tomorrow, as I have been today."

"There, have some of mine. I always carry them with me and to their head-clearing qualities I owe much of my success---in fact it is part of my SYSTEM to use them in my SYSTEM."

The Great Pegram Mystery

Luke Sharp (Robert Barr)

Originally titled "Detective Stories Gone Wrong," this parody appeared May of 1892, the same month as "The Yellow Cockroach," and is usually rated as among the best of Sherlockian parodies. Robert Barr was its anonymous author, writing under the punnish name of Luke Sharp. His humor is less heavy-handed than Rothwell's and more biting

*Robert Barr (1850-1912) was born in Glasgow, educated in Toronto, and like Mary Tyler Moore's Lou Grant, had once been a reporter for the **Detroit Free Press.** They chose him as their correspondent to England, and he liked London so well, he never returned to America.*

*While editing **The Idler** with Jerome K. Jerome, the author of the humorous novel, **Three Men in a Boat,** he wrote this parody. He was already a friend of Arthur Conan Doyle, but that didn't lead him to pull his punches. A few years later he would do a widely reprinted interview of Conan Doyle for **The Idler.***

*Barr later wrote a series of amusing detective stories titled **The Triumphs of Eugene Valmont** which contains a short story often found in anthologies, "The Absent-minded Coterie." He also wrote a less memorable series of parody/pastiches about **Jane Baxter, Journalist** (1899), who after many adventures, predictably outwits The Great Detective, solves the case, and then marries into the aristocracy. Barr also composed a second clever but bitterly biting parody in 1904 that has Conan Doyle murdering Sherlock when Holmes demands some of*

47

the cash that's rolling in after he returned to life and literature.

It is perhaps understandable that other writers of detective stories might be a little ticked off with Conan Doyle's bringing back Sherlock Holmes from oblivion and might consider him a bit on the greedy side.

****

I dropped in on my friend, SherlawKombs, to hear what he had to say about the Pegram mystery, as it had come to be called in the newspapers. I found him playing the violin with a look of sweet peace and serenity on his face, which I never noticed on the countenances of those within hearing distance.

I knew this expression of seraphic calm indicated that Kombs had been deeply annoyed about something. Such, indeed proved to be the case, for one of the morning papers had contained an article eulogizing the alertness and general competence of Scotland Yard. So great was Sherlaw Kombs's contempt for Scotland Yard that he never would visit Scotland during his vacations, nor would he ever admit that a Scotchman was fit for anything but export.

He generously put away his violin, for he had a sincere liking for me, and greeted me with his usual kindness.

"I have come," I began, plunging at once into the matter on my mind, "to hear what you think of the great Pegram mystery."

"I haven't heard of it," he said quietly, just as if all London were not talking of that very thing. Kombs was curiously ignorant on some subjects and abnormally learned in others. I found, for instance, that political discussion with him was impossible, because he did not know who Salisbury and Gladstone were. This made his friendship a great boon.

48

"The Pegram mystery has baffled even Gregory, of Scotland Yard."

"I can well believe it," said my friend, calmly. "Perpetualmotion, or squaring the circle, would baffle Gregory. He's an infant, is Gregory."

This was one of the things I always liked about Kombs. There was no professional jealousy in him, such as characterizes so many other men.

He filled his pipe, threw himself into his deep-seated arm-chair, placed his feet on the mantel, and clasped his hands behind his head.

"Tell me about it," he said simply.

"Old Barrie Kipson," I began, "was a stockbroker in the City. He lived in Pegram, and it was his custom to ---"

"Come in!" shouted Kombs, without changing his position, but with a suddenness that startled me. I had heard no knock.

"Excuse me," said my friend, laughing, "my invitation to enter was a trifle premature. I was really so interested in your recital that I spoke before I thought, which a detective should never do. The fact is, a man will be here in a moment who will tell me all about this crime, and so you will be spared further effort in that line."

"Ah, you have an appointment."

"I did not know until I spoke that he was coming."

I gazed at him in amazement. Accustomed as I was to his extraordinary talents, the man was a perpetual surprise to me. He continued to smoke quietly, but evidently enjoyed my consternation.

49

"I see you are surprised. It is really too simple to talk about, but, from my position opposite the mirror, I can see the reflection of objects in the street. A man stopped, looked at one of my cards, and then glanced across the street. I recognized my card, because, as you know, they are all in scarlet. If, as you say, London is talking of this mystery, it naturally follows that *he* will talk of it, and the chances are he wished to consult with me upon it. Anyone can see that, besides there is always--- Come in!"

There was a rap at the door this time.

A stranger entered. Sherlaw Kombs did not change his lounging attitude.

"I wish to see Mr. Sherlaw Kombs, the detective," said the stranger, coming within range of the smoker's vision.

"This is Mr. Kombs," I remarked at last, as my friend smoked quietly, and seemed half asleep.

"Allow me to introduce myself, continued the stranger," fumbling for a card.

"There is no need. You are a journalist," said Kombs.

"Ah," said the stranger, somewhat taken aback, "you know me then?"

"Never saw or heard of you in my life before."

"Then how in the world---"

"Nothing simpler. You write for an evening paper. You have written an article slating the book of a friend. He will feel badly about it, and you will console with him. He will never know who stabbed him unless I tell him."

"The devil!" cried the journalist, sinking into a chair and mopping his brow, while his face became livid.

"Yes," drawled Kombs, "it is a devil of a shame that such things are done. But what would you? as we say in France."

When the journalist had recovered his second wind he pulled himself together somewhat. "Would you object to telling me how you know these particulars about a man you say you have never seen?"

"I rarely talk about these things," said Kombs with great composure. "But as the cultivation of the habit of observation may help you in your profession, and thus in a remote degree benefit me by making your paper less deadly dull, I will tell you. Your first and second fingers are smeared with ink, which shows that you write a great deal. This smeared class embraces two sub-classes, clerks or accountants, and journalists.Clerks have to be neat in their work. The ink smear is slight in their case. Your fingers are badly and carelessly smeared; therefore you are a journalist.

"You have an evening paper in your pocket. Any one might have any evening paper, but yours is a Special Edition,which will not be on the streets for half an hour yet. You must have obtained it before you left office, and to do this you must be on the staff. A book notice is marked with a blue pencil. A journalist always despises every article in his own paper not written by himself; therefore, you wrote the article you have marked, and doubtless are about to send it to the author of the book referred to. Your paper makes a specialty of abusing all books not written by some member of its own staff. That the author is a friend of yours, I merely surmised. It is all a trivial example of ordinary observation."

"Really, Mr. Kombs, you are the most wonderful man on earth. You are the equal of Gregory, by Jove, you are."

A frown marred the brow of my friend as he placed his pipe on the sideboard and drew his self-cocking six-shooter.

"Do you mean to insult me, sir?"

"I do not---I---I assure you. You are fit to take charge of Scotland Yard to-morrow---. I am in earnest, indeed I am."

"Then heaven help you," cried Kombs, slowly raising his right arm.

I sprang between them.

"Don't shoot!" I cried. "Youwill spoil the carpet. Besides, Sherlaw, don't you see the man means well. He actually thinks it is a compliment!"

"Perhaps you are right," remarked the detective, flinging his revolver carelessly beside his pipe, much to the relief of the third party. Then, turning to the journalist, he said, with his customary bland courtesy---

"You wanted to see me, I think you said. What can I do for you, Mr. Wilber Scribbings?"

The journalist started.

"How do you know my name?" he gasped.

Kombs waved his hand impatiently.

"Look inside your hat if you doubt your own name."

52

I then noticed it for the first time that the name was plainly to be seen inside the top-hat Scribbings held upside down in his hands.

"You have heard, of course, of the Pegram mystery---"

"Tush," cried the detective; "do not, I beg of you, call it a mystery. There is no such thing. Life would become more tolerable if there ever *was* a mystery. Nothing is original. Everything has been done before. What about the Pegram affair?"

"The Pegram---ah---case has baffled everyone. The*Evening Blade*wishes you to investigate, so that it may publish the result. It will pay you well. Will you accept the commission?"

"Possibly. Tell me about the case."

"I thought everybody knew the particulars. Mr. Barrie Kipsonlived at Pegram. He carried a first-class season ticket between the terminus and that station. It was his custom to leave for Pegram on the 5:36 train each evening. Some weeks ago, Mr. Kipson was brought down by the influenza. On his first visit to the city after his recovery, he drew something like 300 pounds in notes, and left the office at his usual hour to catch the 5:36. He was never seen again alive, as far as the public have been able to learn. He was found at Brewster in a first class compartment on the Scotch Express, which does not stop between London and Brewster. There was a bullet in his head, and his money was gone, pointing plainly to murder and robbery."

"And where is the mystery, may I ask?"

"There are several unexplainable things about the case. First, how came he on the Scotch Express which leaves at six, and does not stop at Pegram? Second, the ticket examiners at the terminus would have turned him out if he had shown his season ticket; and all the tickets sold for the Scotch Express on the 21st are accounted for. Third, how could the murderer have escaped? Fourth, the passengers in the two compartments on each side of the one where the body was found heard no scuffle and no shot fired."

"Are you sure the Scotch Express on the 21st did not stop between London and Brewster?"

"Now that you mention the fact, it did. It was stopped by a signal just outside Pegram. There was a few moments pause, when the line was reported clear, and it went on again. This frequently happens, as there is a branch line beyond Pegram."

Mr. Sherlaw Kombs pondered for a few moments, smoking his pipe silently.

"I assume you want the solution in time for to-morrow's paper?"

"Bless my soul, no. The editor thought if you evolved a theory in a month you would do well."

"My dear sir, I do not deal with theories, but with facts. If you can make it convenient to call here to-morrow at 8:00 a.m. I will give the full particulars early enough for the first edition. There is no use taking up much time in so simple an affair as the Pegram case. Good afternoon, sir."

Mr. Scribbings was too much astonished to return the greeting. He left in a speechless condition, and I saw him go up the street with his hat still in his hand.

Sherlaw Kombs relapsed into his old lounging attitude, with his hands clasped behind his head. The smoke came from his lips in quick puffs at first, then at longer intervals. I saw he was coming to a conclusion, so I said nothing.

Finally he spoke in his most dreamy manner.

"I do not wish to seem to be rushing things at all, Whatson, but I am going out to-night on the Scotch Express. Would you care to accompany me?"

"Bless me!" I said glancing at the clock, "you haven't time, it's after five now."

"Ample time, Whatson---ample," he murmured, without changing his position. "I give myself a minute and half to change slippers and dressing gown for boots and coat, three seconds for hat, twenty-five seconds to the street, forty-two seconds waiting for a hansom, and then seven minutes to the terminus before the express starts. I shall be glad of your company."

I was only too happy to have the privilege of going with him. It was most interesting to watch the workings of so inscrutable a mind. As we drove under the lofty iron roof of the terminus I noticed a look of annoyance pass over his face.

"We are fifteen minutes ahead of our time," he remarked, looking at the big clock. "I dislike having a miscalculation of that sort occur."

The great Scotch Express stood ready for its long journey. The detective tapped one of the guards on the shoulder.

"You have heard of the so-called Pegram mystery, I presume?"

"Certainly, sir. It happened on this very train, sir."

"Really? Is the same carriage still on the train?"

"Well, yes, sir, it is," replied the guard, lowering his voice, "but of course, sir, we have to keep very quiet about it. People wouldn't travel in it, else, sir."

"Doubtless. Do you happen to know if anybody occupies the compartment in which the body was found?"

"A lady and a gentleman, sir; I put 'em in myself, sir."

"Would you further oblige me," said the detective, deftly slipping half-a-sovereign into the hand of the guard, "by going to the window and informing them in an offhand casual sort of way that the tragedy took place in that compartment."

"Certainly, sir."

We followed the guard, and the moment he had imparted his news there was a suppressed scream in the carriage. Instantly a lady came out, followed by a florid-faced gentleman, who scowled at the guard. We entered the now empty compartment, and Kombs said;

"We would like to be alone here until we reach Brewster."

"I'll see to that, sir," answered the guard, locking the door.

When the official moved away, I asked my friend what he expected to find in the carriage that would cast any light on the case.

"Nothing," was his brief reply.

"Then why do you come?"

"Merely to corroborate the conclusions I have already arrived at."

"And might I ask what those conclusions are?"

"Certainly," replied the detective, with a touch of lassitude in his voice. "I beg to call your attention, first, to the fact that this train stands between two platforms, and can be entered from either side. Any man familiar with the station for years would be aware of that fact. This shows how Mr. Kipson entered the train just before it started."

"But the door on this side is locked, I objected, trying it."

"Of course. But every ticket-older carries a key. This accounts for the guard not seeing him, and for the absence of a ticket. Now let me give you some information about the influenza. The patient's temperature rises several degrees above normal, and he has a fever. When the malady has run its course, the temperature falls to three-quarters of a degree below normal. These facts are unknown to you, I imagine, because you are a doctor."

I admitted such was the case.

"Well, the consequence of this fall in temperature is that the convalescent's mind turns toward thoughts of suicide. Then is the time he should be watched by friends. Then was the time Barrie Kipson's friends did not watch him. You remember the 21st, of course. No? It was a most depressing day. Fog all around and mud under foot. Very good. He resolves on suicide. He wishes to be unidentified if possible, but forgets his season ticket. My experience is that a man about to commit a crime always forgets something."

"But how do you account for the disappearance of the money?"

"The money has nothing to do with the matter. If he was a deep

57

man, and knew the stupidness of Scotland Yard, he probably sent the notes to an enemy. If not, they may have been given to a friend. Nothing is more calculated to prepare the mind for self-destruction than the prospect of a night ride on the Scotch Express, and the view from the windows of the train as it passes through the northern part of London is particularly conducive to thoughts of annihilation."

"What became of the weapon?"

"That is just the point on which I wish to satisfy myself. Excuse me for a moment."

Mr. Sherlaw Kombs drew down the window on the right hand side, and examined the top of the casing minutely with a magnifying glass. Presently he heaved a sigh of relief, and drew up the sash.

"Just as I expected," he remarked, speaking more to himself than to me. "There's a slight dent on the top of the window-frame. It is of such a nature as to be made only by the trigger of a pistol falling from the nerveless hand of a suicide. He intended to throw the weapon far out of the window, but had not the strength. It might have fallen into the carriage. As a matter of fact it bounced away from the line and lies among the grass about ten feet six inches from the outside rail. The only question that now remains where the deed was committed, and the exact present position of the pistol reckoned in miles from London, but that, fortunately, is too simple to even need explanation."

"Great Heavens, Sherlaw!" I cried. "How can you call that simple? It seems to me impossible to compute."

We were now flying over Northern London, and the great detective leaned back with every sign of *ennui*, closing his eyes. At last he spoke wearily:

"It is really elementary, Whatson, but I am always willing to oblige a friend. I shall be relieved, however, when you are able to work out the A B C of detection yourself, although I shall never object to helping you with the words of more than three syllables.

"Having made up his mind to commit suicide, Kipson naturally intended to do it before he reached Brewster, because tickets are again examined at that point. When the train began to stop at the signal near Pegram, he came to the false conclusion that it was stopping at Brewster. The fact that the shot was not heard is accounted for by the screech of the air-brake, added to the noise of the train. Probably the whistle was also sounding at the same moment.

"The train being a fast express would stop as near the signal as possible. The air-brake will stop a train in twice its own length. Call it three times in this case. Very well. At three times the length of this train from the signal-post towards London, deducting half the length of the train, as this carriage is in the middle, you will find the pistol."

"Wonderful!" I exclaimed.

"Commonplace," he murmured.

At this moment the whistle sounded shrilly, and we felt the grind of the air-brakes.

"The Pegram signal again," cried Kombs, with something almost like enthusiasm. "This is indeed luck. We will get out here, Whatson, to test the matter."

As the train stopped, we got out on the right-hand side of the line. The engine stood panting impatiently under the red light, which changed to green as I looked at it. As the train moved on with increasing speed, the detective counted the carriages, and noted down the number. It was

59

now dark, with the thin crescent of the moon, hanging in the western sky, throwing a weird half-light on the shining metals. The rear lamps of the train disappeared around the curve and the signal stood at baleful red again.

The black magic of the lonesome night in that strange place impressed me, but the detective was a most practical man. He placed his back against the signal-post and paced up the line with even strides, counting his steps. I walked along the permanent way beside him, silently. At last he stopped and took a tape-line from his pocket. He ran it until the ten feet six inches were unrolled, scanning the figures in the wan light of the new moon. Giving me the end, he placed his knuckles on the metals, motioning me to proceed down the embankment. I stretched out the line, and then sank my hand in the damp grass to mark the spot.

"Good God!" I cried, aghast, "what is this?"

"It is the pistol," said Kombs quietly.

"It was!"

Journalistic London will not soon forget the sensation that was caused by the record of the investigations of Sherlaw Kombs, as printed atlength in the next day's *Evening Blade*.

Would that my story ended here. Alas! Kombs contemptuously turned over the pistol to Scotland Yard. The meddlesome officials, actuated, as I always held, found the name of the seller upon it. They investigated. The seller testified that it had never been in the possession of Mr. Kipson, as far as he knew.

It was sold to a man whose description tallied with a criminal long watched in the police. He was arrested, and turned Queen's evidence in the hope of hanging his pal. It seemed that Mr. Kipson, who was a gloomy, taciturn man, and usually came home in a compartment by himself, thus escaping observation, had been murdered in the lane leading to his house.

After robbing him, the miscreants turned their thoughts towards the disposal of the body---a subject that always occupies a first class criminal mind before the deed is done. They agreed to place it on the line, and have it mangled by the Scotch Express, then nearly due. Before they got the body half-way up the embankment the express came along and stopped. The guard got out and walked along the other side to speak with the engineer. The thought of putting the body into an empty first-class carriage instantly occurred to the murderers. They opened the door with the deceased's key. It is supposed that the pistol dropped when they were hoisting the body in the carriage.

The Queen's evidence dodge didn't work, and Scotland Yard ignobly insulted my friend Sherlaw Kombs by sending him a pass to see the villains hanged.

A Study in Red

A. Donan Coyle   (A. Dewar Willock)

*This is the earliest Sherlockian Christmas parody, though it lacks somewhat in the spirit of Christmas charity, perhaps because it was published in July---July 22, 1892.   It appeared in **Fun,** the major competitor of **Punch**.*

The Sherlockian, Edward S. Lauterbach, checked at the Huntington Library in San Marino, California where he was able to identify A. Dewar Willock as its author.

*A. Dewar Willock (1848---?) wrote a good many humor books.   As his middle name may suggest to some of us who are familiar with other exports of his native land, he was a Scot.   He authored such thigh slappers as **Never Hit a Man Named Sullivan!** (John L. that is), **Ally Sloper's Half Holiday,** and **Taradiddles, A Series of Whackers**.   His book **Rosetty Ends, The Chronicles of a Country Cobbler** has recently been re-issued in paperback.*

This was the fifth Sherlockian parody published. It is indicative of what was to follow that this professional humorist so quickly saw the possibilities in Sherlockian parody.

The parody is also notable because it concentrates on the Sherlockian deduction---nothing else, aside from the detective's name and the title, is taken from the Conan Doyle stories---in fact the two men having dinner in a boarding house introduces a novel feature. The surprise ending, of course, required the omission of all Baker Street detail, but others without this excuse soon followed the precedent.

****

We sat at dinner together. It was Christmas dinner; yet there was little about the decorations of the room or of the table to suggest that the glorious time of peace and dyspepsia and goose and good will was with us.

The remarkable man with whom I was dining was not given to the display of sentimental decorative effects. He was practical, intensely practical.

Everything for him had a meaning, and what did not have a meaning had one promptly manufactured to fit into it.

I might have had my dinner at home, or I might have had it in a hotel or restaurant. My reason for having it here, in a plain lodging house, was because I had been asked; had I not been asked I would not have been here; had I not been here I was have missed one of those remarkable manifestations of logical thought which are so frequently exhibited by the remarkable man.

I may state that we had almost dined. We had had soup, we had had a bit of fish with oyster sauce, we had had roast beef; we had dallied with a small bit of fowl, and we were about to deal with plum pudding. It will at once be seen that our dinner was plain, but substantial. It was a dinner which might have been eaten any day---the plum pudding, perhaps, being the only offering which had been made at the shrine of the festive season.

It had been a silent dinner---comparatively. The remarkable man devoted himself to his meal with that intensity which marked his treatment of everything upon which he entered. Only twice had he spoken during the repast. Once he asked me to pass the mustard, and once he had invited me to have more gravy. I saw he was wrapped in thought, and I knew better than to disturb the train of ideas.

As he lifted the second spoonful of pudding to his lips, I observed him suddenly pause. To one who had studied him less than I had, the emotion which passed over his face would have passed unnoticed, but I was at once aware something had happened. Suddenly he raised his hand, and with his finger and thumb he nervously fingered the side of his mouth; then he withdrew his hand, and allowed it to rest a moment by the side of his plate. The action was suggestive that he had laid down something, but I could see nothing.

He rang the bell with a sharp blow, and the obsequious landlady entered the room.

"Mrs. Smith," said the remarkable man, "you have a young girl concealed somewhere about the basement flat.

"Which I won't deceive you, sir, I have," replied the landlady.

"She is untidy---is down at heel," said the remarkable man.

"I am sorry to say she is."

"She is the slavey---the maid of all work."

"She is."

"And she has red hair."

"She has."

"I knew it. Enough! I leave these lodgings at the end of the week."

"I am so sorry," whimpered the landlady, as she left the room.

I looked across for an explanation of the sudden resolve. For answer the remarkable man motioned me to come to the window. As I approached him he extended his open palm towards me, and I saw laying across it a single red hair!

"It was in the first spoonful of plum pudding," he whispered.

The whole affair was simple, and could be seen at a glance, but to make it clear, and draw the proper deductions, it required the intellect of--

Sherlock Holmes!

OTHER SHERLOCKS

A Trip to the Country

Charles Battell Loomis

Here we have what we will call a Sherlockian pastiche, though only Sherlock's spirit hovers over it. Loomis titled it "A la Sherlock Holmes."

*Two friends take a pleasant trip to the country and meet up with a mystery. It was published in **Puck** on February 20, 1895 and later in 1899, Loomis put it in his **The Four-masted Cat-boat and Other Truthful Tales**.*

Charles Battell Loomis (1861-1911) was a well known humorist and lecturer. Like Conan Doyle, after successfully contributing pieces to magazines, he quit his day job, which was in business, to become a writer full time. His pieces continued to appear in almost every major American journal of the day and his books of humor sold well and seem to be still in demand on the internet.

****

Jones and I recently had occasion to take a drive four or five miles in upper Connecticut. We were met at the station by Farmer Phelps, who soon had us snugly wrapped in robes and speeding over the frozen highway in a sleigh. It was bitter cold weather---the thermometer reading three degrees above zero. We had come up from Philadelphia, and to us the extreme cold was a novelty, which is all we could say for it.

As we rode along, Jones fell to talking about Conan Doyle's detective stories, of which we were both great admirers---the more so as Doyle has declared Philadelphia to be the greatest American city. It turned out that Mr. Phelps was familiar with the **Memoirs of Sherlock Holmes**,and he thought there was some "pretty slick reasonin'" in it.

"My girl," said he, "got the book our er the library an' read it about laud to my woman an' me. But of course this Doyle had it all cut an' dried afore he writ it. He worked backwards an' kivered up his tracks, an' then started afresh, an' it seems more wonderful to the reader than it reely is."

"I don't know," said Jones, "I've done a little in the observation line since I began to read him, and it's astonishing how much a man can learn from inanimate objects, if he uses his eyes and his brain to good purpose. I rarely make a mistake."

Just then we drove past an outbuilding. The door of it was shut. In front of it, in a straight row and equidistant from each other, lay seven cakes of ice, thawed out of a water-pan.

"There," said Jones, "what do we gather from those seven cakes of ice and that closed door?"

I gave it up.

Jones waited impressively a moment, and then said quite glibly, "The man who lives there keeps a flock of twelve hens---not leghorns, but probably Plymouth Rocks or some Asiatic variety. He attends to them himself, and has good success with them, although this is the seventh day of extremely cold weather."

I gazed at him in admiration.

Mr. Phelps said nothing.

"How do you make it all out, Jones," said I.

"Those cakes were evidently formed in a hen's drinking pan. They are solid. The water froze a little all day long, and froze solid in the night. It was thawed out in the morning and left lying there, and the pan was refilled. There are seven cakes of ice, therefore there has been a week of cold weather. They are side by side, from this we gather that it was a methodical man who attended to them, evidently no hireling, but the good man himself. Methodical in little things, methodical in greater ones, and method spells success with hens.

"The thickness of the ice proves that comparatively little water was drunk; consequently he keeps a small flock. Twelve is the model number among advanced poultrymen, and he is evidently one. Then the clearness of the ice shows that the hens were not excitable leghorns, but fowl of a more sluggish kind, although whether Plymouth Rocks or Brahmas or Langshans I cannot say. Leghorns are so wild that they are apt to stampede through the water and roil it. The closed door shows he has the good sense to keep them shut up in cold weather.

"To sum up, then, this wide-awake poultryman has had wonderful success, in spite of a week of exceptionally cold weather, from his flock of a dozen hens of some large breed. How's that, Mr. Phelps? Isn't it almost equal to Doyle?"

"Yes, but not accordin' to Hoyle, ez ye might say," said he. "Your reasonin' is good, but it ain't quite borne about by the fac's. In the fust place, this is the fust reel cold day we've had this winter. Secon'ly, they ain't no boss to the place, fer she's a woman. Thirdly, my haouse is the nex' one to this, an' my boy an' hers hez be'n makin' those ice-cakes fer fun in some old cream pans. Don't take too long to freeze solid in this weather, An' las'ly, it ain't a hen-haouse, but an ice-haouse."

The sun rode with unusual quietness through the heavens. We heard no song of bird. The winds went whist. All nature was silent.

So was Jones.

The Whims of Erasmus Tuttlebury

W. Carter Platts

*W. Carter Platts, about whom little is known, wrote a series of books about an Erasmus Tuttlebury. Chapter thirteen of **The Whims of Erasmus** (1902) is titled "Mr. Sherlock Holmes Tuttlebury."*

This very rare parody/pastiche is pretty old fashioned and corny and begins like an old vaudeville routine of George Burns and Gracie Allen. I dug it out at The British Library where it had lain undisturbed for many years.

****

Having successfullycaptured the fancy of the British public, Sir Conan Doyle's famous hero, rather late in the day, perhaps, scooped Mr. Tuttlebury into his band of worshipers.

Hitherto Sherlock Holmes had been but a name to Erasmus Tuttlebury; now that, through a chance volume placed in the latter's hands, he had become intimate with the great detective's marvelous adventures, Sherlock Holmes had become a burning personality---a fascinating reality perched upon a massive pedestal, round which Mr. Tuttlebury crept reverently in his stocking feet, so to speak, as with uplifted eyes he gazed enviously at the great glorious halo of popularity that flamed around the head of the people's pet, and figuratively, dared to wonder if it might not fit himself---that is, of course, if it were filed down to six-and-seven-eighths size.

"Humph! Finest literary creation of the nineteenth century!" he observed enthusiastically to Mrs. Tuttlebury one evening as he closed the book.

"Who?---what?" inquired Mrs. Tuttlebury, dropping half a dozen stitches in her knitting.

"Sherlock Holmes."

"I've some sort of idea that I've heard that name before, Erasmus," chirped Mrs. Tuttlebury. "Oh, I know now! It was in the pantomime of 'Robinson Crusoe'---one of the scenes was laid in 'Sherlock Holmes's cupboard', wasn't it?"

"Cupboard? Sher---? Jee-rusalem, Maria, you mean 'Davy Jones's Locker!'"

"Well, I knew there was a 'lock' and a 'Holmes' or a 'Jones' or something in it!" murmured Mrs. Tuttlebury with a triumphant smile. "Well, dear, who was this Sherlock Jones who had the finest literary cupboard in the last century?"

"Holmes, Maria!---finest literary creation!" cried Tuttlebury. "He was the ideal of cultivated observation---sort of double-barreled human microscope with an X-ray attachment for seeing what was going on in the dark through a brick wall! He was the perfection of inference and the grand master of the science of deduction!"

"What's deduction, Erasmus?"

"Taking---cr---taking one thing from another, Maria."

"Oh, I understand, lisped Mrs. Tuttlebury, cheerfully; "but I didn't recognize it by that name; we always used to call it simple subtraction when I was a girl."

"I wasn't talking about sums," growled Tuttlebury, impatiently. "I was referring to ideas. You see it's like this---suppose I borrow Johnson's copy of **Inquire Within.** There's some trifling peculiarity--- say, an accidental ink-blot---about the book which catches my attention, and from that apparently insignificant point I work back logically, step by step, from effect to cause, through a chain of sequences, until I know what year it was that Johnson's boy had the measles!"

"I don't see how you could possibly do that," ventured Mrs. Tuttlebury.

"It's possible enough."

"But, how can it be possible," persisted Mrs. Tuttlebury, "when he never had the measles! Mrs. Johnson told me so herself. Now, if you'd said whooping-cough---"

"But it was only a supposititious case---entirely imaginary," jerked in Mr. Tuttlebury.

"Imaginary?" echoed Mrs. Tuttlebury, indignantly. "It was a most serious case, and they had to take the poor little chap on to the moors seven times and wheel him down to smell at the gasworks four times before he was better! Mrs. Johnson's mother says it was the worst kind of whooping-cough---"

"Who the dickens was talking about whooping-cough?" roared Mr. Tuttlebury.

"I was," replied Mrs. Tuttlebury, meekly; "and it seems to me, Erasmus, that there's something out at the gathers somewhere about your fancy science that can logically tell from a blot in somebody's book

72

when somebody else had the measles that never had it, and can't tell what I'm talking about when I'm saying it all the time!"

Tuttlebury maintained a brilliant silence for some time after that, while Mrs. Tuttlebury contentedly went on knitting. But his brain was not inactive. He was determined to give her a convincing exposition of the science of deduction; and he watched her narrowly, waiting to pounce upon the first opportunity. It came. Mrs. Tuttlebury, lost in thought, paused in her knitting. Her gaze traveled from one object to another, and became fixed there. Tuttlebury turned on the intelligence department of his brain and set it deducting full steam ahead.

"Yes, they spread out over a good deal of ground," he observed, quite casual like. And Mrs. Tuttlebury dropped her jaw and seventeen stitches in her knitting, as she shot bolt upright in her chair, and gasped,---

"Good gracious, Erasmus! However did you know what I was thinking about?"

"Pooh!" sniffed Tuttlebury, loftily, airily giving space a gentle back-hander with his left hand, "easy enough---mere child's play! They do spread over a lot of ground, eh?"

"Yes," assented Mrs. Tuttlebury, in wonder.

"As a matter of fact," went on Tuttlebury, with refreshing cock-suredness, "they cover nearly an acre."

"Nearly a---" gasped Mrs. Tuttlebury incredibly.

"Yes," he went on serenely, "nearly an acre. To be precise, an acre all but half a rood and thirty-four yards; I've seen the exact measurements today. Now, I'll just show you how I came to know that

73

you were thinking of the new district hospital buildings!"

"But I wasn't thinking of the hospital buildings! I---I---I was only thinking what big feet you got, Erasmus!" blurted out Mrs. Tuttlebury. And when you said they covered an acre all but---"

"You were not thinking of the hospital buildings?"

"No."

"Then you ought to have been doing so, Maria!" snorted Tuttlebury, emphatically. "I saw you notice that mud mark on the carpet, and then you turned your eyes from that to my boots, which ought to have made you ask yourself where I'd got the mud, and that should have caused you to remember that I'd told you. I'd been this afternoon to see the buildings in course of erection, and that the ground was very dirty, and that ought to have set you thinking of the buildings. It's all clear as daylight---couldn't be plainer! It's not the science of deduction that's at fault; it's you Maria!"

And Mrs. Tuttlebury picked up the stitches in her knitting while Mr. Tuttlebury picked up his book.

The following evening Mr. Tuttlebury, who had been detained at his office at Leeds beyond his usual time, burst into the house in a state of white-hot indignation.

"My goodness, Erasmus!   Whatever's the matter?" cried Mrs.Tuttlebury, in alarm.

"Matter!"he exclaimed. "Outrage is the matter! A dastardly outrage has been committed almost at our gate! And the victim an innocent child, too! You know Farmer Gosenford's man, Jim---the one who came to look after our horse while we had him? Well, I came across his little girl close to our gate, crying like---like watering cans---said her mammy had sent her down to 'The Cow and Kettle' with fourpence in a jug for a quart of vinegar, and as she came back past the gap in the hedge just down the road, somebody suddenly clapped one hand over her eyes, and grabbed the jug with the other, and swigged off the whole quart, before thrusting the empty jug back into her hand, and giving her a shove along, so that she had no chance of recognizing her assailant in the dark! Cowardly scamp! I hope he'll suffer the pangs of remorse!"

"I should think he's more likely to suffer the pangs of stomach-ache first. A quart of vinegar!---good gracious!" ejaculated Mrs. Tuttlebury, when her husband suddenly relaxing into something approaching a grin, hurriedly explained,---

"Well, it wasn't vinegar. You see, Maria, Jim told me in confidence once that his wife was a bit of a tartar---'holy terror' he called her---and bossed the show, so that the poor beggar has hardly a soul to call his own; and certainly has no money. She takes jolly good care of that---says he isn't to be trusted with any. Won't let him show his face inside a public-house---says if he must have beer he shall have it at home, when he can't rob his family by running up a score. So about every other evening she sends the girl to 'The Cow and Kettle' for a quart of beer, but for fear the child might get into the way of tasting on the road, she's a private understanding with the landlord that it's to be called 'vinegar,' see?"

"Yes. And what did you do Erasmus?"

"Do? Gave the child fourpence to enable her to go back for some more, and told her to tell her father I'd make it in my way to see the police and put the affair in their hands. And so I will. I'll---But if I do, they'll only make a mess of it. Crustaceous crumpets, Maria, I'll follow this thing up myself! Of all the despicable, sneaking villainies, robbing a kid is about the lowest form! But I'll track the vile brute! Let him beware, for Mr. Sherlock Holmes-Tuttlebury is on his trail!"

"It must have been some low, ignorant tramp! Nobody else would do such a thing!"cried Mrs. Tuttlebury, conclusively.

"My dear, Maria, when shall I ever get you to look at things reasonably," expostulated Mr. Sherlock Holmes-Tuttlebury. "Now the case presents features absolutely staring you in the face, which makes it utterly impossible that your theory can be correct. Let us marshal the facts so far as we know them--- The villainous skunk who committed the outrage was in possession of the knowledge that the child was coming along with the jug, or he would not have been waiting for her. He knew that the jug did not contain vinegar, or he wouldn't have drunk it. It is also perfectly clear that it wasn't money he was in want of, or he'd have waylaid the child on her way to 'The Cow and Kettle,' and collared the coppers. Then too, it's equally clear that the rascal was a man with some reputation for gentility to maintain; that it was solely beer he wanted, and wouldn't risk his reputation by being seen in a local public-house; therefore, he must be someone well known in this neighborhood, and who has at present no beer in his own house."

"It's wonderful however you do it, Erasmus!" gasped Mrs. Tuttlebury, in admiring wonder.

"Tut. tut! It's easy enough. The case is so straightforward so far that it cannot admit of a possible doubt. We have got the field of our investigation narrowed considerably. I must think!"returned Tuttlebury, as he puckered his brows, and stared hard at the back of the fireplace.

When he failed to find the despicable ruffian up the chimney, so to speak, he turned his gaze towards the ceiling, and hunted as unsuccessfully for him round the cornice.

76

"Haven't you got any further yet, Erasmus? Haven't you found out who did it?" asked Mrs. Tuttlebury at length.

"N-o-o," muttered Mr. Sherlock Holmes-Tuttlebury, with cautious deliberation. I've been over the whole line of argument again, and there isn't a flaw in it---not the slightest shadow of room for doubt. I've hunted down the skulking cur into a corner, but I can't just---Good heavens, Maria!" he gasped, as his face suddenly turned a sickly green, and the cold sweat of anguish poured out from his forehead. "We've no beer in the house!---well-known local man!---reputation to maintain!---must have known the beastly stuff wasn't vinegar!---why, that's me!"

"You?" screamed Mrs. Tuttlebury.

"There's nobody else to fit the specification, and I can't find a flaw in the evidence. It's---"

"Jim, Farmer Gosenford's man, to see you particular, sir!" announced the servant, at that moment. And without any ceremony, the man shoved himself awkwardly into the room.

"Mr. Tuttlebury," he began, vigorously wiping the perspiration of embarrassment from his face, "I've come---thank yer on account of my little girl. But for mercy's sake, don't ye put this job into t' police hands! It's---it's--- Well, ye know, what I told yer about my missus sending for t' beer? Well---er---well, I might as well tell yer all. Whenever she sends for any she allus has t' first sup, an' of course, when there's nobut a quart t' start wi' it doesn't give me 'at comes last a fair first sup; an' I waited in t' hedge for my little lass, an' I had t' first sup, without letting her know who it was, so 'at when she got home and told my missus perhaps she send her for some more. An' that's all about it, an' I'll take it very kindly if ye'll say nowt about it. For if it got to my missus's ears she'd wash my head for me, an' no mistake!"

After Jim had gone, Mr. and Mrs. Tuttlebury stood staring blankly at one another. Then, with a sudden hissing growl, like a dog makes when he is about to play at being a rat-trap on the calf of your leg, Tuttlebury snatched up *The Adventures of Sherlock Holmes* from the table, and hurled it into the fire.

"Maria," he observed at breakfast the following morning, "I've come to the conclusion that Sherlock Holmes is a very much over-rated character. The science of deduction has its limitations and its dangers, and to avoid these it is perhaps as well when you see shells to content yourself with merely guessing eggs, without tempting Fate by foolishly attempting to figure out with the sole aid of a bit of shell and a streak of spilled yoke, the pedigree of the hen that laid them to five points of decimals."

MOCKING SHERLOCKHOLMES

A Double-Barrelled Mystery

Mark Twain

Mark Twain, (Samuel Clemens) (1835-1910) subtitled this short novelette, "We ought never to do wrong when people are looking.

Ellery Queen claimed that in this dark tale, published in 1902, Mark Twain was doing a take-off on all detective stories. Maybe so.

The beginning two-thirds of the piece is stuffed full of the passion and revenge, violence, and a wild chase around the world. Here's a sample.

"Get up and dress!"

She obeyed---as always, without a word. He led her half a mile from the house, and proceeded to lash her to a tree by the side of the public road; and succeeded, she screaming and struggling. He gagged her then, struck her across the face with his cowhide, and set his bloodhounds on her. Then tore the clothes off her, and she was naked.

Then he says good bye and lets her there to languish.

So much for satiric melodrama. You may, like me, find it a little too realistic and gamey to seem like much fun.

But finally the tale settles down in a mining camp village in California where a nephew of Sherlock Holmes lives. A murder occurs just after Uncle Sherlock pays his nephew a visit. (He doesn't solve it.) If it makes you feel any better, the victim is the fellow who tied the woman to the tree, and the murderer is put in jail and then allowed to escape since everyone feels he did the public a real service.

But on Holmes's arrival, the more wickedly humorous Mark Twain emerges.

****

Two afternoons later the village was electrified with an immense sensation. A grave and dignified foreigner of distinguished bearing and appearance had arrived at the tavern, and entered his formidable name upon the register:

Sherlock Holmes!

The news buzzed from cabin to cabin, from claim to claim, tools were dropped, and the town swarmed toward the center of interest. A man passing out at the northern end of the village shouted it to Pat Riley, whose claim was the next one to Flint Buckner's.

At that time Fetlock Jones seemed to turn sick. He muttered to himself: Uncle *Sherlock!* The mean luck of it! ---that he should come just when . . . .

He dropped into a reverie, and presently said to himself: "But what's the use of being afraid of him? Anybody that knows him the way I do knows he can't detect a crime except where he plans it all out beforehand and arranges the clues and hires some fellow to commit it according to instructions. . . . Now there ain't going to *be* any clues this time --- so, what show has he got? None at all. No, sir; everything's ready. If I was to risk putting it off --- No, I won't run any risk like that. Flint Buckner goes out of the world tonight, for sure."

Then another trouble presented itself. "Uncle Sherlock'll be wanting to talk home matters with me this evening and how am I going to get rid of him, for I've got to be at my cabin for a minute or two about eight o'clock?" This was an awkward matter, and cost him much thought. But he found a way to beat the difficulty.

"We'll go for a walk, and I'll leave him in the road a minute, so that he won't see what it is I do; the best way to throw a detective off the track, anyway, is to have him along when you are preparing the thing. Yes, that's the safest --- I'll take him with me."

Meanwhile the road in front of the tavern was blocked with villagers waiting and hoping for a glimpse of the great man. But he kept in his room, and did not appear. None but Wells-Fargo man, Ferguson, Jake Parker, the blacksmith, and Ham Sandwich the miner had any luck. These enthusiastic admirers of the great scientific detective hired the tavern's retained baggage-lockup, which looks into the detective's room across a little alleyway ten or twelve feet wide, ambushed themselves in it, and cut some peepholes in the window blind. Mr. Holmes's blinds were down; but by and by he raised them.

It gave the spies a hair-lifting but pleasurable thrill to find themselves face to face with the Extraordinary Man who had filled the world with the fame of his more than human ingenuities. There he sat --- not a myth, not a shadow, but real, alive, compact of substance, and almost within touching distance with the hand.

"Look at that head!" said Ferguson, in an awed voice. "By gracious *that's* a head!"

"You bet!" said the blacksmith, with deep reverence. "Look at his nose! Look at his eyes! Intellect? Just a battery of it."

81

"And that paleness," said Ham Sandwich. "Comes from thought ---
that's what it comes from. Hell! Duffers like us don't know what real
thought *is.* "

"No more we don't," said Ferguson. "What we take for thinking is
just blubber and slush."

"Right you are, Wells-Fargo. And look at that frown --- that's *deep*
thinking --- away down, down, forty fathoms into the bowels of things.
He's on the track of something."

"Well, he is, and don't you forget it. Say --- look at that awful
gravity --- look at that pallid solemness --- there ain't any corpse can lay
over it."

"No sir, not for dollars! And it's his'n by hereditary rights, too; he's
been dead four times already, and there's history for it. Three times
natural, once by accident. I've heard he smells damp and cold, like a
grave. And he ---"

"Sh! Watch him! There --- he's got his thumb on the bump on the
near corner of his forehead, and his forefinger on the off one. His think
works is just *a-grinding* now, you bet your other shirt."

"That's so. And now he's gazing up toward heaven and stroking his
chin slow, and ---"

"Now he has rose up standing, and is putting his clues together on
his left fingers with his right finger. See? He touches the forefinger ---
now middle finger --- now ring finger ---"

"Stuck!"

82

"Look at him scowl! He can't seem to make out *that* clue. So he---"

"See him smile --- like a tiger --- and tally off the other fingers like nothing! He's got it, boys; he's got it sure!"

"Well I should *say!* I'd hate to be in that man's place that he's after."

Mr. Holmes drew a table to the window, sat down with his back to the spies, and proceeded to write. The spies withdrew their eyes from the peepholes, lit their pipes, and settled themselves for a comfortable smoke and talk. Ferguson said with conviction:

"Boys, it's no use talking, he's a wonder! he's got the signs of it all over him."

"You hain't ever said a truer word than that, Wells-Fargo," said Jake Parker.

Ferguson sat silently, then he murmured, with deep awe in his voice:

"I wonder if God made him."

There was no response for a moment; then Ham Sandwich said reverently:

"Not all at one time, I reckon."

Mr. Dooley's Observations

Finley Peter Dunne

Finley Peter Dunne, (1867-1937) grew up in the Irish Catholic community on the west side of Chicago. He was an experienced newspaperman when he invented Mr. Dooley to satirize Chicago politics and life in general. This one he just called "Sherlock Holmes."

Dunne had Mr. Dooley running a saloon out on the West Side Chicago's Archer Road. His weekly observations were made to his customer Hennesey on a variety of current topics, including Sherlock Holmes.

Dooley claimed that the hero of the Battle of Manila Bay, Admiral Dewey, was a cousin whose name had been Americanized. Dooley gained national attention by correctly describing how the Manila Bay naval battle went, days before the full newspaper accounts arrived. Dooley soon became as much a craze in turn of the century America as Sherlock Holmes.

Don't be put off by the dialect spelling.

"Dorsey and Dugan are havin' throuble, said Mr. Hennessy.

"What about?" asked Mr. Dooley.

"Dorsey," said Mr. Hennessy, "says Dugan stole his dog. They had a party at Dorsey's an' Dorsey heard a noise in th' back yard an' wint out an' see Dugan makin' off with his bull tarryer."

"Ye say he see him do it?"

"Yis, he see him do it."

"Well," said Mr. Dooley, "twad baffle th' injinooty iv a Sherlock Holmes."

"Who's Sherlock Holmes?"

"He's th' gr-greatest detictive that iver was in a story book."

"I've been r-readin' about him an' if I was a criminal, which I wud be if I had to wurruk f'r a livin', an' Sherlock Holmes got afther me, I'd go sthraight to th' station an' give mesilf up. I'd lay th' goods on th' desk an' say: 'Sargent, put me down in the hard cage. Sherlock Holmes has jus' see a man go by in a cab with a Newfoundland dog an' he knows I took the spoons.'"

"Ye see, he ain't th' ordh'nry fly cop like Mulcahy that always runs in th' Schmidt boy f'r iviry crime rayported fr'm stealin' a ham to forgin' a check in the full knowledge that someday he'll get him f'r th' right thing."

"No, sir; he's an injanyous man that can put two an' two together an' make eight of thim. He applies his brain to crime, d'ye mind, an' divvie th' crime, no mather how cunnin' it is, will escape him."

"We'll suppose, Hinnissy, that I'm Sherlock Holmes. I'm settin' here in me little parlor wearin' a dhressin' gown an' now an' thin pokin' mesilf full iv morpheen. Here we are. Ye come in. 'Good-mornin',Watson."

"I ain't Watson," said Mr. Hennessy, "I'm Hinnissy."

"Ah," said Mr. Dooley, "I thought I'd wring it fr'm ye. Perhaps ye'd like to know how I guessed ye had come in. "T'is very simple. On'y a mather iv observation. I heerd ye'er step, I seen ye'er refliction in th' lookin' glass; ye spoke to me. I put these things together with me thrained faculty f'r observation an' deduction, d'ye mind. Says I to mesilf: This must be Hinnissy."

"But mind ye, th' chain iv circumstances is not complete. It might be some wan disguised as ye. So says I to mesilf: 'I will throw this newcome, whoiver he is, off his guard, be callin' him be a sthrange name!' Ye wuddn't feel complimented, Hinnissy, if ye knew who Watson is. Watson knows even less than ye do. He don't know anything, an' anything he knows is wrong. He has to look up his name in th' parish raygisther before he can speak to himsilf. He's a gr-reat frind iv Sherlock Holmes an' if Sherlock Holmes iver loses him, he'll find him in the nearest asylum f'r th' feeble-minded."

"But I surprised ye'er secret out iv ye. thrown off ye'er guard be me innocent question, ye popped out, "I'm Hinnissy,' an' in a flash I guessed who ye were. Be th' same process iv raisonin' be deduction, I can tell ye that ye were home las' night in bed, that ye're on ye'er way to wurruk, an' that ye'er salary is two dollars a day. I know ye were at home between ilivin an' sivin, bar Pathrick's night, an' ye'er wife hasn't been in lookin' f'r ye. I know ye'er on ye'er way to wurruk because I heerd ye'er dinner pail jingle as ye stepped softly in. I know ye get two dollars a day because ye tol' me ye get three an' I deducted thirty-three an' wan third per cent f'r police license. 'Tis ver simple. Ar-re those shoes ye have on ye'er feet? Be hivins I thought so."

"Simple," said Mr. Hennessy scornfully; "'tis foolish."

"Nivir mind," said Mr. Dooley. "Pass the dope, Watson. Now bein' full iv th' cillybrated Chow-Sooey brand, I addhress me keen mind to th' discussion iv th' case iv Dorsey's dog. Watson, look out iv th' window an' see if that's a cab goin' by ringin' a gong. A throlley car? So much th' betther. My observation told me it was not a balloon or a comet or a reindeer. Ye ar're a gr-reat help to me, Watson. Pass th' dope.

"Was there a dog on th' car? No? That simplifies th' thing. I had an idee th' dog might have gone to wurruk. He was a bull-tarryer, ye say. D'ye know anything about his parents? Be Mulligan's Sloppy Weather out iv Hannigan's Diana iv th' Slough? Was ayether iv thim seen in th' neighborhood th' night iv th' plant? No? Thin it is not, as many might suppose, a case of abduction. What were th' habits iv Dorsey's coyote? Was he a dog that dhrank? Did he go out at nights? Was he payin' anny particular attintions to anny iv th' neighbors? Was he baffled in love? Ar-re his accounts sthraight? Had Dorsey said anything to him that wud've made him despondent? Ye say no. He led a dog's life but seemed to be happy. Thin 'tis plainly not a case of suicide.

"I'm gettin' up close to th' criminals. Another shot iv th mad mixture. Wait till I can find a place in th' ar-rm. There ye ar-re. Well, Watson, what d'ye make iv it?"

"If ye mane me, Dugan stole th' dog."

"Not so fast," said Mr. Dooley. "Like all men iv small minds ye make ye'ers up readily. Th' smaller th' mind, th' aisier 'tis made up. Ye'ers is like a blanket on th' flure before th' fire. All ye have to do to make it up is to lave it. Mine is like a large double bed, an' afther I've been tossin' in it, 'tis no aisy job to make it up. I will puncture me tire with th' fav'rite flower iv Chinnytown an' go on."

87

"We know now that the dog did not elope, that he didn't commit suicide an' that he was not kidnapped be his rayturnin' parents. So far so good. Now I'll tell ye who stole th' dog. Yesterday afthernoon I see a suspicious lookin' man goin' down th' street. I say he was suspicious lookin' because he was disguised an' looked ivry wan in the face. He had no dog with him. A damning circumstance, Watson, because whin he'd stolen th' dog he niver wud've takin' it down near Dorsey''s house. Ye wuddn't notice the facts because ye-er mind while feeble is unthrained. His coat collar was turned up an' he was whistlin' to himself, a habit iv dog fanciers. As he wint be Hogan's house he did not look around or change his gait or otherwise do anythin' wrong, facts in thimselves that proved to me cultivated intelligence that he was guilty. I followed him in me mind's eye to his home an' there chained to th' bed leg is Dorsey's dog. Th' name of th' criminal is P. X. O'Hannigan, an' he lives at twenty-wan hundhred an' ninety-nine South Halsted sthreet, top flat, rear, a plumber be pro-fission. Officer, arrest that man!"

"That's all right," said Mr. Hennessy; "but Dugan rayturned th' dog las' night."

"Oh, thin," said Mr. Dooley, calmly, "this is not a case iv Sherlock Holmes but wan f'r the polis. That's the throuble, Hinnissy, with th' detective iv th' story. Nawthin' happins in real life that's complicated enough f're him.

"If th' presidint iv th' Epworth League was a safe-blower be night th' man that'd catch him'd be a la-ad with gr-reat powers iv observation an thrained habit iv reasonin.'

"But crime, Hinnissy is th' pursoot iv th' simple-minded---that is catchable crime is a pursoot iv th' simple-minded. Th' other kind, th' uncatchable kind that is took up by men iv intellect is called high finance."

"I've known many criminals in me time, an' some iv thim was fine men an' very happy in their home life, an' a more simple, pasth-ral people I nivir knew. Wan iv the ablest bank robbers iv th' country used to live near me---he owned a flat buildin'---an' before he'd turn in to bed afther rayturnin' fr'm his night's wurruk, he'd go out in th' shed an' chop th' wood. He always wint in th' house through a thransom f'r fear iv wakin' his wife who was a delicate woman an' a shop lifter. An' I tell ye he was a man without guile, an he wint about his jooties as modestly as ye go about ye'ers. I don't think in th' long run he made much more thin ye do. Wanst in a while, he'd get hold iv a good bunch iv money, but manny other times afther dhrillin' all night through a steel dure, all he'd find'd be a short crisp note fr'm th' presidint iv th' bank. He was often discouraged, an' he tol' me wanst if he had an income iv forty dollars a month, he'd retire fr'm business an' settle down on a farm.

"No sir, criminals is th' simplist crather in th' wide wurruld---innocent, sthraight-forward, dangerous people, that haven't sinse enough to be honest or prosperous. Th' extent iv their schamin' is to break a lock in a dure or sweep a handful iv change fr'm a counter or dhrill a hole in a safe or adminisher th' strong arm to a tired man takin' home his load. There are no mysteryous crimes excipt thim that happens to be. Th' ordh'nry crook, Hinnissy, goes around ringin' a bell an disthributin' hand-bills announcin' his business. He always breaks through a window instead iv goin' through an open dure, an afther he's done anything that he thinks is commindable, he goes to a neighborin' liquor saloon, an stands on th' pool table and confides th' secret to ivrybody within sound iv his voice."

"That's why Mulligan is a betther detective thin Sherlock Holmes or me. He can't put two an' two together an' he has no powers iv deduction, but he's a hard dhrinker an a fine sleuth.

"Sherlock Holmes nivir wud've caught that frind iv mine. Whin th'safe iv th' Ninth National Bank was blowed, he wud have put two an' two together an arristed me. But me frind wint away lavin' a hat an' a pair iv cuffs marked with his name in th' safe, an' th' polis combined these discoveries with th' well known fact that Muggins was a notoryous safe blower an' they took him in. They found him down th' sthreet thryin' to sell a bushel basket full iv Alley L stock.

"I told ye he was a simple man. He ralized his ambition f'r an agracoolchral life. They give him th' care iv th' cows at Joliet."

"Did he rayform?" asked Mr. Hennessey.

"No," said Mr. Dooley, "he escaped. "An'th way he got out wud baffle th' injinooty iv a Sherlock Holmes."

"How did he do it?" asked Hennessey.

"He climbed over th' wall," said Mr. Dooley.

Scotland Yard Responds

Sir Basil Thomson

It must irritate Scotland Yarders to be asked about Sherlock Holmes so often. Once at a meeting where it occurred, I observed a Chief Inspector respond with a kind of patient tolerance, out of politeness, not wishing to insult his hosts.

At least four Scotland Yarders, somewhat less restrained, have written out their views. As early as 1903, Sir Robert Anderson, Head of the Criminal Investigation Department (CID) of Scotland Yard, had already expressed himself on the subject in print, in 1905 John Sweeny, Detective Inspector of Scotland Yard, wrote much along the same lines, and much later in 1974, so too did Sir Robert Mark, Commissioner of Police for London. And no doubt there were others.

Their basic argument is that Sir Arthur Conan Doyle cooked the books.

But Sir Basil Thomson is the only one we know of who also expressed his views through Sherlockian parody. His remarks may be found in Wilfred Whitten (John O'London) **Unposted Letters Concerning Life & Literature.**

During World War I, Sir Basil Thompson, Chief of the Special Department of Scotland Yard gave a speech to the Royal Society of Arts, and included this take on Sherlockian methods.

****

I have often asked myself, when I have had a particularly difficult problem to solve, what Sherlock Holmes would have done in such a case. I imagine him, for instance, examining with his piercing gaze, a bit of mud on a gate---the only clue to a crime.

I see him go to a cupboard where he keeps samples of the mud of every street in London. He scrutinizes each sample intently, and ponders for a space of a few seconds. Presently he turns to Dr. Watson, who is standing in open-mouthed wonder beside him, and, with a significant puff at his pipe, says casually---

"Watson---I am now going out to arrest the Archbishop of Canterbury!"

Picklock Holes and The Samovar Diamond

Rudolph Chambers Lehmann

*Picklock Holes is a ricochet Sherlock Holmes, a really bent detective. He arrived in **Punch** on August 12, 1893. The series of his adventures continued for eight episodes, ending with the presumed death of Sherlock at Reichenbach. Picklock Holes suffers a similar fate in the Serpentine, but clasped in the arms of his nemesis, Sherlock Holmes. Three weeks after the return of Sherlock Holmes in 1903, the first of eight new adventures of Picklock Holes appeared in **Punch,** titled "Picky Back." And in 1918, a last single episode parallels what the author thought was the last bow of Sherlock Holmes.*

Picklock Holes is bad, bad, bad. He is a four-flusher and charlatan, a liar who manufactures clues, plants evidence so he can later solve the crime, always claims he was just about to say whatever brilliant comment anyone else makes, and offers wild deductions with ludicrous and convoluted logic. Only missing in this episode, but found in another, is Picklock hiring criminals who he can later catch.

But in this episode he provides us with a new and interesting word game.

The writer, Rudolph Chambers Lehmann (1856-1929), was a journalist and Liberal party member of Parliament. Two collections of Picklock Holes adventures were published by the Aspen Press of Tom

93

and Enid Schantz.

****

Everybody must remember the apparently causeless panic that seized the various European governments only a few years ago.

It was the dead season. Members of Parliament were all disporting themselves on the various grouse-moors which they specially reserved for that August legislative body in order that there may be no lack of accuracy in the articles of those who imagine that the 12th of August brings to every M. P. a yearning for the scent of heather and the sound of breach-loading guns.

Suddenly, and without any warning, a great fear spread through Europe. Nobody seemed able to state precisely how it began. There were, of course, some who attributed it to an after-dinner speech made by the German Emperor at the annual banquet of the Bosewitzers, the famous Cuirassier regiment of which the Grand Duke of Schnupftuchstein is the honorary commanding officer. Others again saw in it the influence of M. Paul Deroulede, while yet a third party attribute it with an equal assumption of certainty to the fact that Austria had recently forbidden the import of Servian pigs.

They were all wrong.

The time has come when the truth must be known. The story I am about to tell will show my extraordinary friend, Picklock Holes, on an even higher pinnacle of unmatchable acumen than that which fame has hitherto assigned to him. He may be vexed when he reads my narrative of his triumphs, for he is as modest as he is inductive, but I am determined that, at whatever cost, the story shall be made public.

It was on one of those delightful evenings for which our English

94

summer is famous that Holes and I were as usual sitting together and conversing as to the best methods of inferring an archbishop from a hatband and a commander-in-chief from a penny-whistle. I had put forward several plans which appeared to me to be satisfactory, but Holes had scouted them one after another with cold impassivity which had not failed to impress me, accustomed though I was to the great man's exhibition of it.

"Here, said Holes eventually, "are the necessary steps. Hatband, bandmaster, mastermind, mind-your-eye, eyeball, ball-bearing, bear-leader, Leda and the Swan, swan-bill, bill-post, post-cart, cart-road, roadway, Weybridge, bridge-arch, archbishop.

"The inference of a commander-in-chief is even easier. You have only to assume that a penny-whistle has been found lying on the Horse-Guards Parade by the Colonel of the Scots Guards and carried by him to the office of the Secretary of the State of War. Thereupon you subdivide the number of drummer boys in a regiment of Goorkhas by the capital value of a sergeant's retiring pension, and---"

But the rest of the marvelous piece of concise reasoning must remain forever a secret, for at this moment a bugle call disturbed the stillness of the summer night, and Holes immediately paused.

"What can that mean?" I asked, in some alarm, for Camberwell (our meeting place) is an essentially unmilitary district, and I could not account for this strange and awe-inspiring musical demonstration.

"Hush," said Holes, with perfect composure. "It is the agreed signal. Listen. The great Samovar diamond, the most brilliant jewel in the turquoise crown of Hungary, has been lost. The Emperor of Austria is in despair. Next week, he is due at Pesth, but he cannot appear before the fierce and haughty Magyars in a crown deprived of the decoration that all Hungary looks upon as symbolic of the national existence.

95

"A riot in Pesth at this moment would shake the Austro-Hungarian Empire to its foundations. With it the Triple Alliance would crumble into dust, and the peace of Europe would not be worth an hour's purchase. It is, therefore, imperative before the dawn of the next Monday the diamond should be restored to its wonted setting."

"My dear Holes," I said, "this is more terrible than I thought. Have they appealed to you, as usual, after exhausting all the native talent?"

"My dear Potson," replied my friend, "you ask too much. Let it suffice that I have been consulted, and that the determination of the question of peace or war lies in these hands." And with these words the arch-detective spread before my eyes those long, sinewy, and meditative fingers which had so often excited my admiration.

Our preparations for departure to Hungary were soon made. I hardly know why I accompanied Holes. It seemed somehow to be the usual thing that I should be present at all his feats. I thought he looked for my company, though his undemonstrative nature would never have suffered him to betray any annoyance had I remained absent. I judged it best not to disturb the even current of his investigations by departing from established precedent. I therefore departed from London---my only alternative. Just as we were setting out, Holes stopped me with a warning gesture.

"Have you brought the clue with you?" he asked.

"What clue?"

"Oh," he answered, rather testily, "any clue you like, so long as it=s a clue. A torn scrap of paper with writing on it, a foot-print in the mud, a broken chair, a soiled overcoat---it really doesn't matter what it is, but a clue of some kind we must have."

"Of course, of course," I said, in soothing tones. "How stupid of me to forget it. Will this do?" I continued, picking up a piece of faded green ribbon which happened to be lying on the pavement.

"The very thing," said Holes pocketing it, and so we started.

Our first visit on arriving in Pesth was to the Emperor-King, who was living incognito in a small back alley of the Hungarian capital. We cheered the monarch's heart and proceeded to call on the leader of the opposition in the Hungarian Diet. He was a stern man of some fifty summers, dressed in the national costume. We found him at supper.

Holes was the first to speak. "Sir," he said, "resistance is useless. Your schemes have been discovered. All that is left for you is to throw yourself on the mercy of your king."

The rage of the Magyar was fearful to witness.

Holes continued inexorably. "This piece of green ribbon matches the color of your Sunday tunic. Can you swear it has not been torn from the lining? You cannot, I thought so. Know then that wrapped in this ribbon was found the great Samovar diamond, and that you, you alone, were concerned in the robbery."

At this moment the police broke into the room.

"Remove his Excellency," said Holes, "and let him forthwith expiate his crimes upon the scaffold."

"But," I ventured to interpose, "where is the diamond? Unless you restore that---"

"Potson," whispered Holes, almost fiercely, "do not be a fool."

As he said this, the door once again opened, and the Emperor-King entered the room, bearing on his head the turquoise crown, in the center of which sparkled the great Samovar, the moon of brilliancy, as the Hungarian poets love to call it.

The Emperor approached the marvelous detective. "Pardon me," he said, "for troubling you. I have just found the missing jewel under my pillow."

"Where," said Holes, "I was about to tell your Majesty that you would find it."

"Thank you," said his Majesty, "for restoring to me a valued possession and ridding me of a knave about whom I have long had mysuspicions."

The conclusion of the speech was greeted with loud *"Eljens,"* the Hungarian national shout, in the midst of which we took our leave.

That is the true story of how the peace of Europe was preserved by my wonderful friend.

****

SHERLOCK STUMBLES

The Adventure of the Stolen Doormat

Allen Upward

---

*This adventure is a chapter in a larger series of episodes in the life of Ebenezer Lobb as chronicled in **The Wonderful Career of Ebenezer Lobb,** published in 1900. H-lm-s was then still considered dead in Switzerland.*

*Allen Upward (1863-1926) was a renaissance man---poet, novelist, politician, lawyer, and most of all saw himself as a thinker of great thoughts. He believed he deserved the Nobel Prize for his book **The New Word**. He is thought to have committed suicide because the award went instead to George Bernhard Shaw.*

Upward was no slouch. He wrote two books of poetry and one of his poems was included in an imagist collection edited by Ezra Pound. He wrote close to a half dozen novels and an autobiography, and translated from the Chinese the sayings of Confucius as well as writing an anthropological study of Christian mythology. He ran for parliament as a Liberal/Labor candidate but lost. And he once served as a judge in Kenya for the British Foreign Office.

And he also wrote this funny little Sherlockian parody, which sadly is probably the one piece of his output that is still to be read and enjoyed.

****

The harsh duty is cast on me of exposing a charlatan who, after trading for a long time on the credulity of the public, has now gone to his long account.

A Roman poet has declared that we should speak no evil of the dead; but on the other hand a modern writer, the author of **Odgers On the Law of Libel and Slander,**has pointed out that there are certain disadvantages in speaking ill of the living. On one side there is the maxim---*De mortius nil nisi bonum,* on the other, the maxim---*Actio personalis moritur cum persona.* If both these writers had their way, Judas Iscariot would go scot free. On the whole it seemed to me that the advice of the Roman *litterateur* may be more safely ignored than that of his English successor. I therefore withheld this memoir from the press during the lifetime of the specialist.

Now that he is no more, having met with a fatal accident while traveling in Switzerland, I have decided, at whatever risk of causing pain to the sorrowing relatives, that I must go through with my distasteful task.

I was sitting over breakfast in the *Dovecote* one morning when Susan rushed into my presence, all tear-stained and disheveled, and exclaimed;

"If you please, sir, the doormat's gone!"

This doormat, destined to such celebrity in the annals of crime, I should explain, was a prized gift from my dear Aunt Penelope. It was made of india rubber, and bore the inscription WELCOME, in large capitals. During the day time it occupied a position on the top of the steps outside the front door. Every night it was my custom to bring it inside before locking up, and in the morning it was Susan's duty to

100

restore it to its place.

Susan is a female. She might be pardoned for giving away under the stress of misfortune. But such weakness was not for a man. Without permitting myself to waste the precious moments in idle grief, I resolved on instant action.

"Bring me a telegraph form," I commanded the agitated girl. "I will wire at once to a criminal specialist in Baker Street who, without a doubt, will be able to solve this dark problem and recover my missing property."

"Yes sir. Shall I tell a policeman?" asked Susan.

I have had cause ere now to suspect that Susan is not such a stranger to the Constable on duty in Camberwell Grove as she would have me believe. I am not easily deceived, and when a constable is constantly haunting the pavement outside my front gate, and greeting me with effusive familiarity every time I go in or out, I draw my own conclusions. On this occasion I fixed a sternly searching gaze on Susan, under which she quailed, as I responded:

"It can do no harm to communicate with the police. But I will not have the *Dovecote* overrun by officers on the pretext of making inquiries about this crime---you understand?"

The crimson flushwhich mantled in her cheek showed that she did.

The wire was despatched, and within an hour I got the following response:

ARRIVE NEXT TRAIN. PUT NO TRUST IN POLICE.

H---LM---S

101

He was as good as his word. Within five minutes of the arrival of his wire he was seated before me, clad in the well-known ulster and traveling-cap without which he never went anywhere, even in the hottest weather. As he explained to me, it was his uniform, and if he had not worn it, the public would not have recognized him at a glance in the illustrations.

Along with him the celebrated expert brought a rather insignificant, stupid-looking man whom he introduced as Dr W---. I received the doctor coldly.

"Pardon me," I said to his principal, "if I remark that I expected to see you here alone, Mr. H----s. The very distressing crime which has plunged my household into grief, and stirred Camberwell to its depths, is not one to be laid bare to every stranger's eye."

The medico blushed, but his friend took up the cudgels on his behalf.

"I know it looks like bad taste," he said, "but I have to cart him about with me in order that he may write an account of my investigation, for publication in a well-known magazine." He drew me aside and added in a whisper, "Poor fellow, although he has been through so many of my cases with me, and seen so much of my method, he still remains as simple and credulous as a child, and every fresh case comes as a complete surprise to him. He is no use in my work, but he gets money by reporting my doings, and I get reputation so I put up with him as best I can."

While he was speaking he glanced once or twice round the room, and played with the leaves of a photograph album on the table.

"Well, of course, if it is your custom, I will say no more, but I should have thought it would be far more convenient to leave your friend at home, and tell him all about it when you get back. Now to come to this case. The facts are extremely simple."

He stopped me with a gesture.

"My dear Mr. Lobb! that is just what I have to explain to my friend W---It is precisely the cases which appear extremely simple which present the greatest difficulties. Give me a really bizarre crime like a murder by a Mormon or an Andaman Islander, and I can dispose of it without leaving my room, whereas with a thoroughly ordinary affair like this of yours, I find myself all at sea."

"Well let me tell you how this case stands so far. Susan---"

He interrupted me again.

"Susan? Who is that?

"Susan is my general.

"Ah!" He looked round at the doctor. "Make a note of that W----. Yes?"

"She has been in my service eleven years and two months. During that time I have found her faithful, honest and obliging. Her habits are clean, she is an early riser, and a regular attendant at Divine Service."

The expert shook his head doubtfully.

"All that tells me nothing. Has she any followers?"

I hung my head. I saw the net was closing round the unsuspecting girl, and that unless I were careful she would be lost.

"No," I answered uneasily, "at least I have sometimes thought that the policeman on the beat---"

Mr. H----s threw up his hands.

"Always the police!" he cried. "They meet me at every turn! When was this policeman seen last?"

"Susan tells me she saw him this morning, and gave information of the robbery. He is now on the track of the criminals."

The specialist lay back in his chair and smiled a smile of supreme scorn.

"He has got a clue," I continued. "Two gipsies were seen passing down the Grove this morning, and they afterwards went off along the Peckham Road. The officer has gone in pursuit of them."

"Really, Mr. Lobb, I am ashamed of you. The idea of supposing that the stupid brains of the regular police could possibly fathom an inscrutable affair like this. This tale about gipsies is clearly a blind. I am glad the police are out of the way, however, as I can now pursue my own inquiry undisturbed. What kind of mat was it?"

Before I could answer, Dr. W---- hurriedly leant over and murmured something in his friend's ear.

"Oh, ah, I forgot!" said Mr. H----s. And turning to me he remarked; "My friend here reminds me that I have forgotten the usual preliminary demonstration. I have first to give you a specimen of my detective powers. Let me tell you then, that I have already discovered you to be a man of independent means, not following any regular profession, but occupying yourself with literary pursuits, and particularly the study of poetry; you hold Evangelical views, are a teetotaler, have a quarrelsome disposition, and were formerly friendly with a clergyman of the Church of England from whom you are now estranged."

I was stupefied. As soon as I recovered breath I cried out;

"You must be a necromancer! a Mahatma! Except the quarrelsome disposition, which is false and will lead to unpleasantness between us if repeated, you speak as if you had known me all my life."

Dr. W----, who had taken out a notebook and was writing hard, looked up and smiled admiringly on his friend, who turned to him, and asked;
"Now, can you explain how I found all that out, W----?"

The doctor shook his head.

"Dear me, you never get any brighter," muttered the expert in a tone of disappointment. Then he turned to me.

"I will explain. From your being at home in the middle of the morning I inferred that you had no regular profession, and therefore that you must have private means. Your literary pursuits and their direction, were revealed to me by that bulky manuscript on your desk, which bears the title *The Principles of Shakespearean Punctuation.* On your wall hangs a text, which leads me to suppose you are Evangelical; and as the words of the text are *Blessed are the Meek,* I conclude that it was given to you by some friend who had observed your failing and wished to correct it. [This was nasty, The text was given me by my own sister. I have returned it to her.] I judge you to be a teetotaler, because my friend and I have been in your house half an hour, and you have not offered us a drink. That you were once friendly with a clergyman is proved by this photograph in your album, below which is written--- 'With the Vicar's Compliments'---and that your friendship has met with interruption I gather from the fact that a pencil has been drawn through those words, and has written beneath them the word---'Serpent.'"

105

I could hardly help laughing as he finished.

"Really, Mr. H----s, you must excuse my saying so, but all that is so childishly simple, that I am afraid I can't give you credit for much astuteness in finding it out. But if you meant it merely as a hint that you are thirsty; why---"

I got up and went to the sideboard.

As soon as the refreshments had been disposed of, the specialist rose to go out to the scene of the crime, accompanied by his medical friend. I was coming too, but he waved me back.

"Your presence would only distract me, he said. "I am about to make a microscopic investigation outside, and I wish to be alone, so that my brain may work freely, and my reasoning powers have full play."

I heard them open the front door and pass outside. Tortured by curiosity I went to the window and tried to see what they were doing. I could just catch a glimpse of the celebrated detective's legs. He appeared to be kneeling on the steps, going over every inch in search of those minute indicia which escape the notice of ordinary minds, but which reveal a whole complicated tragedy to the trained intellect of a literary detective. The foolW---- was standing on the garden path, notebook in hand, looking on with an expression of childlike reverence, and every now and then taking down something which fell from his friend, but in accents too low for me to overhear.

At last I could bear the suspense no longer. I had come out into the hall, resolved to find out what they had discovered, when my wish was anticipated by Mr. H----s stepping softly in, followed by the inevitable W., and closing the door behind him.

106

The great expert's look was grave, almost to weeping. An expression in sycophantic imitation was assumed by the tiresome doctor.

"Well, have you found out anything?" I asked with a beating heart.

"Everything!" was the solemn answer. "Prepare for the worst. You have been boldly and shamelessly robbed by one who is evidently numbered among your most intimate friends, who had supper here only last night, and went away at twelve o'clock, in a partially intoxicated condition, dressed in a covert coat and gaiters, and smoking Pioneer tobacco in a shilling briar. He is five feet eleven inches in height, aged thirty-eight, wears No. 9 boots, and earns a precarious livelihood on the Stock Exchange."

"*Johnson!*" I wailed, and sank senseless on a chair.

My cry brought Susan from the kitchen with a rush. She was closely followed by a police-constable, who was hurriedly passing the sleeve of his coat across his mouth.

The Baker Street consultant glanced at him with ineffable scorn.

"What are you doing here?" he demanded, with ill-concealed jealousy.

"I came here about Mr. Lobb's mat," stammered the officer. "It's all right. I caught the gipsies the other side of New Cross."

The specialist gave a lordly wave of his hand.

"So much for the intelligence of the police," he sneered. "Where is Mr. Lobb's mat, pray?"

"I brought it back with me, sir."

107

I sprang to my feet, darted to the front door, and flung it open. There, in its familiar spot, with the dear old WELCOME staring on its honest face, it smiled up at me like an innocent child.

The mat had been lying there for the last hour!

I was disappointed in Mr. H----s. In the reports in the magazine his language has never been other than that of a gentleman and a philosopher. I am sorry to say my experience puts him in a far less favourable light.

P. S.---I had the greatest difficulty in restraining Johnson, when he heard of the affair, from going into Baker Street to "have it out with that beggar, H----s.

The Mysterious Glove

Anonymous

Swatson finds a glove. Herlock Sholmes deduces the identity of its owner.

What more do you need to know?

*It appeared in **Snap-Shots** on June 30, 1903 as "Herlock Sholmes Again", just as the public was celebrating the Return of Sherlock Holmes.*

****

"This glove," said Herlock Sholmes, the great detective, "this glove speaks to me of a great mystery."

"I knew it would," said Swatson,who had brought the glove to him.

"Yes," said Sholmes, lighting a cigarette and putting his feet on the mantel. He puffed in meditative silence for some minutes. "Now," he resumed, "the question is---"

"The question is when and where the murder was committed," interrupted Swatson, with the keen haste of a man who delights in anticipating the thoughts of a great personage.

"No, that is not the question," replied Sholmes, while Swatson shrank swiftly into his natural state of subjection. "The question is shall we work it up into a hundred-and-fifty-thousand-word novel, or merely make a short sketch of it."

Swatson vouchsafed no reply, save to motion to his empty pocket.

"Ah, we need the money at once," smiled Sholmes. "Then it shall be a short sketch, for cash comes more quickly from the magazines than from the royalties on a book."

For some moments he pulled at his cigarette, and then laid the glove on the open palm of his right hand.

"This glove," he deduced, "was worn by a young woman who belongs to the best of families. How do I know that? Because she was on the way to the manicurist's. How do I know that? Because you picked it up in front of the manicure-shop across the way. I saw you. Very well. I know she was going there because she was in a hurry, and drew the glove from her hand before she entered, in order to save time. She had an engagement for the theatre. How do I know that? They all have. Yesterday she bought a copy of **Lady Rose's Daughter** at the book-shop in Main-Street. How do I reason that out? The newspapers advertised a special sale of the story at that shop for that day. She plays golf. I deduce that because she plays bridge-whist. I am positive of that because she has a lap-dog. I am sure of that because she is a pianist. I discover that because of the shape of the fingers of the glove. I venture the opinion as to the other attributes of her elevated station because she also drives a motor-car."

"Smell the glove," commanded Sholmes.

Swatson did so. The smell of gasoline was overpowering.

110

"Now, Swatson," kindly said Sholmes, "Don't you see how I did it all? I smelled the glove first and then deduced all the rest. I have cultivated the hab---"

"Excuse me, Mr. Sholmes," spoke a slender lady who had entered unnoticed, "but I took the liberty of running up here to ask if Mr. Swatson did not pick up my glove. I thought I saw him do so, and I knew I would find him here. I had cleaned the gloves with gasoline and hung them up on my window-ledge to dry and one of them fell."

She took the glove, smiled her thanks, and left.

"Do you know who she is?" asked Sholmes, after the door had closed.

"Yes," replied Swatson. "She is the manicurist."

Baffled!!

Another Adventure About that Dear Old Has-Been, Sherlog Combes

Anonymous

*A broken-down Sherlock Holmes faces up to a burning issue of post war Britain and fails. This anonymous parody was in the June 7, 1919, **London Opinion**, another of the discoveries of Robert C. S. Adey.*

****

The aged detective affixed his signature to the Unemployment Benefit form; and, wrapped in reverie and a dressing gown, sank back in his chair. His violin lay amongst the littered breakfast dishes. A quid of cocaine, or a wad or tumblerfull of it---I forget exactly how you take it--- stood at his elbow. The hound of the vilkerbaskes wearing a bird-cage in lieu of a muzzle, spread itself over most of the hearth-rug. All these properties had to be there. How otherwise would you have recognized Sherlog Combes, the greatest living---if only just living---detective? His brow, like his financial outlook and the whiskey he is drinking, was clouded. He had not had a case for years (like the wine and spirit merchants).

Suddenly a jarring tintinnabulation shattered the sylvan calm of Baker Street. An ordinary mind would have imagined that the belfry in a neighboring church had fallen into the road, but to Combes' trained

112

intelligence it could mean but one thing; the front-door bell. He removed his feet, and incidentally an oleograph of the Relief of Lucknow, from the mantelpiece. His hawk-like eyes glinted. His hawk-like nose quivered. His hawk-like ears---no. Sorry, that won't do.

A lady entered hurriedly, without waiting to be announced. Her skirt and blouse were in the height of fashion, but her countenance was in the depth of despair.

Her voice was deeply agitated. "My husband"---she began.

"I understand perfectly," interrupted Combes. "You wish to tell me that your husband has disappeared. Maddened by the horrors of the super-tax he has probably"

"Nothing of the kind," said the lady. "My husband and I---"

"Say no more. I see it all. Home troubles. Domestic affliction. You are being blackmailed by a former admirer, who holds the billets doux which you, as a schoolgirl, flicked across the aisle to him in church."

"No, much worse. My husband and I and our baby---"

"Heavens!" cried Combes. "Your angel-child has been kidnapped. Four masked bandits, I presume, drove up in a black bassinette---"

"Please let me finish. We have been searching all over for---"

"Why didn't you say so at first?" snapped Combes. "A jewel robbery, of course, Madam, confide in me. It was I who discovered the great Carbuncle in the Duchess's powder-box. It was I who---"

"No, not that."

113

"Well, what can I do for you? Perhaps your uncle has been found lying dead in the conservatory with an aspidistra embedded in his brain?"

"No, no. Listen," said the lady in a weary voice. "I have simply come to ask you to find us a house."

"A house!" The detective's jaw dropped; not on the floor, you understand it just dropped.

"Madam," he quavered in a voice broken with failure, "you demand the impossible. I have been a match for all the murderers, blackmailers, forgers and master-criminals in the world, but even I dare not tackle a modern landlord. I dabble every day in fabulous fortunes and missing millions, but London rents are beyond me. I can find diamonds and rubies as easily as a conjurer fetches rabbits out of a hat; I can produce coronets and tiaras as quickly as a politician can abstract coin from a taxpayer's pocket; I admit my powerlessness. I cannot find you a house."

With a low, gurgling cry, reminiscent of the last half-inch of water bidding a reluctant farewell to a bath, the lady fell forward in a swoon.

Combes gently raised her, and laid her on the sofa.

He swallowed the quid, wad, or bucketful of cocaine at one gulp, and, taking his violin from under the butter-dish, he drew forth, with ineffable pathos and a bow that needed rosin, the first haunting notes of, "There's nae luck aboot the hoose."

The lady swooned again. You cannot blame her.

Motoring with Sherlock

Croton Oyle

Chess Clubs, crossword puzzlers, early radio fans searching out faraway station call letters, and even motor buffs all had to get into the Sherlockian act. And with a pretty good Sherlock Holmes parody in this case. It was titled, "The Affair of The Lost Compression"

The anonymous author passed up the chance to sign himself as Motor Oyle or Castor Oyle (see the early Popeye Thimble Theater), but perhaps he or she chose Croton because this product, the internet informs us, was made from seeds of an Indian tree and was then given medicinally in small doses to cause diarrhea.

*The parody appeared in **The Car Magazine** in 1903 and was rescued by George Locke of Ferret Fantasy.*

This is one of those "hey sonny, go fetch me a left-handed monkey wrench" things.

****

"I am about to be visitedby a motorist," said Romes as I entered his room on full morning in a November. My wife was away on a visit to some friends, and I was spending a few days with my old friend.

He was curled up in his big, easy-chair, puffing moodily at a very old and foul pipe. I could see no indication whatever which could lead him to anticipate such visit.

"I know you will have a simple explanation of the mystery," I said; "but I cannot fathom it," and I looked inquiringly at him. I might have guessed, but to do so would not be acting up to approved methods. The public loves consistency; to alight upon an explanation by a mere guess would, in a way to defraud them of their rights.

"You are right, my dear Scotson; it is quite simple," laughed Romes, "And anyone who understands my methods could arrive at it by an easy course of deduction; but as much as no such person exists, I must give you the clue to the chain of reasoning which led to my statement."

"A moment before you entered the room," he continued, "I heard a noise of a train passing through a tunnel, then I noticed several women look out interestingly from the window opposite at an object which could not have been a burst main, a cab accident, a barrel organ out of gear or a dog fight---"

"But," I interposed.

"And finally," Romes continued, "I heard the toot-toot! of a motor horn, and the confirmatory 'pip-pip!' of a small boy."

Even as he spoke, there was a knock at the door, and a young man was ushered in.

He had a leather cap in his hand, and wore a large motor coat. His face was pale and he was of medium height. I tried in vain to form some idea of his occupation or character.

Romes motioned him to a chair.

116

"You are a motorist, is it not so?" he asked, quietly.

The young man started in surprise. "How did you find that out?" he gasped.

Romes smiled slightly and pointed at his boot.

"There's a viscid, oleaginous speck on the upper of your right foot," he said quietly. "Probably you have not read my little monograph on lubricants, which was withdrawn from circulation some years ago? No? Well, it dealt with 1,765 varieties of oils, and gave, amongst other secrets, an infallible test by which parafin could be distinguished from olive oil."

"Marvelous!" cried the young man.

"Yes," mused Holmes, "It was bought up by the Anglo-American Oil Company after that little adventure which my friend Dr. Scotson has so well told under the title of '680.'"

"Yes---Yes," said the young man, "I know that story."

"I see," continued Romes, "that you drive a fast car."

The young man smiled.

"Every motorist does---until stopped by the police."

"Then there are the marks of goggles on the right side of your nose," explained Romes, "which indicate the wind pressure caused by high speed they also show the wind pressure was on your right side. You come from Surrey, if I mistake not?"

"Well, I was born there, certainly," said the young man; "but I came from Norfolk today."

"Ah," said Romes calmly, "the wind has changed!" and sank into a deep reverie.

"Oh Mr. Romes!" broke in the motorist, after a few moments of painful waiting. "I have come to you for aid. My case is a desperate one!"

"Go on, my friend," spoke Romes soothingly. "I knew you were in trouble. Tell your story and if it is of sufficient interest, my good friend, Dr. Scotson, will give it full publicity at the usual rates. Go on, fear nothing. The laws of copyright are sacred."

"I am a motorist," spoke our visitor, with deep emotion. "I am young, I am wealthy, but I am deeply unhappy!"

"Fallen into a police trap, have you?" I asked quickly, resolving to score before Romes this time.

"Worse!" I've fallen in love!

"Ah, I knew there was a woman in the case," said Romes. "Wherever there are motors, there are women," he added sententiously.

"I am in love," said the young man. "My name, I should tell you, is Gerald Goodley, and the lady I love is Miss Seebrighte."

"And the other man?" queried Romes, with another flash of his marvelous intuitive powers.

"Ah, how did you guess there was another man?" said the motorist, deeply impressed. "Certainly there is; his name is Ferdinand Smickton, confound him! He is a motorist also. The lady is romantic and unable to decide between her two suitors, and declared her hand should be given to the winner of a motor race between us. I at once bought the guaranteed fastest car in Europe, and Smickton bought another, which he declared was quite as fast. The race was to take place in a few days' time. It would have been a neck and neck contest; but this morning , as a result of foul play, my car has been tampered with and has lost its compression!"

The young man paused to give the full weight of the horror of this terrible revelation; glanced searchingly from Romes to me, and the muscles of his face twitched.

Romes, leaning back in his chair, his eyes fixed on a spot on the ceiling, his long fingers meeting, made no remark.

Mr. Goodley resumed: "Now the car runs dead slow. I shall be beaten. No one else has been able to help me. In deep despair I appeal to you, Mr. Romes."

"Lost your compression," said Romes slowly, "that's serious! By-the-by, for Dr. Scotson's information, you might tell him what you do with the compression when you have it. When did you see it last? Did you notice any peculiar habits in it? Have you a photograph of it?"

"No," said the poor young fellow, disconsolately. "You see it's in the engine---inside, don't you know! I've never seen it, but my man tells me that unless it's there the engine won't go!"

"But can't you buy a new compression?"said I, venturing, as I thought, a safe question, for I did not care to be thought entirely ignorant of motoring. The young man's features contracted painfully.

119

"No, my mechanic has tried everywhere; he has done everything...all in vain! The affair was wrapped in mystery, and up to this morning I had not the faintest clue. Then I discovered a peculiar hobnail on the road fifty yards from the motor house; and on the panel of my racing car I found the following mysterious word cut with some instrument, which, from the nature of the incision, could only have been accomplished by a fine cutting tool used exclusively by surgeons."

"Ha!" said Romes, "that may be an important clue. Is your rival a doctor?"

"No, but his grandfather was an apothecary."

"Good! that's important! It may be the first link in our chain. What was the word?"

"It is a strange one and it appears to be 'Watoe'.I can make nothing of it. I knew at once, however, that it had some connection with the injury done to the engine. The discovery of the hobnail strengthened this belief."

"You are a very intelligent man, Mr. Goodley."

"Ah, I study your methods closely, Mr. Romes."

"Could you tell me some more about this compression?" asked Romes.

"Well, it's inside the engine, don't you know, and it helps it to go!"

"Compresses something, no doubt."

"Yes, that's it!---that's it!" And both Goodley and myself were amazed at the deep knowledge which Romes evidently possessed of motor cars, a subject which I thought he had never taken up.

"Well, good-by Mr. Goodley, for the present. Kindly give me your address and that hobnail. I shall visit you this evening and inspect the place. By tomorrow I shall restore that lost compression."

"Oh, how can I thank you, Mr. Romes?"said the young man, in a burst of gratitude, "I owe you more than my life! I am certain now to win the race, and with it the sweetest girl in England!"

Since my solitary patient who keeps me going did not require me that afternoon, I determined to accompany Romes, and so, taking the train from St. Pancras, we reached the country house where Mr. Goodley and his aged mother dwelt. Romes, with his microscope examined three acres of ground surrounding the motor house, took a casting and a photograph of the mysterious word 'Watoe' scratched on the car, discovered several fingermarks on the engine, and interviewed the servants---all of whom looked equally guilty.

During the railway journey back to town Romes spoke very little; but I felt sure he had a clue.

"The culprit," said he, after a long silence, "is a stout man, with a slight halt in his left leg; he has served in the army, and lives in London."

Not another word did he utter, and thus I left him on reaching his rooms.

Late that evening, after four hours smoking, Romes came to me and said, "If you are not tired, Scotson, we will go out. Put a few revolvers in your pockets. As I anticipated, this simple affair is going to be serious. You must have noticed that all the simple affairs I took part in have become serious also."

I assented and watched my gifted friend prepare for the night's work.

Having disguised ourselves as seafaring men (Romes looked the part to the life, with his keen, intellectual face and long, white hands), we journeyed into the East End, and after a long walk called at a villainous little public-house well known to Romes as the habitual resort of criminals.

"Tom Fowler is to meet me here," he said in a low voice. "He's the most dangerous man in London; but I have him under my thumb. He was once a policeman, but was dismissed from the force for prosecuting horse-drivers who exceeded the legal limit! At first, it was thought that he was insane, but afterwards, his extraordinary behavior was traced to drink and a desire to tell the truth. He went to the bad after this disgrace, and became a notorious criminal---his knowledge of police traps standing him in good stead. He has a strong taste for motoring, and now I believe acts as a 'fence' for receiving stolen motor cars---S-s-h! here he comes."

A low-sized, square-jawed man entered the room cautiously and hobbled towards us.

"Evenin' mate!" Romes said gruffly, and then lowering his voice to its natural tone, asked: "How's the rheumatism, Tom?"

"Bad, sir! ---bad!" he said. "Curse them traps!"

"Got his rheumatism from sleeping in traps," Romes explained to me aside.

"Well now, Tom, I want your help," he continued, "and, of course, no tales will be told. A motoring friend of mine has lost a valuable compression. It was an heirloom. I fancy; of no use except on its own special motor. Now this Compression was stolen some days ago and I want it back."

Fowler screwed up his face in a rather funny way, and at first I fancied he was restraining himself from laughing.

"This Compression," went on Romes, "was stolen from my friend's car by a stout man who has a halt in his left leg, and who was in the army. I want his address and you shall come to no harm. If not---" and Rome's eyes glittered with that hard look which readers of the magazines know so well.

"I know the man, sir, and you shall have his address, Mr. Romes," said Fowler meekly. "What's more, sir, I'll ask him to put that compression back at once and make it better than ever. But I warn you, sir, he's a desperate man. He's injured several police before he gave up motoring."

"I come well prepared," said Romes quietly.

"Well, sir, you know your own business best," replied Fowler. "By the way," he added, "I'm a poor man, Mr. Romes sir, and information"

They moved away to a distant part of the room, and I could not catch their conversation, but I heard the clink of money, and I saw a smile of satisfaction on both their countenances, Fowler slipping something into his trouser pockets, while Romes carefully placed a dirty card into his case.

The interview over, Romes and I hurried to a cabstand, and there my friend said, as he took my hand, "This promises to be one of the most serious adventures of my life, Scotson, and I must go into it alone. You are married, and I cannot allow you to share the risks. I am inflexible on that matter. Go home, and await me. I shall be back by dawn if all is well. Good night old man. Give me all the spare revolvers you have."

I parted from him sadly and went home, racking my brain over the terrible adventure he had undertaken, and wondering what dangers the fates had in store for him that night.

I went to bed soon after reaching the house, and many troubled dreams came to me in the long watches of that awful night. After many hours of broken sleep, I must have fallen into a deep slumber. Some street noises awoke me about six o'clock next morning. At last in my anxiety, and I hurried to Rome's room. Thank heaven, he was sleeping peacefully in bed!

On his pale, intellectual face there was a placid yet weary look, which told me that he had triumphed, but after desperate perils, perhaps only after a life and death struggle; goodness only knew what he must have gone through during that awful night!

On the floor lay a greasy book, the cover of which bore the title, "The Principles of the Motor Car." It was ear-marked at a chapter headed, "Compression." Beside the book was a dirty card---the card which Fowler had handed to Romes on the previous night. This card bore the legend, "Johnson Digby, Motor Car Expert and Engineer, Burrow Lane, London SE."

He was the culprit, no doubt. Romes had run his man to earth.

I stole from the room and returned to bed, happy at the success of my old friend.

At breakfast Romes was more than usually reticent. For a long while he seemed wrapped up in the *Police Intelligence.* For some time I curbed my curiosity; but at length, unable to restrain my patience, I

124

broke the silence.

"Any report of the adventure in the paper?" I asked.

"Adventure! what adventure?" he asked abstractedly.

"Why, about The Affair of the Lost Compression."

"No," replied Romes abruptly, "there isn't."

"Your methods are wonderful!" I said. "No doubt Digby saw the game was up immediately you appeared on the scene."

Romes looked at me enquiringly---indeed almost suspiciously.

"What do you know about Digby?" he said.

"Ah, my dear fellow, I was too anxious about your safety to wait for news until breakfast time. I crept into your room early this morning with bated breath, and you can imagine my joy when I found you peacefully sleeping."

"And on the floor you saw the card?"

"Exactly. Tell me what happened. Did the man show fight?"

A slight frown passed over Rome's features.

"Will you never learn my methods, my dear Scotson?" he asked. "You may be quite sure if Digby had been the guilty party I should not have gone to work as I did. Frankly, Scotson, in spite of your assumed knowledge yesterday, admit that you are quite ignorant of what a 'Compression' is."

What foolishness to attempt to deceive Romes! I admitted it.

"If you had owned it at the time matters would have gone very differently."

"Then you have failed?" I asked.

"It has been entirely profitless," was the enigmatical reply; "and as such I do not regret the case."

"But what of Mr. Goodley? Will he be able to race after all?"

"Goodley!" said Romes, his eyes flashing, "Goodley is a young man of depraved morals, consequent, I suppose on his being a motorist. Here is a book called 'The Principles of the Motor Car.' Principles! Motor cars may have principles, but I am quite sure motorists of Goodley's type have not. Turn to the chapter (page 156) on 'Compression' and read it."

I did so. When I finished the mystery was solved. I looked at my friend, who with closed eyes was sucking philosophically at another very foul old pipe.

"What a ruffian," I said, "to play a practical joke on you."

For a few minutes no words were spoken. At length Romes opened his eyes.

"Scotson," he said, "if you must publish this adventure to the world, I would be greatly obliged if you used assumed names."

And so I have.

How It Plays in Peoria

Frank E. Kellogg

Frank E. Kellogg (1880-1923) died at the early age of 43. He wrote books for juveniles but has two other books of humor still being sold on the internet.

*This parody is found in **Flip Flap Fables: A Bunch of Twenty-Seven Tales Concerning Animals of Various Kinds from Which May Be Deduced Many Morals** (1907). It was titled "The Great Detective Who Unearthed Things."*

Sherlockian collector, Marv Epstein discovered this parody and used it as his Christmas keepsake to friends.

****

Once there was a Great Detective. He was very great. From a professional point of view, he was "Two Looks high, and still climbing." He could detect anything. He had been known to locate a wobbly-legged calf that the old cow had hidden so effectively she couldn't find it herself.

He came on deck after the Hoopskirt Age and before the dress pocket was abolished, and it had passed into History he once found his

127

wife's dress pocket in forty-five minutes by the parlor clock. But of course he couldn't do that every time; not without straining himself. He also did a fairly good Stunt on Collar Buttons. Could generally locate one in about thirty minutes if the dust wasn't too thick under the dresser.

His long suit, however was in putting the Tag on aspirants for jobs in the State Government Works at Peoria, and in that particular field he was on the 400 class, batter up.

One day a roughly-dressed, stocky man walked into the office, and, Squatting on a Chair without waiting for an invite, remarked:

"Say, pardner, be you the Brass Collared Detective we hear so much about, nowadays?"

"The same. Have you something in my line? I can give you ten minutes," and the Great Detective fished out a note-book and began whittling the end of a Pencil.

The Stocky One pulled out a slab of tobacco the size of a six-inch section of 2x4 scantling, and detaching a chunk big as a piece of pie with his eye teeth, remarked:

"Ten minutes will do, I guess, if you're drawing as many Loads as they say. I am a farmer---"

The Great Detective interrupted him with a wave of the hand and smiled. "It is not necessary to inform me of that Fact, my Dear Sir. You live on a farm seventeen and a quarter miles north of here. Your farm is Part Clay and part a Sandy Loam."

The Stocky One appeared to be greatly impressed, and said:

"Well, I'll be switched. How did you get into that?"

128

The Great Detective smiled in a patronizing, indulgent way.

"We do not generally make a practice of Exhaling state secrets, but as you are a simple-minded farmer the knowledge will go no further, so I don't mind telling you. You started out this morning with a fresh plug of tobacco, did you not?"

"Yep."

"You have taken just Chews enough to go seventeen and a quarter Miles."

"Good Guess. But why north?"

"The wind is in the west and there is more dust in your right ear than in your left. The nature of the soil on your farm I detected instantly by the different shades of dust on your Collar, which are easily noted and classified by an expert."

"Say, but you're onto your job all right, pardner. You make me ashamed of myself. Now I'll shoot my wad and give you a chance to meditate."

The Great Detective once more waved his hand.

"Wait. You keep seven horses and nine cows."

The Stocky One stared and scratched his head.

"I've evidently come to the right party, but what's your recipe for the last batch of wisdom?"

"Simple again, when you know how. There are seven different

distinct equine smells on your garments and nine separate and clearly-defined odors from the cow. Every animal has an odor peculiar to itself. Now tell your business."

The Stocky One changed his quid to the other side and said with some unction, "Say, you're a Peach. If anybody ever intimates that your Garret is Dusty, just refer them to me."

"Now I'll speak my piece. My name is Jake Jagpole. You see, my Aunt Sarah Watkins dropped off rather sudden, and some of us got it into our nut that there was crooked work. After bothering over it for a spell, I happened to think maybe you could help us out."

The Great Detective raised his hand.

"Wait. That is sufficient." Then turning to a pigeon-hole in his desk he looked over some papers for a moment and said:

"Your Aunt Sarah Watkins was a widow and lived alone."

"Yep."

"She was near-sighted."

"Yes, awful. Why, I've seen her set down to a carpenter's work bench and try to milk it, thinking the darn thing was a cow."

"Exactly. Set your mind at rest. There was no foul play. Your aunt died from eating some Embalmed Beef that she chopped in the hash by mistake owing to the defect in her vision. Is that all you wish to know?"

The Stocky One arose and observed with some emotion:

"Yes, that's all. Much obliged. What's the damage?"

"Oh, the service was so slight: Twenty dollars."

The Stocky One handed over a twenty and turned to go; halted a moment, faced about, and remarked:

"Pardner, you're the smoothest event that ever occurred. You're a Ten Wheeler with 200 pounds of steam. I'm glad I came. I'm a V to the Good, besides a whole lot of valuable information.

"You see, on the run in yesterday I bet my head brakeman---by the way, I'm a freight conductor on the P. D. Q. & T. S. Never was on a farm in my life, and never had an Aunt Sarah Watkins, or any other kind of Aunt. But that doesn't alter the fact that you have given me the worth of my money."

"As I was saying, I bet the head brakeman twenty-five dollars that you could ferret anything whether it happened or not. As you see, I have won out. I started to tell you I was a farmer-looking chap, but you jumped in and took my run, and when I saw I was Swiped a trip I kept quiet."

"So long. We'll have a good time with the other five."

MORAL

When you know the other fellow is bluffing, it's like money from home.

Curses!AnotherOne of Those Gifted Amateurs!

Oswald Crawfurd

*Oswald Crawfurd (1834-1909) was a turn of the century British theater critic and writer of light romances. His mystery, **The Revelations of Inspector Morgan**, describes four cases of his fictional detective. In the American edition only, (1907) Crawfurd inserted this parody and titled it "Our Mr. Smith.".*

He wished to "establish the professional detective police of my own country in that position of superiority to the mere amateur and outsider." Ironically the first of his own Inspector Morgan's cases is about how Morgan, as an amateur and outsider, discovers he is gifted with deductive skills superior to the local police---and then he enters the professional force.

Crawfurd blames an American for inventing this notion of the gifted amateur sleuth and the writer he holds responsible is Edgar Allen Poe, whose detective was M. C. Auguste Dupin.

But it isn't Poe's Dupin that he goes after here.

****

After a hard day's professional work, I was sitting in my little room in Baker Street, deeply meditating on a subject very long absent from my thoughts.

Reader, you can guess what that subject is. I was considering the marvelous analytical faculty of my friend Purlock Hone, when the door opened and Purlock Hone, himself, appeared on the threshold. In my accustomed impulsive and ecstatic way, not unmingled with that humour which I am proud to say tempers the veneration I feel for that colossal intellect, I was beginning with the trivial phrase, "Talk of the ---" when my friend cut me short, with, "Sh," and put his finger on his lips.

He sat down by the fire without a word, depositing his hat, gloves and handkerchief in the coal scuttle (I have before referred to my friend's untidy habits) and reached to the mantelpiece for my favorite meerschaum. He filled the pipe with long cut Cavendish, and sitting with knotted brows, smoked it to the end before he spoke a word. Then he said,

"Humph!" It was little enough, perhaps, but from Purlock it meant volumes.

"Well," I said, "Go on."

He did. He filled the pipe anew, and, for a second time smoked it to the bitter end.

"Your pipe, Jobson, wants cleaning!" and he gently threw it upon the fire, from which I rescued it before the flames had done it too much injury. From anyone else this action had seemed hasty, if not inconsiderate, in this gifted and marvelous being it betokened a profound train of abstract and analytical meditation. I waited patiently for some revelation of the subject of his thoughts.

I need not remind the reader that in the spring of this year, the world

133

of international politics was gravely agitated. Menacing rumours were about everywhere, the international atmosphere was electrical and mutterings of the tempest were to be heard on every side, but no one could divine where and when the storm would burst---on whom the bolt would fall.

Mysterious messages were daily passing between the Dowager Empress of China and Kaiser William; what did they portend? President Castro of Venezuela was known to be in secret communication with the Dalai Lama. Our eminent statesman, Mr. Kier Hardie, was said to have despatched an ultimatum to the Emperor of Japan and an identical document to President Roosevelt. The aged wife of the Commissionaire at the Foreign Office (Irish by birth and convivial habits) had made compromising revelations of the policy of the government in a tavern in Charles Street, Westminster, and the Cabinet of St. James was already tottering to its fall!

I eagerly recapitulated to my friend these various sources of disquietude in the nation, to Europe and the World and urged him eagerly to enlighten me as to which of these great world problems he was preparing to solve. His answer was characteristic of this remarkable man, characteristic at once of his geniality, his simplicity, his wonderful self control, his modesty, and at the same time of his refusal, even to me, to commit himsclf to an avowal.

"Any one of them, or no one - or all; I cannot guess," said Purlock Hone.

My friend could not guess! I forbore from speech, but I smiled when I reflected that I was in the presence of the man who had more than once interposed to save a British Ministry from defeat, who had maintained the balance of power in Europe by discovering a stolen naval treaty, nay, of the man who had restored the jeweled crown of England when it had been lost for nearly three hundred years!

134

"A penny for your thoughts," said Purlock Hone gaily. "Or, come, you shall hear them from me for nothing."

"I defy you to know what I was thinking of," I said impulsively, but a moment later that defiance seemed to me rash, as in truth it proved to be.

"My dear, Jobson," said this greatest of clairvoyants, "if you wanted me not to guess your thoughts you should not have smiled and looked towards the portrait of the late Premier. That told me, as clearly as if you had spoken, that you were recalling my little service to the late Unionist Government. I suppose you are unconscious of the fact, but you distinctly hitched the belt of your trousers as you crossed the room, with a sailorlike roll in your walk; what more was needed to tell me your thoughts were of my modest success in the matter of the lost naval treaty?"

"Amazing! And the recovery of the Crown of England?"

"You have tell-tale eyes, Jobson, and you rolled them regally as you directed them to the print of His Gracious Majesty over the mantelpiece."

"Wonderful man! Stupendous perspicacity!" I muttered.

Purlock Hone filled my rescued pipe for the third time and resumed his smoking. As in most other things, as in his taste for tobacco he resembles no other human being. I happened to know that he had not touched a pipe, a cigar, or a cigarette for a month before.

"Smoking, Jobson, in one of the world's follies. No ordinary man needs tobacco. It is poison!"

135

"Yet you smoke, Hone, even to excess at times," I said.

"I said no ordinary man, Jobson," retorted my friend.

I quailed under the justice of the reproof. Any other man would have pressed his victory. He generously forbore.

"I smoke only when some very heavy work is before me," he went on, "not otherwise."

Then I had guessed alright! He had some great work in hand. Never before had I seen so deep a frown between those sagacious eyes, never had the thoughtful face been so pale, the whole physiognomy so enigmatic. Never had so thick a cloud of tobacco smoke issued from between those oracular lips.

"I expect a visitor," he observed presently, between two puffs of tobacco smoke.

"Where? I asked.

"Here," said Hone simply. "I left word at home that anyone who called at my place was to come on here. Read this!" He tossed a letter across the table. I read aloud:

"Dear Sir: I will do myself the pleasure of waiting upon you between 5 and 6 today.

Yours faithfully,

John Smith.

"A pregnant communication, Jobson, eh?"

"I dare say, but I confess I don't see anything peculiar about it. I looked again at the letter. It seemed to me as plain an epistle as any man could write. A dunning tradesman might have written it---a tax collector might have subscribed it."

"What do you make of those t's, Jobson? Does the spacing of the words tell you anything? Are those w's and l's there for nothing?"

"To me, Hone, they are there for nothing, but then--- I am not a Purlock Hone."

He smiled as he regarded me with pity, and cocked his left eye, using one of those fascinating and favourite actions of his that bring him down to the level of our common humanity.

"It is a disguised hand, Jobson, and do you observe the absence of an address?"

The lucid and enlightened explanation that I expected was cut short by a ring of the door bell. Immediately afterwards the maid announced Mr. Smith. A little man with grey side whiskers, a neat black frock coat and carrying a somewhat dampish silk umbrella, entered the room.

"Be seated, ---Mr. Smith." The slight pause between the last two words of Hone's sentence was eloquent.

"Which of you two gentlemen is Purlock Hone, Esq?" The accent on which 'Mr. Smith' spoke was cockney and the tone depreciating.

I looked to Hone to answer. He smiled upon the stranger. It was a smile of complete approval.

"Admirable!" said my friend. "Pray go on, sir."

The visitor was viably taken aback.

"I asks a plain question, and I looks to get a plain answer."

"It does you the greatest credit, my dear sir," said Hone. "It would pass almost anywhere."

The little gentleman with grey side whiskers got red in the face and his eyes grew round. He was obviously angry, or was he only acting anger?

My friend, Purlock Hone, as I think I have observed before in the course of these memoirs, often smiles, but seldom condescends to laugh.

Our visitor coloured violently and struck the end of his umbrella on the floor. "Look here," he said, "play acting is play acting, but I comes here on business; my name is John Smith, and I don't want none of your chaff."

"Capital! Capital! Go on Mr.---Smith!"

"I will do so, sir, if you please!" The little gentleman put his hand in the inner breast pocket of his coat and produced there from a blue envelope; a quick glance at the superscription showed me that it was addressed to my friend and was written in that bold, regular, cursive hand which is characteristic of the man engaged in commercial pursuits. My interest was now strongly roused. I waited eagerly for developments.

The mysterious visitor looked from one to the other of us. "As you gentlemen refuse to say which of you is Hone, Esq., I'll make as bold to read this communication to the two of you."

"You may do so with perfect safety, Mr.---Smith. My friend is in my confidence."

The little gentleman cast a puzzled look at us both and read as follows: "To Porlock Hone, Esq., Dear Sir---account already rendered and which you have no doubt overlooked. Early attention to the same will oblige."

The reader paused and looked at my friend. I, too, looked. His face was inscrutable, his lips were grimly closed. My curiosity---shall I say my indiscretion?--- got the better of me.

"And whose Mr. Smith may you be, sir?"

The little man glibly read out the conclusion of the letter; "Yours obediently, Dear Sir, Jones & Sons, Hatters, Oxford Street. And here is the bill, gentlemen. To one fancy broad brimmed silk hat; cathedral style;---To one clerical soft felt bowler;---To one slouched Spanish sombrero; To one---"

Purlock Hone raised his hand as if deprecating a list of further items, and Mr. Smith stopped and stared at him.

"What!" I thought. "Is it a real account for hats---after all? For I remembered these unusual forms of head-covering having formed parts of the various disguises in which my friend had walked the streets of London, incognito. No! There must be some deep diplomatic secret behind the seemingly simple transaction!"

"What is the total amount, Mr. Smith?" asked my friend in muffled tones.

"Nine, eleven, four, sir."

Without another word Hone walked across to my writing table, took his check book from his pocket, sat down, and wrote and signed a cheque for nine pounds, eleven shillings, and four pence.

139

"There you are, Mr. Smith. No---don't trouble to give me a receipt. The cheque is to order and Jones & Sons' endorsement will be as good as a receipt."

Mr. Smith rose quickly as my friend pronounced these, no doubt, pregnant words, bowed, and took his departure ,with a, "I wish you good-morning, gentlemen." He preserved the deprecating attitude and the cockney accent of a small tradesmen to the very last.

Purlock Hone preserved a pregnant silence. He slowly filled my pipe for the fourth time with strong Cavendish tobacco. I struck a match and handed it to him. It was my tacit tribute of admiration to the skill with which this mysterious scene, of evidently the highest diplomatic tension, had been played through without a hitch by the two great actors concerned. Words would have failed me---had I attempted to use them. My friend held my wrist while he lit his pipe at my match. His hand did not tremble more than mine---indeed not so much.

"Purlock Hone!" I cried with rising enthusiasm, "If I did not know that a great thing had passed and that Mr. Smith was an emissary of some great European Power and the bearer of some deep international secret, and that you have conveyed a secret reply to some European potentate under the pretense of writing a cheque on your banker, I could have sworn that Mr. Smith was a dunning hatter's assistant, and that you had paid an over-due bill."

"Jobson, you know I make it a rule never to take you in--- everyone else, but not you. Mr. Smith was in point of fact an emissary, but only from Jones & Sons of Oxford Street, and I have paid their bill."

Purlock Hone is one of the few men who can afford to tell the plain truth when it is against him. He is great even in defeat.

A Sherlockian Parody?

Percie W. Hart

*This one appeared in **Puck** on February 19, 1896. It was titled:*

"The Sherlock Holmes Theory"

Here is the ultimate Sherlockian parody---no Sherlock, no Watson, no Moriarty. Just a title. But it aims at the essenceof the Conan Doyle stories in a kind of subtle way.

****

Two-thirds of a cigarette lay on the station platform, unheeded by the passing throng.

They still had two minutes to wait before the 5:10 train for Mudhunk would be ready.

"See!" said Charlie Breakhearts; "the lady came sooner than he expected. He wouldn't have bothered lighting it for such a short smoke."

"You're way off!" cried John Butterfingers; "he dropped it and was ashamed to be seen picking it up."

"Both wrong!" laughed Willy Knowitall; "he was a beginner and he

141

felt himself sick, and so he stopped."

Then began a friendly argument that developed into a heated debate, as each one put in new reasons for the support of his theory.

"What's de matter wid dem gents?" queried the gatesman of the newsboy.

"Aw! der fightin' over a cigarette stump," he replied; "the dude saw it foist, but de udders was on him before he could swipe it."

SHERLOCK TRIUMPHS

The Adventure of Two Santa Clauses

by B. L. T. (Bert Leston Taylor)

*Bert Leston Taylor (1866-1921) was a newspaper man who spent most of his career on the **Chicago Tribune**, where he put together a widely read column called, "A Line O'Type or Two." But this is one of four Sherlockian parodies he wrote for **Puck** as a young journalist of 28. His identifier brings you up a little short, since each of these four parodies he signed only with his initials, now more familiar as a bacon, lettuce, and tomato.*

This Sherlockian parody was published December 28, 1904 at the height of the Christmas season. It was discovered by Sherlockian H. B. Williams. Actually Taylor titled it as "The Adventure of the Double Santa Claus.

The squeamish may assume that the Sherlock Holmes corpse was one of Sherlock's wax figures.

****

"Twas the night before Christmas. Prey to a depression I could not shake off. I sat alone in my old lodgings in Baker Street. I had not seen Holmes for six weeks, and I feared the worst. Holmes, I knew, had received a letter from Dr. Conan Doyle, threatening him with death, but he treated it lightly. Doyle had threatened him before, and it had come to nothing.

143

"Watson," he said with his enigmatic smile, "Watson, I am immortal."

I was unable to share his optimism. Dr. Conan Doyle was a desperate man, who harassed by editors, would stop at nothing. As the weeks passed, and no word of Holmes reached me, suspicion that my friend was no more grew into certainty, and I mourned for him in the laboratory where so often I had watched him busy over test tubes.

Never again, I thought, should I hear his familiar sharp indrawing of breath; never again should I meet him at Paddington for the 11:15 train, or run about London to insert want ads in the newspapers at his command; never again to hear him say, "Watson, there has been devilish work here," or "Come Watson, our work is finished," or "You remember, Watson, what Goethe said," or, "Can your patients spare you for a few days, Watson?"

I glanced moodily at the Persian slipper in which Holmes kept his tobacco; at the wash pitcher which held his supply of matches. I was even sharply reminded of his absence by the reflection that my medical practice was picking up again.

A rap at the door cut short my meditations. Hopefully, I sprang up, only to taste disappointment. An expressman had arrived with a trunk. On it was tacked a card, a message in Holmes' handwriting. It read:

"In case of accident notify Dr. Watson, Baker Street, London."

One glance at the contents of the trunk, and I fell back with a cry of horror. What seemed to be a human body, horribly mangled, as if by an explosion of dynamite, was before me! Dr. Conan Doyle had kept his word! He had blown up Sherlock Holmes; and he had made a complete job of it.

Sick with horror of the thing, I staggered toward the whiskey, and was in the act of taking the bottle from the coalscuttle when a familiar chuckle caused me to wheel about.

SHERLOCK HOLMES STOOD IN THE DOORWAY!

"Tush, Watson, I tell you I am immortal," replied my friend.

"Holmes! Holmes!" I gasped. "or, merciful jove! is it his ghost?"

"And this? - I indicated with shaking finger the gruesome trunkful."

"My most original disguise; a little surprise for you, Watson. You see, by an unfortunate mistake Dr. Doyle blew up the wrong man. Hist!"

A timid knock at the door. I pushed the trunk into the laboratory while Holmes responded to the summons. A little girl entered.

"Please, sir, I wish to see Mr. Holmes," she said gravely. "Are you Mr. Holmes? Oh, sir, I am so glad I have found you. I am in great distress. Would you tell me whether there really IS a Santa Claus? I feel sure there is, but HE says Santa Claus is only a myth."

"He? He? Who is He?" asked Sherlock Holmes, patting the child's head. "Who has been poisoning your mind, little girl?"

"Professor Moriarty," she replied, sobbingly.

"By heaven, Watson! That fiend again!" cried Holmes. "There, there, little girl, don't cry. Tell Dr. Watson where you live and then run along home. Of course there is a Santa Claus, and Sherlock Holmes will find him for you."

While I noted the tot's address and dismissed her with a lollipop Holmes busied himself in the laboratory, and presently appeared with a complete Santa Claus disguise.

"Watson," said he, "can you leave your practice for a few hours?"

I replied that Anstruther could probably look after it.

"Good," he said, "At midnight, then, we start."

Holmes ascended to the roof by means of a scaling ladder, drawing me up after him from sill to sill. He then examined the chimney.

"Rather narrow," he muttered: "but we will make it. Would you mind going down first, Watson?"

He fastened a rope about my waist and lowered me to the hearth; then he secured the rope to the chimney pot and slid himself down. Fortunately the fire was out.

"Remain here, Watson," he whispered, and shouldering his pack of toys he stepped into the room. A match flared. Holmes lighted the gas. At the same instant he uttered a cry, and peering forth I saw a remarkable picture.

Two men disguised as Santa Claus, each with a pack on his back, confronted each other; while in the doorway, candle in hand, stood a night-robed figure, the little girl who had visited our lodgings!

Instantly the men recognized each other. The sudden sharp indrawing of the breath betokened Sherlock Holmes. The cold, steely glitter of eye could belong to none other than Professor Moriarty. Holmes hurled himself upon his ancient foe with the force of a catapult, and the two rolled on the floor. The little girl vanished with a scream that awakened the entire household.

I sprang forward to lend my friend a hand, but even as I left the chimney I saw Moriarty, escaped in some way Holmes' tigerish clutch, rise from the floor. He dashed by me and disappeared up the chimney, employing the rope by which we had descended.

"After him!" cried Holmes, beginning to ascent. But Moriarty, reaching the roof, cut the rope, and we fell back on the hearth, with his malicious laugh ringing in our ears. At the same instant the room filled with people in various stages of dishabille, and a police officer followed in and laid hold of us. It was Lestrade!

"Oh, see what Santa Claus brought me!" piped the little girl, rummaging in Holmes' pack of toys.

"Oh, my silver!" shrieked a woman, opening a pack which Moriarty had dropped. "They were carrying it off!"

"Hardly a fair exchange," said Lestrade, advancing with handcuffs. Holmes removed his cotton whiskers, and the police officer fell back, gasping: "Sherlock Holmes!"

"Lestrade," said Holmes, "I turn this case over to you. I desire no glory, and request you keep my name out of it."

"Thank you, Mr. Holmes," replied Lestrade gratefully. Holmes turned to me.

"Come, Watson; our task is finished."

The Mysterious Ink Blots

Anonymous

The famous Egyptologist, Professor Wilfred Bulkeley, has disappeared!. His wife is frantic, sure that the Copts got him after all that fuss about opening the tombs of those musty old pharaohs.

*This piece appeared in **Punch** on May 11, 1927 as "The Velvet Blotting Clue." .John Bennett Shaw rescued it.*

******** ********

"Mr. Holmes!" cried the elderly lady who had burst so unceremoniously into our little flat in Baker Street. "He's gone. Vanished! Oh, what shall I do?"

With a gesture of admirably concealed *ennui*, Holmes motioned me to provide a chair. Then he bent on her the penetrating gaze that has probed to the heart of so many a tragic mystery.

"I presume, madam," he said at length, "that you refer to Professor Wilfred Bulkeley, the eminent Egyptologist. You are Mrs. Bulkeley of 19 Cranford Gardens, West Kensington."

I drew in a sharp breath of astonishment. This is incredible. Was there nothing he did not know?

"I had the honour," Holmes continued inexorably, "of dining at your house last Tuesday. I never forget my hosts. Professor Bulkeley, then, has vanished. *Excell*---too bad, I mean, ---too bad!"

"Perhaps you had better recount the story from the beginning."

I felt my face become grave as she complied. She had left her house at eleven that morning, when her husband had been in his study correcting the proofs of his latest book. At one o'clock she had returned; had vainly searched the house for her husband. The servants knew nothing. No one had called, or been heard to go out.

There was not the smallest trace of the husband she had left, apparently happy and in perfect health---nothing---except the sinister message she was now waving in the imperturbable Sherlock's face.

"Pinned to the mantelpiece?"

"Yes!" she cried, for Holmes had snapped out one of his terse, illuminating questions, "pinned with a pin. It's those awful Copts! You know the fuss there was about that Luxor tomb. And ever since we've been back, the queerest people have called. Dark-skinned people! I always *knew* they were only waiting . . ."

Holmes took the missive from her trembling fingers, and with one nervous stride was at the window. Even from where I stood, I could see that the paper he held to the yellow, evening light was of no ordinary sort. It was thick/ and of a curiously soft texture, like velvet; and the writing---could it indeed be Coptic, as Mrs. Bulkeley suggested?

It *looked*, I thought like Coptic.

Holmes was back in his chair, and his tones had now that decisive ring I knew so well.

"Madam," he said, "it is well you came to me. The police---but no matter. Professor Bulkeley is safe. He is at present with friends, and if you care to meet the 2:35 train from Edinburgh tomorrow, you will find him, I am sure, little the worse for his experiences."

When Mrs. Bulkeley, almost hysterical with relief, had left the room, and I had found my breath, I turned to my friend, "Holmes!" I ejaculated, "you astound me! How on earth---"

Holmes had sunk back in his chair as though unspeakably weary. "Blotson," he said, "you know my methods. Look at this paper. Examine its texture, note its unusual purity. Does it suggest nothing to you? Imagine the professor at work on his proofs. It suddenly becomes necessary---for reasons that will be apparent in a moment---that he should instantly proceed to Edinburgh."

"He scrawls a note to his wife, blots it carefully, and then . . .*Hold the paper to the light, Blotson.* The words 'Craig's Velvet Blotting' are visible, are they not? To the trained mind, what does that convey? Blotting paper. And---for I have given some little time to this subject--- the *best* blotting paper.

"Probably, since the paper was used for the first time, its property of perfect absorption will reveal something further. It does, you say? And to end our conjectural scene---the professor absent-mindedly puts the note back in the drawer of his desk, pins the blotting paper to the mantelpiece, and runs out into the street for a hansom. . . ."

I read what he read when you turn the paper and hold it up to the light.

"Holmes," I cried, "this isn't marvelous at all! You don't astound me in the least! Why, I myself---"

"Could have solved the mystery?" Holmes coldly suggested. "And did you?"

"No," I replied after a moment's thought.

There crept into his voice that testiness with which my friend was only too apt to receive the gentlest of reproofs.

"Well, then, shut up!" said the Great Detective.

Decoding An Adolescent Daughter

Anonymous

This brief parody appeared first in the American humor magazine **Judge** *and was republished in the* **Pittsburg** *(sic)* **Chronicle** *on August 13, 1921. It's original title was "All the Symptoms." Another Shaw entry.*

Fathers, even back in 1921, sometimes also found adolescent daughters a somewhat bewildering offspring.

Sherlock Bones comes to the rescue

****

Sherlock Bones, the celebrated detective, looked at his visitor.

"What can I do for you?" he asked kindly but severely.

"My daughter, Phyllis, is worrying me. She has lately been in a highly nervous state. She throws her arms and kicks and throws back her head disdainfully. She bangs things down on the floor and shrieks and hollers. I can't---"

"Really, sir, this sounds most distressingly," wisely remarked the great detective.

152

"Yes," continued the distracted father, "And that isn't all, she cries out to imaginary people: 'Go!'·'Go!' and then points to the door and cries, "Oh, come back! Oh, come back! I do not mean it!' Mercy!"

The great detective smoked his pipe in silence for a few minutes.

"And does your daughter do all this before a large mirror?" he asked at last.

"Yes, come to think of it she does."

"And does she go to the movies every evening?"

"Um, yes, every night."

"Then cheer up. Your daughter is only training herself to become a movie actress.

"My fee is $100."

"Thank you," said the father fervently, as with great pleasure he paid up.

The Mysterious Incident at PortlandAcademy

Anonymous

*Here we have a parody that **The Troubadour,** the student newspaper of The Portland Academy in faraway Oregon, published. It's anonymous so we don't know whether a faculty member or a student wrote it. My guess is a faculty member, but you may think differently.*

And it is raining in Portland, a touch of reality.

It appeared in two parts in April and May, 1905. It's topical, but unlike most pieces from little known places, this one is nicely done with a feel for the Conan Doyle stories. Its original title was "Sherlock Holmes at Portland Academy."

****

It was in the winter Sherlock Holmes spent in Portland that the case of the five empty peanut shells occurred. In looking over my papers I find it followed shortly after the mystery of the lost class pin, the peculiar circumstances surrounding the incident of the duplicate topic papers, the disastrous results following the research into the numerals on the roof, and several other interesting episodes connected with the same school.

But this case presents several unique points such that it may be of some interest to the public.

One rainy Wednesday, as we were passing by Portland Academy, we decided to take refuge there from the coming storm. It chanced to be the day of the Rhetoricals, so we went up to the chapel and took a seat near the back. Just as the exercises were about to begin, a small girl with red hair announced that two of her rings had been stolen and that she could not speak without them. As she was the first one on the program, this, of course, put a stop to the exercises.

One of the principals turned to us and said: "Perhaps you will help to solve this mystery," Mr. Holmes.

Holmes said he would do all in his power, and required an interview with the girl, in order to ask her some questions.

"When did you first miss these rings?" asked my friend.

"Just before chapel," said the girl nervously.

"Are you sure you put them on this morning?"

"Oh yes, I am sure I had them when school began."

Then she gave a description of the rings, and told us where she had been each hour that morning, saying, however, that she had no idea where she was robbed.

Holmes paced up and down the room in deep thought for a short time, then asked suddenly, "Do you like peanuts?"

"No," said the girl, deeply startled. "I can't bear them. They make me sick."

"That will do. You may go."

It was evident that Holmes was somewhat puzzled, but I had no doubt that he was on the track. He wore that alert look, always his, when he is deeply interested.

He turned to me and said: "You see, no doubt the importance of that last remark in the case? No? I may be mistaken, of course, but it seems to me to throw a great deal of light on the case. Come, Watson, let us take a walk down the hall."

He led the way slowly, looking about him keenly in the now deserted hall.

"Ah, what is this?" he said, suddenly, stooping down and picking half the inside of a peanut off the floor. Not one only, but as many as four or five did he find nearby. Then he searched the floor narrowly for footprints, rising soon with a smile of satisfaction.

"We are beginning to see the light, hey Watson?"

"I confess I do not see the bearing these nuts have upon the case," I answered.

"Oh, Watson, you are hopeless. But, no doubt all will be revealed shortly."

END OF PART ONE---MYSTERY SOLVED NEXT ISSUE!

Holmes would say nothing more. Then his curiosity seemed to be aroused by the sight of a small black box, similar to a mailbox fastened to the wall. A boy passing that way informed us that it was a box for contributions to the school paper.

"Oh, I see, and who has the key, may I ask?"

"I have," and smiling at our surprise the boy explained he was editor of the paper.

"But no one ever opens it any more. There is never anything in it but old transfers and stamp-pictures and chalk. Certainly I will open it if you wish."

He drew a much rusted key from his pocket and applied it to the dusty lock. After some difficulty, the door swung suddenly open. As was foretold, there were no contributions in the box, but numerous other things. Holmes gathered them all carefully in his handkerchief, much to the boy's amazement, and my own as well. He then left us, and I saw no more of him for an hour.

At two we went into the office, and requested that the girl be summoned.

Soon she came eagerly in, and asked, "Have you discovered who has my rings, Mr. Holmes?"

"I have."

"Who? Who?" we all asked, much surprised that the mystery was solved.

"You, yourself, my young lady," was the grave answer.

"I? Absurd!" she said turning white.

"Say no more. I know all. This morning, fearing to speak in chapel, you conceived the idea of hiding your rings and having the exercises stopped on account of a supposed robbery. While considering a hiding place for them, you thought of the *Troubadour* Box as the last place one would look, so hid them there."

"It is true! I confess," cried the now hysterical girl, eyeing Holmes with looks of fear.

We returned the rings to the unfortunate owner, and slipped quietly out, leaving the repentant girl to the mercies of the kind-hearted principals.

"A very simple case, Watson, but with some points of interest," Holmes said on the way down to the car. "It all hinged upon the peanuts. When the girl first came into the room with me, I noticed morsels of peanuts on her dress, and as I knew that girls with that particular shade of red hair rarely ate peanuts, I was puzzled, I admit. When I found out by asking her that she never ate peanuts, the only thing to do was to trace the peanuts.

"As you remember, I saw the insides of several peanuts in the hall. Then I understood that her object was the shell. By examining the floor with a magnifying glass, I discovered the print of a pointed-toe shoe like the one she wore. What more simple piece of reasoning than that she wished the peanut shells to conceal something in, and that something was the lost rings? The most conspicuous place is the best hiding place, and the *Troubadour* Box was seldom disturbed. As I expected, among the buttons, advertisements, scrap paper, transfers, and other similar articles, I found five peanut shells, in two of which were the lost rings in place of kernels.

"A little observation, Watson, is all that is necessary to solve the most bewildering of mysteries."

The Decline of Southern Chivalry

O. Henry

O. Henry wrote three parodies of Sherlock Holmes. Most Sherlockians consider this to be his best. They were published in newspapers or magazines in the early 1900s, and appeared in book form much later. This one was published on February 7, 1904 as "The Adventures of Shamrock Jolnes."

William Sydney Porter (1862-1910) grew up in North Carolina, moved to Texas, and worked at various jobs including as a journalist and then as a bank teller. The casualness of his bookkeeping methods led to his being found guilty of embezzlement. He denied his guilt and fled to Honduras. He later returned learning of his wife's terminal illness. In 1898 he was tried and sentenced to five years and served his time in an Ohio prison, where he began writing short stories. After his release in three years, he moved to New York City, arriving in 1902. He lived alone, drank a quart of whiskey a day, and wrote a weekly short story for a newspaper syndicate.

He had adopted the pseudonym O. Henry after jumping bail and leaving the country. His trademark was the surprise ending, as in the present item.

****

I am so fortunate as to account Shamrock Jolnes, the great New

York detective, among my muster of friends. Jolnes is what is called the "inside man of the city detective force. He is an expert in the use of the typewriter, and it is his duty, whenever there's a murder mystery to be solved, to sit at a desk telephone at Headquarters and take down the messages of "cranks" who phone in their confessions to have committed the crime.

But on certain "off days" when confessions are coming in slowly and three or four newspapers have run to earth as many different guilty persons, Jolnes will knock about the town with me, exhibiting, to my great delight and instruction, his marvelous powers of observation and deduction.

The other day I dropped in at Headquarters and found the great detective gazing thoughtfully at a string that was tied tightly around his little finger.

"Good morning, Whatsup," he said, without turning his head, "I'm glad to notice you've had your house fixed up with electric lights at last."

"Will you please tell me," I said in surprise, "how you knew that? I am sure I never mentioned the fact to anyone, and the wiring was a rush order and not completed until this morning."

"Nothing easier," said Jolnes genially. "As you came in I caught the odor of the cigar you are smoking. I know an expensive cigar, and I know that not more than three men in New York can afford to smoke cigars and pay gas bills too at the present time. That was an easy one. But I am working just now on a little problem of my own."

"Why have you that string on your finger?" I asked.

"That's the problem," said Jolnes. "My wife tied that on this morning to remind me of something I was to send up to the house. Sit down, Whatsup, and excuse me for a few moments."

The distinguished detective went to the wall telephone, and stood with the receiver to his ear for ten minutes.

"Were you listening to a confession?" I asked, when he had returned to his chair.

"Perhaps," said Jolnes, with a smile, "it might be called something of the sort. To be frank with you, Whatsup, I've cut out the dope. I've been increasing the quantity for so long that morphine doesn't have much effect on me anymore. I've got to have something more powerful. That telephone I just went to is connected to a room in the Waldorf where there's an author reading in progress. Now, to get at the solution of this string."

After five minutes of silent pondering, Jolnes looked at me with a smile, and nodded his head.

"Wonderful man!" I exclaimed. "Already?"

"It is quite simple," he said, holding up his finger. "You see the knot? That is to prevent me from forgetting. It is, therefore, a forget-me-knot. A forget-me-not is a flower. It was a sack of flour I was to send home!"

"Beautiful!" I could not help crying out in admiration.

"Suppose we go out for a ramble," suggested Jolnes.

"There is only one case of importance at hand just now. Old man McCarty, one hundred and four years old, died from eating too many bananas. The evidence points so strongly to the Mafia that the police have surrounded the Second Avenue Katzenjammer Gamberinus Club No. 2, and the capture of the assassin is only a matter of a few hours. The detective force has not yet been called on for assistance."

Jolnes and I went out and up the street toward the corner, where we were to catch a surface car.

Halfway up the block we met Rheingelder, an acquaintance of ours, who held a City Hall position.

"Good morning, Rheingelder," said Jolnes, halting. "Nice breakfast that was you had this morning."

Always on the lookout for the detective's remarkable feats of deduction, I saw Jolnes's eyes flash for an instant upon a long yellow splash on the shirt bosom and a smaller one upon the chin of Rheingelder---both undoubtedly made by the yolk of an egg.

"Oh, dot is some of your detectiveness," said Rheingelder, shaking all over with a smile. "Vell, I pet you trinks and cigars all round you cannot tell vot I haf eaten for breakfast."

"Done," said Jolnes. "Sausage, pumpernickel and coffee."

Rheingelder admitted the correctness of the surmise and paid the bet. When we had proceeded on our way I said to Jolnes:

"I thought you looked at the egg spilled on his chin and shirt front."

"I did," said Jolnes. "That is where I began my deduction. Rheingelder is a very economical, saving man. Yesterday eggs dropped in the market to twenty-eight cents per dozen. Today they are quoted at forty-two. Rheingelder ate eggs yesterday, and today went back to his usual fare. A little thing like this isn't anything, Whatsup, it belongs to

162

the primary arithmetic class."

When we boarded the streetcar we found the seats all occupied---principally by ladies. Jolnes and I stood on the rear platform.

About the middle of the car there sat an elderly man with a short gray beard, who looked to be the typical well-dressed New Yorker. At successive corners other ladies climbed aboard, and soon three or four of them were standing over the man, clinging to straps and glaring meaningfully at the man who occupied the coveted seat. But he resolutely retained his place.

"We New Yorkers," I remarked to Jolnes, "have about lost our manners, as far as the exercise of them in public goes."

"Perhaps so," said Jolnes lightly: "but the man you evidently refer to happens to be a very chivalrous and courteous gentleman from Old Virginia. He is spending a few days in New York with his wife and two daughters, and he leaves for the South to-night."

"You know him, then?" I said in amazement.

"I never saw him before we stepped on the car," declared the detective, smilingly.

"By the gold tooth of the Witch of Endor!" I cried, "if you can construe all that from his appearance you are dealing in nothing else than black art."

"The habit of observation---nothing more," said Jolnes. "If the old gentleman gets off the car before we do, I think I can demonstrate to you the accuracy of my deduction."

Three blocks along the gentleman rose to leave the car. Jolnes addressed him at the door:

"Pardon me, sir, but are you not Colonel Hunter, of Norfolk, Virginia?"

"No suh," was the extremely courteous answer. "My name suh, is Ellison---Major Winfield R. Ellison, from Fairfax County, in the same state. I know a good many people, suh, in Norfolk---the Goodriches, the Tollivers, and the Crabtrees, suh, but I never had the pleasure of meeting your friend, Colonel Hunter. I am happy to say, suh, that I am going back to Virginia to-night, after having spent a week in yo' city with my wife and three daughters. I shall be in Norfolk in about ten days and if you will give me your name, suh, I will take pleasure in looking up Colonel Hunter and telling him that you inquired after him, suh."

"Thank you," said Jolnes; "tell him Reynolds sent him his regards, if you will be so kind."

I glanced at the great New York detective and saw that a look of intense chagrin had come upon his clear-cut features. Failure in the slightest point always galled Shamrock Jolnes.

"Did you say your *three* daughters?" he asked of the Virginia gentleman.

"Yes, suh, my three daughters, all as fine girls as there are in Fairfax County," was the answer.

With that Major Ellison stopped the car and began to descend the step.

Shamrock Jolnes clutched his arm.

"One moment, sir," he begged, in an urbane voice in which I alone detected the anxiety "am I not right in believing that one of the young ladies is an *adopted* daughter?"

"You are, suh," admitted the Major, from the ground, "but how the devil yo' knew it is more than I can tell."

"And mo' than I can too," I said, as the car went on.

Jolnes was restored to his calm, observant serenity by having wrested victory from his apparent failure; so after we got off the car he invited me into a café promising to reveal the process of his latest wonderful feat.

"In the first place," he began after we were comfortably seated, "I knew the gentleman was no New Yorker because he was flushed and uneasyand restless on account of the ladies that werestanding, although he did not rise and give them his seat. I decided from his appearance that he was a Southerner rather than a Westerner.

"Next I began to figure out the reason for his not relinquishing his seat to a lady when he evidently felt strongly, but not overpoweringly, impelled to do so. I very quickly decided on that. I noticed that one of his eyes had received a severe jab in one corner, which was red and inflamed, and that all over his face were tiny round marks about the size of an uncut lead pencil. Also upon his patent-leather shoes were a number of deep imprints shaped like ovals cut off square at one end.

"Now there is only one district in New York City where a man is bound to receive scars and wounds and indentations of that sort---and that is along the sidewalks of Twenty-third Street and a portion of Sixth Avenue South of there. I knew from the imprints of trampling French heels on his feet and the marks of countless jabs in the face from umbrellas and parasols carried by women in the shopping district that he had been in conflict with the Amazonian troops. And as he was a man of intelligent appearance, I knew he would not have braved such dangers

165

unless he had been dragged thither by his own women folk. Therefore, when he got into the car his anger at the treatment he had received was sufficient to make him keep his seat in spite of his traditions of Southern chivalry.

"There had to be daughters," said Jolnes, calmly. "If he had only a wife, and she near his own age, he could have bluffed her into going alone. If he had a young wife she would prefer to go alone. So there you are."

"I'll admit that," I said; "but, now, why two daughters? And how. in the name of all the prophets, did you guess that one was adopted when he told you he had three?"

"Don't say guess," said Jolnes, with a touch of pride in his air; "there is no such word in the lexicon of ratiocination. In Major Ellison's buttonhole there was a carnation and a rosebud backed by a geranium leaf. No woman ever combined a carnation with a rosebud into a boutonniere. Close your eyes, Whatsup, and give the logic of your imagination a chance. Cannot you see the lovely Adele fastening a carnation to the lapel so that papa may be gay upon the street? And then the romping Edith May dancing up with sisterly jealousy to add her rosebud to the adornment?"

"And then," I cried, beginning to feel enthusiasm, "when he declared he had three daughters---"

"I could see," said Jolnes, "one in the background who added no flower; and I knew she must be---"

"Adopted!" I broke in. "I give you every credit; but how did you know he was leaving for the South to-night?"

"In his breast pocket," said the great detective, "something large and oval made a protuberance. Good liquor is scarce on trains, and it is a

166

long journey from New York to Fairfax County."

"Again, I must bow to you," I said. "And tell me this, so that my last shred of doubt will be cleared away; why did you decide that he was from Virginia?"

"It was very faint, I admit," answered Shamrock Jolnes, "but no trained observer could have failed to detect the odor of mint in the car."

The Disappearance of the President's Whisker

Anonymous

Sherlock Gnomes is in South Africa during the Boer War investigating spies and such whileTotson is there with the Army Medical Corps. Eight parodies detailing their adventures were printed weekly with these intriguing titles:

The Adventure of the President's Whisker (March 10, 1900).
The Adventure of the White Spot (March 17, 1900).
The Adventure of the Mysterious Corset (March 24, 1900).
The Adventure of the Missing Link (March 31, 1900).
The Adventure of the Artificial Teeth (April 14, 1900).
The Adventure of the Pink Pearl (April 28, 1900)
The Adventure of the Missing Flag (May 12, 1900).
The Adventure of the Grange Mystery (May 26, 1900).

The plots are full of what the author calls "out of the ordinary mysteries solved though out of the ordinary coincidence."And they show acquaintance with the Conan Doyle stories. The pieces use South African terms, such as vrow for Dutch woman, as well demonstrating a knowledge of battles then taking place. This one has the charm of a quaint period piece.

*They were published in **Scraps** (James Henderson=s Penny Weekly).*

I'm indebted to Robert C. S. Adey for copies of all eight.

****

"This climate puts me in mind of my past experiences in India," I said to Gnomes, as we strolled along the harbour at Capetown after disembarking from our transport just out from England.

"No doubt," laconically replied my friend, as with his pipe in his mouth, his long lean arms hanging loosely over the rear of his khaki tunic, with his head bent slightly forward in his old introspective manner, he was taking more observation of the moving crowd than of my remarks.

This trip was semi-professional in both our cases. Gnomes had volunteered for the front that his talents might have a larger field among the disloyal, the contraband, and the spy, while I had become attached to an army hospital corps which was to move up country on the following day.

"I have been thinking," said Gnomes, suddenly wakening out of his reverie, "that although there is much here worth studying, especially in the methods of the native police, I shall entrain with you tomorrow, after all."

"I am certainly glad to hear that," I replied, "as I shall be interested in your doings---or rather undoings would perhaps be more appropriate. In the meantime, don't you think we could profitably study the interior of a restaurant?"

"With all my heart, Totson, but hadn't we better ask that policeman to direct us to a good place?"

"What policeman? I don't see one," I said confusedly.

"Well, he's right in front of you."

"I can only see a gentleman in khaki," I replied---"one of the R.H.A."

"Precisely, but can't you deduce the policeman? See the way he leans contentedly against the lamp-post, and though he is not now in his regulation boots, observe how he conscientiously endeavours to cover up the street. No doubt he is a reservist, lately joined."

"Well, Gnomes, you are really too bad," I exclaimed. "Your reasoning is as usual unanswerable. But let us approach and see."

We did and obtained the needful information, together with the first problem my friend was destined to unravel. Drifting from the subject to the front, so to speak, our quondam constable informed us, that amongst other events, he had passed through a season of imprisonment (which was truly a reversal of things for him) at Pretoria, and that the President of the Transvaal Republic, hearing that he was an accredited member of the B Division of London Police, revealed to him the circumstances of a terrible loss; in fact no less than the loss of a favourite whisker, a single hair, it is true, but the longest that he grew, the favourite of his wife and, in fact, the pride of the whole community. It had mysteriously disappeared from the left side of his face.

The officer concluded by saying the President had questioned him as to whether Sherlock Gnomes had arrived, for it seems he knew of the great detective's departure from England, and he was willing to spare no expense in the matter if he could obtain his services.

"Totson," said my friend, as we strolled on towards our dinner, "this is indeed fortunate. A case out of the ordinary will supply the needful tonic to counteract this climate."

"Soup, sir!" grunted the black-and-white waiter a few minutes afterwards, as we were sitting opposite one another at a really smart buffet up town. And a very good soup it was, though Holmes seemed to be prying round his plate in a dissatisfied manner. Spasms of joy and doubt appeared on his eager countenance as with his spoon and fork he deftly fished something from the liquid, and, holding it up muttered one word with intense delight:

"Found!"

"What?" I exclaimed.

"The President's whisker!"

"Now Gnomes, this is too much. You don't suppose that I'm going to swallow that---"

"Not the hair, certainly," he replied, "but the fact of my discovery is beyond doubt."

Saying which he held the whisker up to the point of his nose and sniffed exultantly, then bringing forth his powerful lens, he took a long and careful survey, and finished with a grunt of satisfaction.

"Well, what do you deduce from it?" I inquired.

"Oh, it's perfectly simple, after all. The problem is scarcely as complicated as I hoped, hardly, in fact, worthy of my reputation."

He was now getting into his usual habit of self-adulation, which I have often noted, but I did not interrupt him as I was intensely interested in all his theories.

"This hair," he continued, "came down in a coal truck from Pretoria,

171

and is from the left side of the face."

"Here, that will do," I interrupted. "How in the name of---"

"Easily enough, my friend," said he, "you remember, reading an article in the **Cape Argus** to me, one of the papers which we purchased at such an exorbitant price on the arrival of our transport---that the President a week ago had a bad attack of neuralgia in the left side of his face, and that he was presented by an English officer, at Pretoria, with a bottle of Elliman's Embrocation, which gave him considerable relief. Now, there is a very strong odour still upon this whisker of turpentine, a constituent of the Embrocation, also, I observe very minute particles of coal clinging to it in places, besides which, the colour, its extreme length, and, finally, being as it is impregnated with peculiar tobacco known to be used by the President, puts it beyond all doubt."

"My dear Gnomes, it is plain as day."

Beet Sugar and Reciprocity

William L Riordan

Only one of the four hundred plus parodies I collected contained racial slurs. The offending piece was insulting to African Americans with all the negative stereotypes clear through from beginning to end. Only three had anti-Semitic or ethnic slurs. More though turned to commonly held stereotypes about women. But, say three or four, used the mentally challenged as the butt of humor.

This parody treats with the actions of a developmentally disabled offspring. But in this case a father's has humane concern for a cherished son.

*The author of this and two other parodies, was William L. Riordan, (1861-1909), a **New York Times** reporter, in whose paper the piece appeared on October 25, 1903, during the height of a New York mayoral election. It was titled "Bedlamite.|*

*Riordan is well known to political junkies for his book **Plunkitt of Tammany Hall,** in which a ward boss gives the journalist some good "practical" political advice such as knowing the difference between honest graft and dishonest graft. Boss Plunkitt said his motto was, "I seen my opportunities and I took 'em."*

****

173

"Observe that man walking ahead of us," said Padlock Jones, as we turned into Candlestickmaker Street on the way to our lodgings.

"I say observe the man," he continued. "Don't merely look at him; that will tell you nothing. Observe him and tell me what you make of him."

"He seems to be an ordinary portly business man, rather in a hurry." I ventured, "but we would meet a dozen such men in two or three blocks. I notice nothing peculiar about him."

"You mean to say that you cannot even say where he comes from?" asked Padlock Jones, gazing at me with unaffected surprise.

"I cannot," I replied, rather nettled.

"Well, well, Jotson, I fear I will have to give you up as a pupil in the science of deduction. I thought I observed in you signs of almost human intelligence in that little affair of the stolen diamonds, but it seems that even I can be mistaken. Anyhow, I will try you once more. Now, observe that man again. Can't you see that he is from Brooklyn?"

"I can't say I do," I answered.

"Ha, ha!" laughed Padlock Jones. "This is an example of the A B C of my science. Don't you see how he walks with squared elbows, as if he were trying to force his way through a crowd? Now, nobody does that except a football player in daily practice or a man who is accustomed to cross the Brooklyn Bridge in the rush hours. His age and build would preclude the idea that he plays football now, whatever he may have done a quarter century ago. Isn't the deduction plain?"

"But that is not all. Put on your glasses and look at the seams of the man's coat. Don't you see that they are stretched almost to the bursting

174

point and that the coattails are perceptibly dragged down? That is an infallible indication of recent and regular participation in Brooklyn Bridge crushes. It is possible to be mistaken once in a hundred times about the elbows, but you can't be mistaken about those seams and coattails. If I were asked in a court of Justice to give still further proof I would say confidently, 'Let that man remove his shirt and you will find bruises under his fourth rib and',---but hello! our Brooklynite is making for our den!"

So he was. A few minutes later he was standing before us in Padlock Jones's study, saying, "I have come to see you, Mr. Jones, about a painful matter. I am John W Hawkins---"

"Of Brooklyn," my friend interrupted.

"Ah, you have heard of me?" queried our visitor.

"Never," replied Padlock Jones. "Only one of my little deductions. Now, what can I do for you?"

After an embarrassing silence, Mr. Hawkins said: "I have a son, just of age; a handsome boy, but he has been---er---feeble-minded from boyhood. About two months ago I was advised to send him to a sanitarium near Central Park---here is the address---and I determined to try it. I received somewhat favorable reports of his condition till this morning, when the physician in charge of the sanitarium telephoned me that the boy had disappeared. I did not care for the publicity that would attend a police search, and I thought that such a search would be fruitless anyhow. So having heard of your marvelous success in finding the elusive north pole without leaving your room, I come to you for help. The boy is altogether harmless, but I fear he may come to harm in this great city after having lived so long in the quiet glades of Brooklyn."

"Pass the thinker, Jotson," was Padlock Jones's only comment, as he bared his arm for the cocaine. Having taken in the usual supply, he yawned, threw his feet over the desk, and said, "Come in at 8 o'clock this evening, Mr. Hawkins, and I will lead you to the boy all right. No, not a word now, Good day."

At the appointed time Mr. Hawkins was on hand. Padlock Jones led us to the street, hailed an automobile, pushed us in, and called out, "To the Circle!"

Within a few minutes he called a halt, and we found ourselves on the edge of a crowd, with open umbrellas, listening to a spellbinder, who was shouting something about beet sugar and reciprocity. It was raining freely, and the cold blasts of wind made me shiver from head to foot as we stepped from the automobile.

"I didn't know we had come out to attend a political meeting," said I huffily, my teeth chattering.

"Didn't you?"laughed Padlock Jones. "I'm afraid you're not a good party man, Jotson. But now to business. Mr. Hawkins, go up on that stand where that fellow is yelling and take a careful look over the crowd. We will wait here."

Mr. Hawkins made his way to the stand with difficulty and peered about anxiously. Suddenly his face lighted up, and he sprang from the stand into the crowd. A minute later he emerged, leading a young man whose clothes were soaked and whose lips were blue with cold. "It's my boy!" he exclaimed.

"Get in the automobile and take him home right away," said Padlock Jones, stopping a flow of thanks. "You may drop in to-morrow morning, if you wish."

"But how could you know that---"

176

"It is no time for questions now," said Padlock Jones sternly. "If you are curious about a very simple matter, come to me in the morning and I will try to satisfy your curiosity."

Early in the morning Mr. Hawkins was in our rooms.

"How could you guess---" he began.

"Guess! guess! Why will everybody, even you Jotson, talk about my making guesses?" Padlock Jones interrupted impatiently. "I never guess; I deduce. There is no guessing in mathematics, is there? Well deduction is just as exact a science."

"When I heard that this feeble-minded young man had escaped from a sanatorium I considered where he was most likely to go. It was reasonable to assume that, after having been cooped up for two months, he would seek some entertainment adapted to his intellect."

"At first it occurred to me he would steer straight for one of the new plays at certain Broadway theatres. In fact, I was about to make a round of those theatres, but, knowing by experience that hasty action is not wise action, I went over the field again and asked myself, 'Is there any other place to which a feeble-minded man would be more likely to go under the circumstances?'"

"While I was thinking, my glance fell on a newspaper on the table, and I saw an advertisement of this open-air meeting. All at once it occurred to me that if there was one place in New York to which a feeble-minded person would go on a blood-chilling night like this it was to an open-air political meeting and as this one was to be held not far from the sanitarium I decided to try it first. When I heard the speaker talking beet sugar and reciprocity in a municipal campaign I was sure I had struck the right place."

177

"No particular mystery about all this, is there? It is simplicity itself. Just one more jab of the needle, Jotson. Won't you have one, Mr. Hawkins? It's great. No? well, good night."

Sherlock Among the Spirits

Anonymous

As soon as Conan Doyle revealed in 1917 his belief in Spiritualism, "Other World" Sherlockian parodies began to appear. Three even were published in a Spiritualist magazine having Sherlock come to the defense of Spiritualists, something Conan Doyle never made him do.

This one is an anonymous parody that turned up in a magazine edited by G. K. Chesterton (1878-1936), titled only as "From the Diary of Dr. Watson." It bears the marks of Chesterton himself, for unlike most parodies, it is a little more serious in tone. To the writer, Spiritualism seems to be more than just a bad joke.

Chesterton began as an illustrator but soon was drawn into journalism. He wrote over 80 books, 200 short stories, 4000 essays, plus numerous poems and plays. One book was a well received study of Charles Dickens. And he created one of the major detectives of the classic period---Father Brown, a Roman Catholic priest.

His greatest influence though was as a witty literary and social critic and an apologist for orthodox Christianity. He loved to turn common ideas on their head with paradox and this occurs frequently in his series of detective stories about the Father Brown.

In his early years he too was fascinated by the occult and experimented with the Ouija board. This was published in **G. K.'s Weekly** on August 15, 1925.

****

The Spiritualist Séance, which my friend Conan Doyle had induced me to hold in my old rooms in Baker Street, was just over. It had been a tremendous revelation. The medium, Dr. Magog, whom I assumed from the first to be a charlatan (for my training had been strictly scientific and rational), because of his long white hair and beard and his Lithuanian name, astounded me with the accuracy of his suggestions. He even converted Sir Arthur's other friend Dr. Challenger, whom readers of the **Strand Magazine** may remember as having discovered a world of prehistoric animals, whose manners and demeanour he seemed to share. He had begun by having grave doubts, which he expressed by hurling the table to the end of the room and dancing on several the enquirers after truth; but half way through the proceedings he burst into sobs that shook the building.

I could understand his feelings. The medium mentioned things that could only be known in the innermost domestic circle; such as a knock given to a girl when she was a child, now recalled by the spirit of her brother killed in the war. Sometimes this intimacy was even distressing; as in the picture called up before us of a girl sobbing in a remote chateau in France, and the gloomy admission by a young man present that the memory moved him to remorse. Perhaps the most remarkable case was that of the spirit of a daughter who told her father not to neglect his appearance from grief at her death, seeing that the Shining Ones liked to see him in a single eyeglass and spats. Now the man in question was indescribably shaggy and shabby, but he admitted that he had indeed been thus adorned in happier days.

I was brooding on these things after the others had left, when I heard a step on the stair that told of one of them returning. Dr. Magog himself hurriedly re-entered the room, saying: "I had forgotten my hat. Interesting occasion, wasn't it?"

"You absolutely amazed me," I answered.

"You have often told me so, my dear Watson," he replied.

I sprang to my feet and stood stiffened with incredulous stupefaction, for I had caught a note of something more marvelous than any psychical marvels.

He seated himself languidly and removed the white wig, showing the unmistakable frontal development of the greatest detective in the world. "If you had used my methods, Watson," he said, "you would have known that a man never forgets his hat except when he is wearing a wig. It was a deplorable lapse. Well, you see, I converted Challenger."

"A wonderful achievement," I said, "The discoverer of the prehistoric world."

"A very appropriate occupation Watson," he said. "I should say Dr. Challenger's powers of scientific observation were just about equal to noticing one of the larger Plesiosauri a few yards off. With a little more attention to minutiae he might even see a mammoth on the mat."

"But how on earth did you manage it?" I asked. "How did you know of that nursery incident, for instance?"

"The girl was good looking and healthy and she had false teeth. More probably she had them knocked out; and who should knock them out if not her brother?"

"And what about the eyeglass and spats," I demanded.

"I have myself written a little monograph on 'The Monacle of Crime,' and we saw something of its devastating effect when we looked into that little problem of the Haunted Hat Peg. The man had different markings in the two eye sockets, in a way only produced by the single eyeglass. Did you ever know a shabby, unshaven man wear a single eyeglass? His beard bristled like that of all men who were once clean shaven. I guessed the spats; but I was careful only to say that the higher intelligences would like to see them. There is no accounting for taste."

"And how did you know," I asked, lowering my voice, "that the young man had broken the heart of a lady in a chateau?"

"He hadn't," replied Sherlock Holmes, "but I could see by his face he would be the last man to deny it. Rather too obvious, Watson. Will you pass me my violin?"

The Model T Mystery

E. H. Soans

This is an English mystery taking place at the height of World War I. Alice Nosegay, "the only woman that Sheerluck Jones had ever betrayed the slightest affection for," has disappeared.

*This appeared in **The Ford Times** of August 1916 as "The Disappearance of Alice Nosegay," and is another Shaw discovery.*

****

Rain was falling steadily as I emerged from the bowels of the earth, and there, outside the tube station stood Sheerluck Jones.

Buttoning up my coat I fell into step with the great detective, wondering what surprise he had in store for me.

It was not long before I was enlightened. "My dear What's On, disaster has overtaken us. I will not tax your brain with deductions but simply state fact. In a few words: Alice Nosegay has disappeared."

This was indeed disaster, because, as all the world knows, Alice was the only woman that Sheerluck had ever betrayed the slightest affection for.

"No clue?" I ventured.

"None whatsoever," he vouchsafed, "she has disappeared as completely as if she had never existed."

He walked moodily on, never speaking a word until, turning into Piccadilly, he surprised me by singing at the top of his voice:

"Of all the gir-ir-ir-irls that are so sweet,
There's none so sweet as Al-lus;
She is the dar-ar-ar-aling of my heart,
And lives by the Crystal Pal-lus."

I looked at him, wondering if the shock had turned his brain.

A policeman attracted by the singing, came up prepared to remonstrate, but when he saw who the singer was he became subservient in a moment, and remarked with a smile, "Ha, Mr. Jones, working out another tick-lish case, I observe."

The astute detective threw him under the wheels of an on-coming motor bus and passed on, while I followed closely in his footsteps.

He was making for Butcher Street, so I did not disturb him by talking. I knew he would think things over when we were there.

He took a seat by the fire that was blazing merrily. Noticing how distrait he was, I said;---"Why don't you compose yourself, Sheerluck?"

"Ah, me, how can I?" he more sobbed than said.

"Yiddle on your fiddle," said I.

"Good idea, What's On, I'll yiddle." Which he did, sucking a nob of resin the while. I left him, knowing full well that his brain was intent on discovering Alice, even though he was weaving such subtle melodies.

About a week after, we were sitting at breakfast, when he told me that he had recently called at Alice's home, and found that though she was still missing he has discovered there some correspondence that would help him solve the problem. What that correspondence was he would not for the moment say.

Realising that I could not render any assistance I went out.

After wandering about for an hour or so, I dropped in a café and was enjoying a cup of coffee and a cigarette, when I was surprised to see a figure enter clad in a suit of armour.

After looking around for a few moments the person thus garbed made for the table where I was seated, and, taking a chair, said in a sepulchral voice, "Do you know me?"

I confessed I did not.

The mysterious one then asked me to guess.

Nothing loth, I ventured, "Oliver Cromwell."

A scornful laugh greeted me, then: "My dear What's On, I am Sheerluck."

"But why this get up?" I queried.

"I am on the track of her whom I most desire to find."

"Well," said I, "with what result?"

"To-night's the night, What's On," he answered. "Be at our rooms by seven o'clock." With which he glided away.

I was there well before the appointed hour and found Sheerluck minus his suit of armour, idly figuring on a piece of paper.

"You will observe, my dear What's On, that this case has been one of peculiar intricacy, complex enough to baffle the best men of Scotland Yard," he said.

Really it had not struck me like that, but to humour him I answered, "Yes."

"I shall, however," he continued, "take you to-night to the spot where she is whom we seek. See to it that our car is ready for the journey. You may go."

Thus dismissed I went to the garage, filled up with petrol, oil, and water, giving the tyres the attention they needed.

The night was perfect, the starlit heavens cast an irradiating light over all, while the new moon, suspended crescent like, added her lustre to the beauty of the night. A slight frost tinged the air, adding a piquancy that made motoring a delight.

Cars a-many have I known; cars a-many do I know, but my present 20 hp, known to you as well as me, is indeed IT.

"Speed up a little," Sheerluck at my side remarked.

I gave her a little more, and the sharp sibilant hiss of the carburetor told us how well the car answered, as did our increased speed.

Through the Surrey lanes we sped, never stopping, but making for our goal with unerring precision.

186

Presently a large house, silhouetted against the sky, caused Sheerluck to cry---"Throttle down, we are there."

I brought the car to a standstill and leaped out beside the great man.

Instead of going to the house, he made for a building a little way off, which proved to be a garage. A tiny stream of light filtered through a crack in the door, to which Sheerluck applied his eye.

He turned round to me, perspiration oozing from every pore, and said; "Look!"

I did so. There was she whom we sought, gazing fondly at a new Ford car.

We tarried no longer but burst in, Sheerluck crying as we did so: "Found at last, dear heart."

With a glad cry of delight, she ran to him, when he put his arms around her, a noise like a back fire, broke the silence. He had kissed her, Alice Nosegay, on the lips.

Little more remains to be told.

Sheerluck had found in Alice's rooms a copy of the **Ford Times**, which gave him the lead, as it were.

Close by was a receipt for a new car, and a letter from the village where we found her, complaining to her mother of the petrol shortage.

Sheerluck saw the thing in a moment. He knew a Ford could only be hung up through want of petrol, and realized it was only a question of time before he found her.

As he told me later---

"You see What's On, really she never disappeared at all."

"No," I echoed, "not really."

MIXED RESULTS

Those Shocking Wellesley Women!

A. Cannon Doily

Sherlock Holmes takes up the complaints of a local editor about those careless female students at Wellesley College in Massachusetts.Holmes is shocked, shocked, shocked!by what he finds.

This is a somewhat querulous and not very appealing Sherlock. Those Twentieth Century "New Women" seem to have really gotten under the skin of the editor of **The Townsman.** *The piece was titled "Sherlock Holmes Redivivus."*

****

Sherlock Holmes, who had just returned from an extended tour of the globe, met Dr. Watson by appointment at the Wellesley Inn.

After lunch the two old friends started for a walk about the village, renewing acquaintance after their long separation. Sherlock Holmes at once fell into his former habits of observation and investigation, stopping to pick up all sorts of objects that attracted his attention as he walked along. The friends had turned into the college grounds and had reached the borders of the lake before Holmes suggested resting for a few moments while he sorted out his collection.

"I am glad to note,"said Dr. Watson, "that you have abandoned the use of your hypodermic. Do you find your faculties of close observation and intuitive reasoning in any measure impaired in consequence?"

Holmes did not answer the question, but remarked, as he looked up at the college buildings, "I was never in Wellesley before. I observe that it is a woman's college."

"What led you to that conclusion?" asked the doctor.

Sherlock Holmes selected from his collection three hair pins that he picked up in his walk from the Inn, remarking as he placed them in the doctor's hand, "Watson, why don't you put that mind of yours to the task of why women who jab these pins in their head with such ferocity, do not get them in far enough to stay put?"

Dr. Watson entered a memorandum in his note book.

"It was said of Thoreau," continued Holmes, "that in his walks along the shores of his beloved Walden Pond he could at any time uncover an Indian arrow head with a random kick of the soil. Some future Thoreau will uncover hair pins by the dozen anywhere within Wellesley village limits in the same way."

"I also observe," said Holmes, "that the young men who visit the young women at the college prefer the 'Mecca' brand of cigarettes, though the 'Sweet Caporal' and 'Turkish Trophies' have their advocates."

Before Dr. Watson could express his surprise at the great detective's wonderful powers of divination Holmes handed him half a dozen empty cigarette wrappers from his collection made in this brief morning walk.

"But there is a coarser streak in some of the men," said Holmes sententiously, as he passed the doctor a soiled Sensible Chewing Plug wrapper.

190

"I thought college girls preferred Page and Shaw's confections,"remarked Sherlock a moment later. "My collection indicates, though Somerset and Shrafft's are close second and Peter's Milk Chocolate seem to be neck and neck in the race, and he handed to the doctor an assortment of wrappers of various forms and colors."

Dr. Watson was so amazed at these exhibitions of his friend's wonderful powers he could hardly speak as he watched the world's greatest detective continue the work of sorting out the results of his morning's walk.

"Watson, the girls out here haven't learned that it is an exploded idea that fish is a brain food," continued Holmes as he handed the doctor an empty tin can stamped Parsifal Brand, Norway and Scottish Fish. "But they do accept your theory, doctor, that the grained and shredded breakfast foods, that must be thoroughly masticulated, are to be preferred to those that are swallowed whole as they come from the double boiler, and Holmes produced a pasteboard box that had once contained a dozen "Shredded Wheat" Biscuits.

Sherlock Holmes was in a seriously thoughtful mood as he selected the remnants of soiled paper bags and pasteboard boxes from his collection and asked the doctor if he wondered that the students sometimes broke down in their efforts to assimilate so much cake and fudge and so many eclairs and doughnuts with philosophy and psychology and ancient history and what not.

The great detective had that faraway look in his eyes as he took in the broad expanse of the lake and was about to continue his walk when he picked up a little blue box which he handed to the doctor with the remark, "I had overlooked this Parlor Safety Match box. It is a delusion, Watson, there is no safety in any kind of match."

Poor Sherlock Holmes! He had become a Pessimist during his wanderings abroad.

Dr. Watson, however laughed uproariously for he had contracted a happy marriage during his old friend's absence in foreign countries.But what a conglomerate mess must litter the streets of Wellesley to produce such results in a short morning walk.

Sherlock in *Oklahoma!*

Sir Arthur Cannon Ball

This anonymous parody appeared in **Sturm's Oklahoma Magazine** *in September 1905, as"Hurlock Shoams – One of His Adventures."*

Oklahoma was then still a Territory, would not reach statehood for two more years. And when you think of it, that's a pretty amazing reach for Sherlock all the way from London.

The time and place are about the same as in the famous Rodgers and Hammerstein musical, and it begins with some of the same words. Still it may be a little difficult to imagine Poor Judd and Curly and the gang chuckling over it.

More than a curiosity, this parody contains a good many nice touches and an accurate knowledge of incidents in the Conan Doyle stories.

Its discoverer, Sherlockian Dick Warner, suspects that a journalist of the day, Walter Ferguson, was the author.   Ferguson was a Republican in a then Democratic state who quit journalism to get himself elected to the Oklahoma Senate. He then left politics to become a successful banker. His wife was also a journalist and was syndicated in the Scripps-Howard newspapers.

****

193

One beautiful summer morning, after the successful completion of "The Adventure of the Three Deviled Crabs, my friend Hurlock Shoams and I were sitting in our apartments in Beaker Street, smoking, when suddenly we were startled by a violent ring at the door bell.

"What deductions do you make from that?" said I, taking out my note book, prepared to get material for Sir Arthur Cannon Ball's next story.

Shoams buried himself in thought for a moment and then replied, "I should say that there is a man at the door, that he is a tall man and that he wears a light suit of clothes and carries a cane."

"And how did you know that?" I asked in amazement.

"Saw him as he came up the steps," answered the great detective, briefly.

I was astounded at my friend's cleverness. Never before had I had a more striking illustration of those powers of logical deduction which have made him so deservedly famous.

"I may say further," continued Shoams, "that he appears to be in a hurry. I infer from the fact that he has already rung the bell eleven times. Perhaps you had better let him in."

I made haste to do so.

"Mr. Shoams," began the visitor, before he was fairly seated, "I have a matter of utmost importance to entrust to you. Let me first tell you who I am and---"

"Hold on! Wait a minute!" cried Shoams excitedly. "Don't you do anything of the kind or you will spoil everything. Think how much more effective this story will be if you give me a chance to display my powers of deduction at this point. Your name, if I am not mistaken, is Cortwright, you are a manufacturer by profession, but have taken considerable interest in music. Furthermore, you are married and have a small boy whose age is somewhere between ten and fifteen."

The visitor was almost overcome. "How did you know all this?" he gasped.

"Your name and profession I got from your business card which you handed to me when you entered the room. I infer your interest in music from the bass drum you are carrying under your arm. The fact that you are married is evident from the most superficial glance at your clothes. No man would choose a neck tie like that for himself. I learned of the existence of your son when you took off your hat and allowed a baseball bat, a kite, and eleven marbles and a toy pistol to fall out."

"Good heavens," Mr. Shoams, exclaimed the bewildered Cortwright, "nothing can be hid from you. I have no doubt that you already know my business as well as I do myself."

"Possibly I do," returned Shoams, with his characteristic modesty, "but for the benefit of the readers it may be well for you to state it. Otherwise they might not understand the story."

"Well," said the visitor, thus admonished, "I have been married for twelve years and am deeply attached to my wife and my only son, who was eleven last month. The thought that they may be involved in the terrible fate that now threatens me drives me almost to despair."

In his agitation he pulled out several handfuls of his rich auburn hair and laid them on the table. "But to get down to the point," he continued, "last Christmas my wife, as a token of her love, and devotion, purchased

195

a present for me (with money furnished by myself) a box of cigars, each and every one tied with a beautiful bow of pink ribbon. I never saw finer pink ribbons in my life. I was deeply touched by the evidence of conjugal affection. I told my wife with tears in my eyes that after such love and thoughtfulness on her part, it would be a crime for me to smoke the cigars, and I vowed to her as long as I lived I would keep them as my most cherished possession."

"That was six months ago. Yesterday I happened to go to the box to look at them, and imagine my consternation on raising the lid to find one of them missing. I knew that no one could have taken it to smoke. They are not that kind of cigars."

"Clearly it was a deliberate plot against me and my family. The theft of the cigar was merely a preliminary warning of greater dangers in store for us. The villain had taken this method of adding additional horror to his dastardly schemes. I shall not worry you with an account of the anxious hours I passed after making this fearful discovery."

"Suffice it to say that this morning another of the cigars was missing. I could endure the strain no longer and came straightway to you and put myself under your protection---and, oh, Mr. Shoams," he ended pathetically, "I look to you alone to save my family and myself from the awful fate that threatens us."

During this terrible narrative Shoams had listened with feverish attention. His agitation, as it drew near its close, had become so great that he had bitten his pipe in half and put the lighted end in his mouth.

"You have not come a moment too soon, Mr. Cortwright," he said, "In all the experience I have had in the three books and numerous short stories that Mr. Cannon Ball has written about me I have never encountered such a fiendish plot as this. We must make haste before it is too late. Come, Dr. Squatson, get the pistols and your notebook and

196

we will follow Mr. Cortwright at once."

We soon arrived at the gentleman's house. Shoams with his characteristic energy began a thorough search of the premises. "I have a hundred and fifty three hypotheses," he said, "any one of which would fit the facts so far as we know them at present. But what we need is more data to work upon. We can not build bricks without straw."

Suddenly he paused. "I think," he said, "that we have arrived at that part of the story when a clue is in order. Let me see, now, what shall it be? Ah, this will do!" he cried, as he stooped down and picked out of one of the flower-beds a half smoked cigar with a bow of pink ribbon.

Cortwright and I were astounded by his cleverness. Shoams shook his head. "That knocks out sixty-nine of my hypotheses," he said, "leaving me, if I am not mistaken, a total of eighty-four to work on."

"But we have even a more subtle opponent to deal with than I supposed. He is trying to throw us off the track by making us believe he really smoked the cigar. Clever fellow."

His eyes sparkled. "Ah Squatson," he said enthusiastically, "this time we have a foeman worthy of our steel. Unless I am very much mistaken this will be one of my best cases." But now, turning to Cortwright, "let us see the box of cigars."

"Well," he said finally, after examining them, "I think I have enough clues to work on for the present. Dr. Squatson and I will be back this evening at seven. Have a ladder against the side of the house and a rope hanging down the chimney. It would never do for us to be seen entering by the door. Somebody might suspect."

We took our departure, and my friend busied himself unsuccessfully for the rest of the day in chemical analysis of a boarding house mince pie.

At seven o'clock we made our way to the Cortwright residence. Shoams disguised as Julius Caesar and I as Davy Crockett, so as not to attract attention. We were both armed to the teeth and in addition carried with us a dark lantern, a wheelbarrow, a fire extinguisher and a lawn mower, so as to be prepared for all possible contingencies.

Sliding down through the chimney cautiously, we took our position in the room in which the cigars were kept, and disposed of our paraphernalia around the room so as to look as natural as possible. Then Shoams took from his pocket a portable canvas tent which he erected in the center of the room. "We shall conceal ourselves in this," he said, "and wait for our man. Above all, we must keep strict silence. And he fired off his pistol twice to make sure that it was working properly."

Scarcely had we arranged ourselves comfortably when the door opened and the villain entered the room. "Sh-h-h!"cried Shoams, directing his lantern on the intruder. "We must not let him suspect our presence."

As he spoke his face grew white with fear. Accustomed though he was to face perils of all sorts, his iron nerve almost failed him as he saw the desperate character who was his adversary.

"Cortwright's son!" he gasped. "Squatson, if he sees us we are dead men!" All we could do was wait and hope. At last, after what seemed ages of suspense, we saw him take one of the cigars, light it and begin to smoke.

Our task was now completed. We had succeeded in laying bare one of the most villainous plots ever conceived by mortal man. It only remained to make good our escape. "Quick," shouted Shoams, "before it is too late."---and seizing me in his arms he leaped gracefully through the window.

"Squatson," he said solemnly, when we had landed safely head downward in a rosebush, "that was the closest call we have had yet. If we had delayed one moment longer we would have been lost. And now that success has crowned our efforts, what do you say to a friendly little pistol duel? I think that after the excitement and danger we have gone through this evening it would have a soothing effect on our nerves."

The Railway Station Sandwich Case

Wex Jones

A few parody writers carried the burlesquing of the whole Sherlockian enterprise to the absurd. In this competition, Wex Jones, a writer for the Hearst syndicate, held the prize.

One of his parodies had Hawkshaw send Holmes a fake telegram from West Upper Tooting "to show what a chump he is." The message was, "Pinky Pink may I call on you hinky dink?" It was signed "Doodlebug Dingbat,"and was sent collect.

*Here is one of Wex's tamer ones from his series of short squibs titled, **Morning Smiles**, most featuring Timelock Foams and Potson.*

They appeared between 1914 and 1916, in the Hearst newspapers, a discovery of Bill Blackbeard.

****

We had twenty minutes to wait for the train which was to take us to Little Stoke Pogis by the Pond, whither the great detective had been summoned to investigate the murders which had set the town all agog.

"Potson, my dear chump," said Foams, "you had better get a bite to eat while we are waiting for the train. There will be dangerous work ahead for us when we reach Little Stoke Pogis by the Pond, and there will be no time to think of food."

I spoke to the tall, languid goddess in black and ordered two ham sandwiches.

"Two?" said Foams.

"Yes, one for you," I replied. "As a medical man I insist upon your eating something. You haven't had a real meal for ten days, and if you become interested in this Little Stoke Pogis case, you won't eat until it's finished, so I insist upon your eating one of these sandwiches I just ordered."

"My dear, Potson," said Foams, "In addition to being a chump you are a tyrant."

The goddess in black placed the sandwiches on the counter, and I saw Foams stiffen all over like a pointer on the scent of birds.

"Potson," he hissed, "do you notice anything about those sandwiches?"

"No," said I, after studying them for several minutes, "they look like two good ham sandwiches to me."

"Good!" Foams fairly ground out the word through clenched teeth. "Good!"

"Yes," said I, "there's a nice thick piece of ham in each."

"A nice thick piece of ham in each," continued Foams. "And do you notice that the bread is fresh? Did you ever see fresh bread in a railway sandwich before?"

When reminded of this I had to confess that such a thing was absolutely unknown.

"This is Moriarty's work," said Foams. "He expected we would wait to eat such good sandwiches and thus miss the train to Little Stoke Pogis, his confederates there escaping in the meanwhile. But he didn't reckon with the intellect of Timelock Foams. I saw through his plan. We do not eat the sandwiches and we catch the train."

But we found the train had gone while Foams was deducing.

A Lesson in Handwriting Analysis

Ring W. Lardner

*Ring Lardner (1885-1933) was born in Niles, Michigan and covered sports for several Indiana newspapers before ending up as a sports writer on the **Chicago Tribune.** He was one of the first to realize that the Chicago White Sox were throwing the World Series in what came to be known as the Black Sox scandal of 1919.*

*Lardner's sports column, "In the Wake of the News" was syndicated to over a hundred newspapers. He would gain further fame with a humorous book of fictional letters a bush league baseball player wrote his friend, Al. The book was published in 1916 as, **You Know Me, Al.** This and subsequent short stories, such as "Haircut,"generally featured midwestern Americans. All have a sharp satirical bite.*

This appeared as the Wake of the News column on March 16, 1915, as "A Study in Handwritiing."

.

****

"I cannot rejoice over the ever-increasing popularity of the typewriter," said Sherlock Holmes, as he lounged in the most comfortable chair provided by our landlady, and refilled, for the sixth time within an hour, a particularly malodorous pipe. "It is spoiling one of the most absorbing ways of studying the human race.

"One can judge from a typewritten letter very little concerning its author; merely whether or not he is an expert with the machine. But a man's handwriting will tell a careful student a writer's likes and dislikes as plainly as he could state them himself, to say nothing of his occupation, his characteristics, his immense thoughts, his---"

"Do you mean to state," I interrupted, "that you can accurately describe a man's vocation, his traits, his opinions, by a study of his handwriting?"

"Just so," returned my companion with a smile, "and if you would look into it, I am sure you would find it as interesting a study as your medicine and surgery."

"I am sure I would find it all bosh," I returned shortly.

"Try it and see," said Holmes, and thrusting his long tapering fingers into the inside pocket of his lounging coat, he drew forth a letter. "Glance at this," handing it to me, "and tell me what you learn of the writer."

I spread the missive on my knee and looked at it for perhaps five minutes. It was written on hotel stationary in a graceful, legible hand, and read:

Editor: Chicago Tribune:

*Of all the silly tommy rot and cheap Barrel House seen or heard, that contained under the heading A*In *the Wake of the News" has them all beat to a frazzle.*

204

It appears to me that R. W. L—— would make a good wit at a real wake and were he the corpse, I'd say thank God.

I've decided to switch to another paper, and talking the matter over with other fellow drummers the general opinion appears to be the same. Namely L—— is a Adead one.

Yours very truly,

XXXXX

"Well," said Holmes at length, "what do you make of him?"

"Nothing," I said, "except that he writes clearly and legibly."

"O. Watson, Watson!" exclaimed my companion, and threw up his hands in mock horror. "Where are your brains?"

"In my head, I hope," I said with some asperity. "But I did not make any ridiculous assertion as to my clairvoyant powers. It was you, I believe, who started the discussion. And it is surely your duty to make good your claim or admit that you were talking nonsense, as I believe to be the case."

Holmes smiled quietly and reaching over, took back the letter he had given me. He pondered it in silence for some moments before he spoke.

"Watson," he said, "it is as far from nonsense as anything could be. This power or knack, or whatever you choose to call it has served me in good stead in some of my most important cases. But I see you are still a skeptic and it is therefore my part to convert you. I have already made my study of this particular letter and will state my conclusions to you as briefly as I can."

"To begin with, I see the writer has recently been in Sheboygan, Wisconsin. He has a bit of spare time on his hands, either while stopping at the Grand hotel, which is centrally located and homelike, owned by R. J. Warner and protected by the electric fire alarm system, or right afterwards. He is not a personal friend of the editor of *The Tribune.* He uses slang. He has no patience with a certain department of *The Tribune* called 'In the Wake of the News.' He is hard-hearted. He is religious. He makes his decisions only after careful thought and discussion. He is democratic. He is interested in the opinion of his fellows and not above talking with them. He is a salesman who travels. He is inconsiderate. I think that is about all. Do you follow me?"

"Holmes, you are wonderful," I exclaimed. "But surely you will tell me how you reached some of your conclusions. For instance, how do you deduce that the writer is inconsiderate?"

"From his handwriting, of course," returned my companion. "Study the formation of the letters in this sentence: 'I've decided to switch to another paper.' If he were considerate of the feelings of others, would he be so blunt with the person addressed? Wouldn't he rather allow the editor to find out gradually that he was no longer a subscriber?"

"It is clear as day," I admitted. "And how long did it take you to master this trick?"

"Trick!" said Holmes, disgustedly scratching the bridge of his aquiline nose with a gold-handled toothpick.

Herlock Shomes In the Trenches

Anonymous

*British soldiers at the front during World War I occasionally liberated a printing press and type, and then published their own unofficial "trench magazines." The best known of such journals was **The Wipers Times,** a cockney pronunciation of Ypres, a Belgian town in Flanders, the site of the fiercest battles of 1914, and those in which poison gas was used in 1915. Each page of this journal had to be handset, printed and then the type redistributed before handsetting the next page.*

***The Wipers Times** published three Sherlockian serials. The first and second each had six parts while the third ended abruptly at three chapters when the press took a direct hit from German artillery.*

"Narpoo Rum. is the only one with some semblance of organization and plot, and it too wanders off into strange places. It concerns the mysterious disappearance the rum ration of the enlisted men. The other two parodies are a series of wild and unrelated episodes In the first, names are listed in the cast of characters at the head of an episode and never appear in the parody while others not listed appear. The name of the detective is changed from Shomes to Sholmes, suggesting the series may have had several authors or the author may just have been following in the casual tradition set by Conan Doyle.

The first concludes with having all the characters killed, some in a bombardment and the rest in a liquid fire attack. The blood and thunder chapters in these Sherlock Holmes parodies reflect life in the trenches--the chaos, random violence and death, and especially the stupidity, a kind of theater of the absurd. There are no heroes. But over it all floats a kind of wry black humor, perhaps the only way the troops or writers could keep relatively sane.

The parodies appeared between February 12, 1916 and early 1918

*A reproduction of all issues of **The Wipers Times** may be found in F. J. Roberts and J. H. Pearson, eds., **The Wipers Times, The Complete Series of The Famous Wartime Trench Magazine.**London: Eveleigh Nash & Grayson, June 1930.*

A Glossary

Estaminet--- a café
Hooge---village east of Ypres
Narpoo---there is no more
Vermoral Sprayer---sprayer used to neutralize poison gas
Very Lights---colored flares fired from a gun
Whizz-bang---German field artillery

****

OUR   SPLENDID
NEW
SERIAL

"NARPOO RUM"

BY THE AUTHOR OF

208

"SHOT INTHE CULVERT"

DRAMATIS PERSONAE

Cloridy Lyme---A Sanitary Inspector
Madaline Carot---A French Girl
Intha Pink---A Pioneer
General BertramRudolph de Rogerum---The Earl of Loose
Lord Reginald de Knellthorpe---His Son
Q. Wemm---A Storekeeper
L. Plummernapple---A Soldier
Herlock Shomes---The Great Detective
Dr. Hotsam---His Admirer

CHAPTER 1. (December 1, 1916)

"My dear Hotsam, nothing of the kind, I assure you," said Shomes, in his comfortable dug-out in Quality Street. "My methods are based on deduction. For instance, you hear someone coming up the stairs. Well, that is all the untrained ear can hear, but I know it's a soldier with many ribbons, an Irish accent, and a friend named Reggie. How do I know? My dear fellow – "

At that moment the door opened, and General Bertram Rudolph de Rogerum entered. Casting himself in a chair he demanded a cocktail, "Well, my dear General," said Shomes, placing his finger tips together, "how can I help you?"

"What? You know me?" gasped the general.

"Oh yes!" said Shomes, as he tilted his vermoral sprayer and squirted a quart into his left arm. "Well," said the general, "I have come about a very mysterious affair. Three nights running the Brigade rum ration has disappeared."

"Good heavens!" ejaculated Hotsam.

"Aha!" said Shomes, "this promised to be a most interesting case."With that he picked up his violin, and proceeded to play dreamily. "Now I am ready General, tell me all about it."

"Well," said the General, "as you know, my men mostly dislike rum, so that when it comes up I have it put in one of the outhouses. Three mornings ago, when my son, a priceless lad, if I may say so and above suspicion, went to look at it, he found it had disappeared. This is happened on both the following nights, and so I thought you might be able to help us."

"Have you no clue at all?" snapped the great detective.

"Only that Wemm's store seems to be more popular with the soldiers than formerly," said the general.

"Leave the matter in my hands, general, I will find your rum," said the detective.   With that the general went off jauntily whistling, "Another Little Drink Wouldn't Do Any Harm."

Immediately he had gone Shomes sprang up. "Now Hotsam, we must to work! Hastily throwing off his smoking jacket, he donned a tin-hat, mackintosh and gum-boots, and disappeared into the night.

Meanwhile in the lovely French evening, Plumernapple was paying court to Madeline Corot, the pretty daughter at the local estaminet. "Well, it's only 'arf past eight," he murmured, "and there ain't no perlice corprel about."

"No compris," she gurgled, as she made to shut the door. Picking up his A frame, he sadly made his way along the road.

At Wemm's store a very merry party was in progress, and Hotsam, taking air, strolled across there. Pushing open the door, he saw Q. Wemm entertaining many friends from among the neighboring troops. He was immediately made welcome, and a mug of hot liquid was thrust in his hand. Casting his eyes round, they fell on a heap of jars in the corner. "The Rum!" he gasped.

(WAS IT?)
(to be continued)

Owing to the shortage of paper we have been obliged to restrict this number to 8 pages, so that many things are unavoidably held over. However, we hope that our Grand Xmas Double Number will follow close on the heels of this, and will contain our new competition and many popular features.---(Ed)

CHAPTER 2. (December 25, 1916)

It was Xmas. The sturdy figure of General Bertram Rudolph de Rogerum was plodding along the snow-covered road jauntily whistling a Xmas carol. Every now and then a frown crossed his handsome face as he thought of the missing rum ration, and how the evidence seemed to point to none other than his son, Lord Reginald de Knellthorpe. Had Reggie in a reckless moment stolen the rum? Heaving a deep sigh he fell into a crump hole which had been hidden under the white mantle of winter.

Meanwhile what was happening at Wemm's store? At Hotsam's exclamation "The Rum!" a guilty look spread over Wemm's face, and his assistant guiltily stole through the door. Hotsam sprang in front of the jars, "Open one he thundered. Shakingly Wemm complied, and poured out a glass of the liquid. Hotsam examined this and found it to be a solution of vermoral sprayers. With a nod to Wemm he went out.

On returning to his dug-out he found Lord Reginald de Knellthorpe in possession of the armchair shooting rats.

"Hello, old boy," said Knellthorpe, "what about papa's rum?"

"Look here Reggie," said Hotsam, "Do you know anything about it? Shomes is on the track and you may be able to help him."

Reggie paled, "Shomes," he gasped, picking up his helmet gas. "Shomes! Good heavens, then all is lost." Staggering to the door he disappeared into the night.

Mixing himself a drink Hotsam sat down and began to go over the evidence. Suddenly the door opened, and the Earl of Loose entered. "Good evening general," said Hotsam.

"General be damned,"snapped Shomes' voice, "Has Reginald de Knellthorpe been here?"

"Just this minute gone," said Hotsam.

Dashing to the door Shomes rapidly disappeared, followed by Hotsam. Suddenly two shots rang out, and Shomes dropped in the snow, crying, "Follow him, follow him." Hotsam dashed madly in pursuit, and didn't stop till he fell down the shaft at the Old Fosse.

Picking himself up, Shomes returned to his dug-out and bound up his wrist where the shot had struck him. Baring his forearm he injected a gallon out of his vermoral sprayer and picked up his violin.

Down in the village Madeline Carot sat at the door of her old mother's estaminet. Her face brightened as she saw the sturdy figure of

Intha Pink coming up the road. "Oh Intha," she exclaimed, "I thought you were never coming to see me. Where have you been?"

Hurriedly glancing up and down the road Pink slipped into the estaminet and closed the door. "Rum," he gasped.

Madeline got him a glass of rum which he swallowed in a gulp. "Has Shomes been here?" he demanded.

"Yes," she replied, "he was here this morning and had a glass of rum."

"Then we are lost," shouted Intha, and disappeared through the door.

Hotsam, meanwhile arrived at the bottom of the shaft. Taking his flash lamp from his pocket he proceeded to examine his position. The first thing his light fell on was a pile of jars stacked in a corner. "The rum!" he gasped.

(WAS IT?)
Read next thrilling installment
(To be Continued)

CHAPTER 3. (January 20, 1917)

It was raining. Shomes, who had business of a pressing nature that night, shuddered as he pulled aside the gas curtain of his dug-out, and looked up and down the trench. Dropping the curtain hastily he injected a good dose from his vermoral sprayer, and disguised himself as a sergeant. He then swallowed half a pint of rum and went out into the night, to proceed on an urgent and secret mission to the Culvert Arms at Hooge.

213

Making his way along the duckboards to the waiting aeroplane he jumped aboard and disappeared into the darkness. Meanwhile, the Earl of Loose was in a very troubled state of mind about his son. In addition to the mysterious disappearance of the rum Reggie had been playing fast and loose with the pretty dark-eyed daughter at the neighboring chateau. So much so indeed that the poor Earl was considering the advantages of sending Master Reginald back to school.

Professor Spot had just recently opened a finishing school for young gentlemen in the neighborhood. He had just made up his mind to send Reginald for a course when his eye fell on the young scapegoat ambling along smoking a cigarette, and without his gas helmet.

Choking back a expletive the General hurried after him, and was only just in time to see him disappear into the corner estaminet where Madeline dispensed beer daily. The General stealthily approached, and looking though a back window saw Reginald with the girl in his arms. On the ground was a stack of rum jars at which Reggie was pointing while saying something to the girl. At this sight the General clutched at his collar and swooned.

Hotsam, who on examination, had found all the jars at the bottom of the Old Fosse to be empty and of a condemned pattern, gathered himself together and proceeding by the old workings soon found himself by the corner estaminet. Hearing laughter and voices he made his way to the back and fell over the unconscious form of General Rudolph de Rogerum, the Earl of Loose. Picking himself up he looked in at the window.

"The Rum!" he gasped.

(WAS IT?)
read next thrilling installment
(to be continued)

214

CHAPTER 4.   (March 5, 1917)

THE CLUE OF THE TORN LETTER

Skillfully landing his plane in the Square of the ancient town of Ypres, Shomes resolved to dine at the Hotel des Ramparts before proceeding up the Menin Road to the Culvert Arms. Having partaken of an excellent dinner, Shomes once more donned his tin hat, raincoat and gum boots thigh, and proceeded by way of the Menin Gate up the Menin Road.

As he walked, the fearful events of the last great adventure in that district flashed through his mind with painful distinctness. He was roused from his reverie by the weary whirr of a five-nine, and realized with a start that he had reached his destination. Looking around with a dawning sense of horror he saw that the Culvert Arms was no more. Shomes, amazed, perplexed, but by no means non-plussed hastily injected a double dose from his vermoral sprayer, and sought for a clue.

Down in the deep and muddy ditch where once the ancient hostelry had stood, he passed a few battered stones, and in the dark and sluggish waters found an envelope, muddy and torn, and readable as far as:---

TOR

IMES

TERS (P

Shomes spoke no word, but a close observer would have noted that his face, seen in the white glare of the Very Lights had a look of grim and purposeful satisfaction.

CHAPTER 5.

About the same time as Shomes was making his important discovery at the ruined Culvert Arms, Hotsam was endeavoring to revive the fainting Earl and at the same time to keep a vigilant watch through the estaminet window. The General at length recovered consciousness, and joined Hotsam at the window.

A strange sight met their eyes. Lord Reginald de Knellthorpe stood with his back to the window supporting the fair Madeline, who appeared to be weeping bitterly. Muttering with impotent rage the old Earl thrust open the door, and followed by Hotsam, entered the room. Lord Reggie turned an amazed and tear-wet face towards them, and simultaneously the Earl and Hotsam burst into tears.

Hotsam with alacrity put on his gas helmet, corked up the rum jar, and opened the window. The General drying his tears, furiously asked the weeping son the reason for his presence there. "Well you see, father," said Lord Reggie, "Madeline" (he tenderly wiped the eyes of the beautiful girl) "told me she had seen some rum jars in here, and, thinking they might contain the rum I am suspected of stealing, I came here to examine them. They appear to contain tear gas."

The Earl with a new burst of tears, joined the hands of Reggie and Madeline, and Hotsam feeling that his presence was no longer required, strode out into the night, leaving the Earl and the young lovers smiling through their tears.

CHAPTER 6.

THE END OF SHOMES?

Hotsam, very fatigued, at length reached the comfortable Quality Street dug-out, where he found a signaler, who handed him one of the dreaded pink forms. He resignedly took the wire and read:---

MEET ME AT YPRES AT ONCE
^^^ OBTAIN BUS FROM GEN.
BERTRAM RUDOLPH DE
ROGERUM ^^^ URGENT ^^^
SICK ^^^^^

Hotsam sighed and after much trouble obtained the bus, and eventually reached Ypres. In the Square he found Shomes, seated in his plane.

"Come Hotsam," he cried, "Jump in, there is no time to be lost, they shall not escape us this time." Hotsam obeyed, and Shomes, having started up the motor, jumped in, and they were off.

After some hours in the air, Hotsam shouted, "Where are we going, Shomes?" He could not catch the answer, so was silent. Suddenly a flash! a crash! and the two men and an Archied aeroplane were falling through the night.

CHAPTER 7.

AT LAST?

Intha sat in a large shell-hole in the grounds of Elvarston Castle. He was not happy. He had been knocked down by a G. S. wagon, machine-gunned on the road, whizz-banged in the trench, and, finally, had taken his A frame to the wrong dump.

As he rested he thought of many things. He thought of war, he thought of snow, he thought of rum. Why had he no rum for some days now? Because some scoundrel had stolen the Brigade supply. Suddenly a great resolve grew in the soul of the Pioneer; he would find the missing liquid. Fired with enthusiasm, he arose, and, casting away his now useless A frame, made his way as quickly to the Estaminet of Madeline Corot.

After some protest, Madeline quietly admitted him. "I'm a bloomin' policeman now," he said, "and don't you bloomin' well forget it. I saw a staff-officer leave 'ere at eight-fifteen, wot yer goin' ter do abaht it?"

"You no tell,"said Madeline, "and I give you beer."

"Narpoo!"

"I give you some rum."

"THE RUM!" thought Intha.

(WAS IT?)
(Read next thrilling installment)
(To be Continued)

CHAPTER 8.   (April 10, 1917)

WHAT CLORIDY LYME SAW

Cloridy Lyme straightened his aching back with a groan; and gazed around the stricken streets of Bapaume in the cold gray light of dawn with every appearance of profound distaste.

"When I joined this 'ere mob I 'ad visions of red coats and flashin' bayonets; and now I spends my time spearin' bits o' paper and orange peel on a pointed stick," mused he.

Gazing upwards at the lowering sky, he saw a strange sight. A sausage was drifting by, scarcely clearing the roofs of the ruined houses. Two men hung precariously to the rigging, and a trail rope dragged over the ground. As he watched the rope caught in a tree stump, and the two men, hastily sliding down it, inquired of the astonished sanitary inspector their whereabouts.

On hearing they were in Bapaume, Shomes (for it was none other than he) said calmly, "Just as I thought, my dear Hotsam, my deductions are sometimes at fault but very rarely I think."

Glancing sharply at the pointed stick held by Cloridy Lime, he suddenly seized it, and tore from the end a piece of paper which, after perusing, he handed to Hotsam, saying, "Just as I told you my dear fellow."

Hotsam took the paper and read,

ED!
WIPERS T
SHERWOOD FORES

CHAPTER 9.

"But my dear Hotsam, the whole thing is absurdly simple," said Shomes curling his long wiry body up in his comfortable bunk.

"What! You really have solved the problem of the missing rum?"

"There never was a problem, and the rum was never stolen."

"For heavens sake explain, Shomes, I really cannot follow your abstruse reasoning."

"You surely remember, my good fellow, at the time the rum was supposed to have been stolen, it was almost impossible to buy whiskey in this country."

"Yes, I remember very well indeed, but what has that to do with the question?"

"My dear Hotsam, can't you follow me now?"

"I really cannot, Shomes."

"You met the Earl and his staff many times during these trying days, did you not?"

"Yes I saw them nearly every day."

"Did they strike you as men who had suddenly become total abstainers?"

"No I cannot say they did."

"Well, just think a little, my dear Hotsam, whiskey was unobtainable then, what did they--- Pass the whiskey and put on the gramophone my good fellow. I think we are entitled to a tot."

FINIS

IN AND AROUND BAKER STREET

Even Conan Doyle Wrote Them

Arthur Conan Doyle

This is one of two Sherlockian parodies Conan Doyle wrote. The other was in 1924 for Queen Mary's fabulous doll house. Builders made beds, chairs, etc., to scale, manufacturers supplied rugs and wall paper, artists contributed tiny masterworks to hang on the walls, and many illustrious novelists including Conan Doyle contributed stories that bookmakers published for a library of big little books. The dollhouse is still on exhibit in London somewhere or other.

I think this parody. "The Field Bazaar," is the better or the two in any case. It has a kind of dreamlike charm that takes you back to the Baker Street of the stories.

*The editors of the student newspaper at the University of Edinburgh, his Alma Mater, asked Conan Doyle to submit a piece that could be used to raise funds for a cricket field. He adroitly replies with this parody that was published in the university paper, **The Student,** on November 20, 1895.*

✳✳✳✳✳✳✳✳

"I should certainly do it," said Sherlock Holmes.

I started at the interruption, for my companion had been eating his breakfast with his attention entirely centred upon the paper which was propped up by the coffee pot. Now I looked across at him to find his eyes fastened on me with the half-amused, half questioning expression which he usually assumed when he felt he had made an intellectual point.

"Do what?" I asked.

He smiled as he took his slipper from the mantelpiece and drew from it enough shag tobacco to fill his old clay pipe with which he invariably rounded off his breakfast.

"A most characteristic question of yours, Watson," said he. "You will not, I'm sure, be offended if I say that any reputation for sharpness which I may possess has been entirely gained by the admirable foil which you have made for me. Have I not heard of debutantes who have insisted upon plainness in their chaperones? There is a certain analogy."

Our long companionship in the Baker Street rooms had left us on those easy terms of intimacy when much may be said without offense. And yet I acknowledge that I was nettled at his remark.

"I may be very obtuse," said I, "but I confess that I am unable to see how you managed to know that I was...I was..."

"Asked to help in the Edinburgh University Bazaar."

"Precisely. The letter has only just come to hand, and I have not spoken to you since."

222

"In spite of that," said Holmes, leaning back in his chair and putting his fingertips together, "I would even mention to suggest that the object of the bazaar is to enlarge the University cricket field."

I looked at him with such bewilderment that he vibrated with silent laughter.

"The fact is, my dear Watson, that you are an excellent subject," said he. "You are never blasé. You respond instantly to any external stimulus. Your mental process may be slow but they are never obscure, and I found during breakfast that you were easier reading than the leader in the *Times* in front of me."

"I should be glad to know how you arrived at your conclusions," said I.

"I fear that my good nature in giving explanations has seriously compromised my reputation," said Holmes. "But in this case the train of reasoning is based upon such obvious facts that no credit can be claimed for it. You entered the room with a thoughtful expression, the expression of a man who is debating some point in his mind. In your hand you held a solitary letter. Now last night you retired in the best of spirits, so it was clear that it was this letter in your hand which caused this change in you."

"This is obvious."

"It is all obvious when it is explained to you. I naturally asked myself who the letter could concern which might have this effect upon you. As you walked you held the flap side of the envelope towards me, and I saw upon it the same shield-shaped device which I have observed upon your old college cricket cap. It was clear, then, that the request came from Edinburgh University---or from some club connected with the University. When you reached the table you laid down the letter

223

beside your plate with the address uppermost, and you walked over to look at the framed photograph upon the left of the mantelpiece."

It amazed me to see the accuracy with which he observed my movements. "What next?" I asked.

"I began by glancing at the address. And I could tell, even at the distance of six feet that it was an unofficial communication. This I gathered from the use of the word 'Doctor' upon the address, to which as a Bachelor of Medicine you have no legal claim. I knew that University officials are pedantic in their correct use of titles, and I was thus enabled to say with certainty that your letter was unofficial. When on your return to the table you turned over your letter and allowed me to perceive that the enclosure was a printed one, the idea of a bazaar first occurred to me. I had already weighed the possibility of its being a political communication, but this seemed improbable in the present stagnant condition of politics.

"When you returned to the table, your face still retained its expression and it was evident that your examination of the photograph had not changed the current of your thoughts. In that case it must itself bear upon the subject in question. I turned my attention to the photograph, therefore, and saw at once that it consisted of yourself as a member of the Edinburgh University Eleven, with the pavilion and cricket field in the background. My small experience of cricket clubs has taught that next to churches and cavalry ensigns, they are the most debt-ladden things upon earth. When on your return to the table I saw you take out your pencil and draw lines upon the envelope, I was convinced that you were endeavoring to realize some projected improvements which was to be brought about by a bazaar. Your face still showed some indecision so that I was able to break in upon you with my advice that you should assist in so good an object."

I could not help smiling at the extreme simplicity of his explanation.

224

"Of course, it was as easy as possible," said I.

My remark appeared to nettle him.

"I may add," said he, "that the particular help which you have been asked to give was that you should write in their album, and that you have already made up your mind that the present incident will be the subject of your article."

"But how---" I cried.

"It is as easy as possible," said he, "and I leave its solution to your own ingenuity." In the meantime, he added, raising his paper, "you will excuse me if I return to this very interesting article upon the trees in Cremona, and the exact reasons for their pre-eminence in the manufacture of violins. It is one of those small outlying problems in which I am sometimes tempted to direct my attention."

Sherlock Gossips About The Ladies

Anonymous

This is a few paragraphs of gossip between two old bachelors, Watson and Holmes, as they discuss the ladies. It is a subject most of us would expect Sherlock knows very little about, anyhow not much that is worth listening to. But that doesn't stop him.

*It appeared as an ad, without illustration, on December 28, 1895 in **Tit Bits**, the sister magazine of **The Strand.** It was titled "A Sherlock Holmes Dialogue, with a Moral for the Ladies."*

****

WATSON: Have you noticed my dear Holmes, how charmingly Mrs. Beauty dresses now; how well her house is managed, and how full of pleasant talk she is. She used to be such a dowdy creature, you know.

HOLMES: Yes, I have observed.

WATSON: The little dinners are now most excellent, and her home seems to be brighter and more charming than it used to be. And such lovely hats she wears! What is the reason?

Holmes said not a word, but placing his hand in his overcoat pocket, he pulled out No. 3 of **Woman's Life** and handed it to Watson with a significant look as he turned over the pages.

"Ah," said Watson, "now I understand how it has all come about."

Sherlock Holmes, Dr. Watson, and Mrs. Beauty understood, and we wish all our lady readers to understand that **Woman's Life** is the best illustrated penny magazine for the home ever published.

NO 3. PRICE ONE PENNY. 52 PAGES! 70 PICTURES!
On sale at all bookstalls and news agents.

Some of the contents:

Aristocratic Rocking Horses   A Famous Lady Football Player

Luxuries of Wealthy Babies   Novel Dancing Shoes

New Year's Millinery   A Chat About Lady Londonderry

Costly Curtains   The Best Dresses for Girls

The Latest Up-to-Datest Fashions, etc. Two Short Stories

EVERY TUESDAY. ONE PENNY

The Stolen Cigar Case

Bret Harte

Bret Harte (1836-1902) made his reputation writing about life in the gold rush camps of California, as in "The Luck of Roaring Camp" and "The Outcasts of Poker Flat." Harte moved east and was appointed U.S. consul to Crefeld, Prussia and in 1880 consul to Glasgow. His tour over, he ended up liking Britain so much, he settled there for the rest of his life.

Conan Doyle's first published short stories, such as "The Mystery of Sasassa Valley" and "The American's Tale," were, he confessed in his autobiography, "feeble echoes of Bret Harte." William D. Jenkins points out Conan Doyle may have lifted more than Harte's style, that the plot of "The Noble Bachelor" closely follows that found in a poem of Bret Harte's, "Her Letter." He suggests that perhaps Harte chose Sherlockian parody as a mild form of literary revenge.

Many think this the best of all Sherlock Holmes parodies and it's certainly a contender. So it seems a shame not to include it even though it has been widely reprinted finding its way into books of otherwise non-

*Sherlockian parody.   It first appeared in December, 1900 in **Pearson's Magazine**and was republished in Harte's **Condensed Novels, Second Series.** (1902).*

   It is seemsappropriate to have one of the best of parodies written by one who was a hands-across-the-sea mixture: a certified American who chose to live out his life in England

****

I found Hemlock Jones in the Old Brook Street lodgings, musing before the fire. With the freedom of an old friend I at once threw myself in my usual familiar attitude at his feet, and gently caressed his boot. I was induced to do this for two reasons---one, it enabled me to get a good look at his bent, concentrated face, and the other, it seemed to indicate my reverence for his superhuman insight. So absorbed was he even then, in tracking some mysterious clue, that he did not seem to notice me.   But therein I was wrong---as I always was in my attempt to understand that powerful intellect.

"It is raining," he said, without lifting his head.

"You have been out, then?" I said quickly.

"No. But I see that your umbrella is wet, and that your overcoat has drops of water on it."

I sat aghast at his penetration. After a pause, he said carelessly, as if dismissing the subject;"Besides, I hear the rain on the window. Listen."

I listened. I could scarcely credit my ears, but there was the soft pattering of drops on the panes. It was evident there was no deceiving this man!

"Have you been busy lately?" I asked, changing the subject. "What new problem---given up by Scotland Yard as inscrutable---has occupied that gigantic intellect?"

He drew back his foot lightly, and seemed to hesitate ere he returned it to its original position. Then he answered wearily; "Mere trifles -- nothing to speak of. The Prince Kupoli has been here to get my advice regarding the disappearance of certain rubies from the Kremlin; the Rajah of Pootibad, after vainly beheading his entire bodyguard, has been obliged to seek my assistance to recover a jeweled sword. The Grand Duchess of Pretzel-Brauntswig is desirous of discovering where her husband was on the night of February 14; and last night---" he lowered his voice slightly "a lodger in this very house, meeting me on the stairs, wanted to know why they didn't answer his bell."

I could not help smiling---until I saw a frown gathering on his inscrutable forehead.

"Pray remember," he said coldly, "that it was through just such an apparently trivial question that I found out Why Paul Ferroll Killed His Wife, and What Happened to Jones!"

I became dumb at once. He paused for a moment, and then suddenly changing back to his usual pitiless, analytical style, he said; "When I say these are trifles, they are so in comparison to an affair that is now before me. A crime has been committed---and singularly enough, against myself. You start," he said. "You wonder who would have dared to attempt it. So did I; nevertheless, it has been done. I have been *robbed!"*

"You robbed! You, Hemlock Jones, the Terror of Peculators!" I gasped in amazement, arising and gripping the table as I faced him.

230

"Yes! Listen. I would confess it to no other. But you who have followed my career, who know my methods, you for whom I have partly lifted the veil that conceals my plans from ordinary humanity---you, who have for years rapturously accepted my confidences, passionately admired my inductions and inferences, placed yourself at my beck and call, became my slave, groveled at my feet, given up your practice except those few unrenumerative and rapidly decreasing patients to whom, in moments of abstraction over my problems, you have administered strychnine for quinine and arsenic for Epsom salts; you, who have sacrificed everything and everybody to me---you I make my confidant!"

I arose and embraced him warmly, yet he was already so engrossed in thought that at the same moment he mechanically placed his hand upon his watch chain as if to consult the time. "Sit down," he said. "Have a cigar?"

"I have given up smoking," I said.

"Why?" he asked.

I hesitated, and perhaps colored. I had really given it up because, with my diminished practice, it was too expensive. I could afford only a pipe. "I prefer a pipe," I said laughingly. "But tell me of this robbery. What have you lost?"

He arose, and planting himself before the fire with his hands under his coat-tails, looked down upon me reflectively for a moment. "Do you remember the cigar case presented to me by the Turkish ambassador for discovering the missing favorite of the Grand Vizier in the fifth chorus girl at the Hilarity Theater? It was that one. I mean the cigar case. It was incrusted with diamonds."

"And the largest one had been supplanted by paste," I said.

231

"Ah," he said with a reflective smile, "you know that?"

"You told me yourself. I remember considering it a proof of your extraordinary perception. But by Jove, you don't mean to say you have lost it?"

He was silent for a moment. "No, it has been stolen, it is true, but I shall still find it. And by myself alone! In your profession, my dear fellow, when a member is seriously ill, he does not prescribe for himself but calls in a brother doctor. Therein we differ. I shall take this matter in my own hands."

"And where could you find better?" I said enthusiastically. "I should say the cigar case is as good as recovered already."

"I shall remind you of that again," he said lightly. "And now, to show you my confidence in your judgment, in spite of my determination to pursue this alone, I am willing to listen to any suggestions from you."

He drew a memorandum book from his pocket and, with a grave smile, took up his pencil.

I could scarcely believe my senses. He, the great Hemlock Jones, accepting suggestions from a humble individual like myself! I kissed his hand reverently, and began in a joyous tone:

"First, I should advertise, offering a reward. I should give the same intimation in handbills, distributed at the 'pubs' and the pastry cooks. I should next visit the different pawnbrokers; I should give notice at the police station. I should examine the servants. I should thoroughly search the house and my own pockets. I speak relatively, I added with a laugh. "Of course I mean your own."

232

He gravely made an entry of these details.

"Perhaps," I added, "you have already done this?"

"Perhaps," he returned enigmatically. "Now my dear friend," he continued, putting the notebook in his pocket and rising, "would you excuse me for a few moments? Make yourself perfectly at home until I return, there may be some things," he added with a sweep of his hand towards his heterogeneously filled shelves, "that may interest you and while away the time. There are pipes and tobacco in that corner."

Then nodding to me with the same inscrutable face he left the room. I was too well accustomed to his methods to think much of his unceremonious withdrawal, and made no doubt he was off to investigate some clue which had suddenly occurred to his active intelligence.

Left to myself I cast a cursory glance over the shelves. There were a number of small glass jars containing earthy substances, labeled *Pavement and Road Sweepings*, from the principal thoroughfare and suburbs of London, with the subdirections *For Identifying Foot Tracks*. There were several other jars, labeled *Fluff from Omnibus and Road-car Seats, Coconut Fiber and Rope Strands from Mattings in Public Places, Cigarette Stumps and Match Ends from Floor of Palace Theatre, Row A, 1 to 50*. Everywhere were evidences of this wonderful man's system and perspicacity.

I was thus engaged when I heard the slight creaking of a door, and I looked up as a stranger entered. He was a rough-looking man, with a shabby overcoat and a still more disreputable muffler around his throat and the lower part of his face. Considerably annoyed at his intrusion, I turned upon him rather sharply, when, with a mumbled growling apology for mistaking the room, he shuffled out again and closed the door. I followed him quickly to the landing and saw that he disappeared down the stairs.

With my mind full of the robbery, the incident made a singular impression upon me. I knew my friend's habit of hasty absences from his room in his moments of deep inspiration; it was only too probable that, with his powerful intellect and magnificent perceptive genius concentrated on one subject, he should be careless of his own belongings, and no doubt even forget to take the ordinary precaution of locking up his drawers. I tried one or two and found that I was right, although for some reason, I was unable to open one to its fullest extent. The handles were sticky, as if someone had opened it with dirty fingers. Knowing Hemlock's fastidious cleanliness, I resolved to inform him of this circumstance, but I forgot it alas! Until---but I am anticipating my story.

His absence was strangely prolonged. I at last seated myself by the fire and, lulled by the warmth and the patter of the rain, fell asleep. I may have dreamt, for during my sleep I had a vague semisciencess of hands being softly pressed on my pockets---no doubt induced by the story of the robbery. When I came fully to my senses, I found Hemlock Jones sittingon the other side of the hearth, his deeply concentrated gaze fixed on the fire.

"I found you so comfortably asleep that I could not bear to awaken you," he said with a smile.

I rubbed my eyes. "And what news?" I asked. "How have you succeeded?"

"Better than I expected," he said, "and I think," he added, tapping his notebook, "I owe much to you."

Deeply gratified, I awaited more. But in vain. I ought to have remembered that in his moods Hemlock Jones was reticence itself. I told him simply of the strange intrusion, but he only laughed.

Later, when I arose to go, he looked at me playfully. "If you were a married man," he said, "I would advise you not to go home until you had brushed your sleeve. There are a few short brown hairs on the inner side of your forearm, just where they would have adhered if your arm had encircled a sealskin coat with some pressure!"

"For once you are at fault," I said triumphantly, "the hair is my own, as you will perceive; I have just had it cut at the barber shop, and no doubt this arm projected beyond the apron."

He frowned slightly, yet, nevertheless, on my turning to go he embraced me warmly---a rare exhibition in that man of ice. He even helped me on with my overcoat and pulled out and smoothed down the flaps of my pockets. He was particular, too, in fitting my arm in my overcoat sleeve, shaking the sleeve down from the armhole to the cuff with his deft fingers.

"Come again soon!" he said clapping me on the back.

"At any and all times," I said enthusiastically. "I only ask ten minutes twice a day to eat a crust in my office, and four hours sleep at night, and the rest of my time is devoted to you always, as you know."

"It is indeed," he said, with his impenetrable smile.

Nevertheless, I did not find him at home when I next called.

One afternoon, when nearing my own home, I met him in one of his favorite disguises---a long blue swallow-tailed coat, striped cotton trousers, large turn-over collar, blacked face, and white hat, carrying a tambourine. Of course to others the disguise was perfect, although it was known to myself, and I passed him---according to an old understanding between us---without the slightest recognition, trusting to

235

a later explanation.

At another time, as I was making a professional visit to the wife of a publican at the East End, I saw him, in the disguise of a broken-down artisan, looking into the window of an adjacent pawnshop. I was delighted to see that he was evidently following my suggestions, and in my joy I ventured to tip him a wink, it was abstractedly returned.

Two days later I received a note appointing a meeting at his lodgings that night. That meeting alas! was the one memorable occurrence of my life, and the last meeting I ever had with Hemlock Jones! I will try to set it down calmly, though my pulses still throb with the recollection of it.

I found him standing before the fire, with that look upon his face which I had seen only once or twice---a look which I may call an absolute concatenation of inductive and deductive ratiocination---from which all that was human, tender, or sympathetic was absolutely discharged. He was simply an icy algebraic symbol.

After I had entered he locked the doors, fastened the window, and even placed a chair before the chimney. As I watched these significant precautions with absorbing interest, he suddenly drew a revolver and presenting it to my temple, said in low icy tones.

"Hand over that cigar case!"

Even in my bewilderment my reply was truthful, spontaneous, and involuntary. "I haven't got it," I said.

He smiled bitterly, and threw down his revolver. "I expected that reply! Then let me now confront you with something more awful, more deadly, more relentless and convincing than that more lethal weapon--- the damning inductive and deductive proofs of your guilt!" He drew from his pocket a roll of paper and a notebook.

"But surely," I gasped, "you are joking! You could not believe---"

"Silence. Sit down."

I obeyed.

"You have condemned yourself," he went on pitilessly. "Condemned yourself on my processes---processes familiar to you, applauded by you, accepted by you for years! We will go back to the time when you first saw the cigar case. Your expressions," he said in cold, deliberate tones, consulting his paper, "were, 'How beautiful!' 'I wish it were mine' to 'I will have it mine' and the mere detail, 'How can I make it mine?' the advance was obvious. Silence!

"But as in my methods it was necessary that there should be an overwhelming inducement to the crime, that unholy admiration of yours for the mere trinket itself was not enough. You are a smoker of cigars."

"But," I burst out passionately, "I told you I had given up smoking cigars."

"Fool!" he said coldly. "That is the second time you have committed yourself. Of course you told me! What more natural than for you to blazon forth that prepared and unsolicited statement to prevent accusation. Yet, as I said before, even that wretched attempt to cover up your tracks was not enough. I still had to find that overwhelming impelling motive necessary to affect a man like you. That motive I found in the strongest of all impulses---love, I suppose you would call it---" he added bitterly "that night you called! You had brought the most conclusive proof on your sleeve."

"But---" I almost screamed.

237

"Silence!" he thundered. "I know what you would say. You would say that even if you had embraced some Young Person in a sealskin coat, what had that to do with the robbery? Let me tell you then that sealskin coat represented the quality and character of your fatal entanglement! You bartered your honor for it---that stolen cigar case was the purchaser of the sealskin coat!

"Silence! Having thoroughly established your motive, I now proceed to the commission of the crime itself. Ordinary people would have begun with that---with an attempt to discover the whereabouts of the missing object. These are not my methods."

So overpowering was his penetration that, although I knew myself innocent, I licked my lips with avidity to hear the further details of this lucid exposition of my crime.

"You committed that theft the night I showed you the cigar case and after I had carelessly thrown it in that drawer. You were sitting in that chair, and I had arisen to take something from that shelf. In that instant you secured your booty without rising. Silence! Do you remember when I helped you on with your overcoat the other night? I was particular about fitting your arm in. While doing so I measured your arm with a spring tape measure, from the shoulder to the cuff. A later visit to your tailor confirmed that measurement. It proved to be *the exact distance from your chair to that drawer!"*

I sat stunned.

"The rest are mere corrobative details! You were again tampering with the drawer when I discovered you doing so! Do not start. The stranger that blundered into the room with a muffler on---was myself! More, I had placed a little soap on the drawer handles when I purposely left you alone.

238

"The soap was on your hand when I shook it in parting. I softly felt your pockets, when you were asleep, for further developments. I embraced you when you left---that I might feel if you had the cigar case or any other articles hidden on your body. This confirmed me in the belief that you had already disposed of it in the manner and for the purpose I have shown you. As I still believed you capable of remorse and confession, I twice allowed you to see I was on your track: once in the garb of an itinerant Negro minstrel, and the second time as a workman looking in the window of the pawnshop where you pledged your booty."

"But," I burst out, "if you had asked the pawnbroker you would have seen how unjust---"

"Fool!" he hissed. "Do you suppose I followed any of your suggestions, the suggestions of the thief? On the contrary, they told me what to avoid."

"And I suppose," I said bitterly, "you have not even searched your drawer."

"No," he said calmly.

I was for the first time really vexed. I went to the nearest drawer and pulled it out sharply. It stuck as it had before, leaving a section of the drawer unopened. By working it, however, I discovered it was impeded by some obstacle that had slipped to the upper part of the drawer and held it firmly fast. Inserting my hand, I pulled out the impeding object. It was the missing cigar case!

I turned to him with a cry of joy!

But I was appalled at his expression. A look of contempt was now added to his acute, penetrating gaze. "I have been mistaken," he said slowly. "I had not allowed for your weakness and cowardice! I thought too highly of you even in your guilt! But I see now why you tampered with that drawer the other night. By some inexplicable means---possibly another theft---you took the cigar case out of pawn and like a whippet hound, restored it to me in this feeble clumsy fashion. You thought to deceive me, Hemlock Jones!"

"More, you thought to destroy my infallibility."

"Go! I give you your liberty. I shall not summon the three policemen who wait in the adjoining room---but out of my sight forever!"

As I stood once more dazed and petrified, he took me firmly by the ear and led me into the hall, closing the door behind him. This reopened presently, wide enough to permit him to thrust out my hat, overcoat, umbrella, and overshoes, and then closed it against me forever!

I never saw him again. I am bound to say, however, that thereafter my business increased, I recovered much of my old practice, and a few of my patients recovered also. I became rich. I had a brougham and a house in the West End.

But I often wondered, if, in some lapse of consciousness, I had not really stolen his cigar case!

Conan Doyle's Favorite Sherlockian Parody

James M. Barrie

*James Barrie found he would have difficulty meeting a deadline for a comic operetta, to be staged at the Savoy Theater by d'Oyly Carte, the producer for Gilbert and Sullivan. He asked Conan Doyle for help which Conan Doyle generously gave. The piece was called **Jane Annie or The Good Conduct Prize.** Despite the skill and fame of its two authors, the piece failed miserably.*

*Barrie wrote this parody shortly after in 1893, and sent it on to Conan Doyle. It first appeared in print in early 1924 and the same year in Conan Doyle's autobiography, **Memories and Adventures.** It was titled "The Adventure of the Two Collaborators."*

It has many excellent qualities, but the last few paragraphs may suggest why, at least why in 1893 when Conan Doyle was busily setting up the Reichenbach drama, this parody of Sherlock Holmes became his favorite.

As far as we know, it seems to be the only parody or pastiche Conan Doyle ever commented on, but it suggests also that he couldn't help reading a few of them.

241

*A sidelight: The Sherlockian, Marvin Kaye, managed to track down a copy of the libretto of **Jane Annie** thinking it couldn't be as bad as reported, given the literary skill of the two authors. However, he found it "unbearably cloying." He offered part of song by Bab "a bad girl" in the appendix of his excellent book on parodies, **The Game Is Afoot.** I give you only a small dose:*

> *Now my figure---once like this---*
> *Droops like autumn berry;*
> *Pity me, my secret is,*
> *Me is sleepy very!*

✱✱✱✱✱✱✱✱

In bringing to a close the adventures of my friend, Sherlock Holmes, I am perforce reminded that he never, save on the occasion which, as you will now hear, brought his singular career to an end, consented to act in any mystery which was concerned with persons who made a livelihood by their pen.

"I am not particular about the people I mix among for business purposes," he would say, "but at literary characters I draw the line."

We were in our rooms in Baker Street one evening. I was (I remember) by the centre table writing out 'The Adventure of the Man with the Cork Leg' (which had so puzzled the Royal Society and all the other scientific bodies of Europe), and Holmes was amusing himself with a little revolver practice. It was his custom of a summer evening to fire around my head, just shaving my face, until he had made a photograph on the opposite wall, and it is a slight proof of his skill that many of these portraits in pistol shots are considered admirable likenesses.

I happened to look out of the window, and perceiving two gentlemen advancing rapidly along Baker Street asked him who they

242

were. He immediately lit his pipe, and twisting himself on a chair into the figure 8, replied: "They are two collaborators in comic opera, and their play has not been a triumph."

I sprang from my chair to the ceiling in amazement, and then he explained:

"My dear Watson, they are obviously men who follow some low calling. That much even you should be able to read in their faces. Those little pieces of blue paper which they fling angrily from them are Durrant's Press Notices. Of these they have obviously hundreds about their person (see how their pockets bulge). They would not dance on them if they were pleasant reading."

I again sprang to the ceiling (which is much dented), and shouted: "Amazing! But they may be mere authors."

"No," said Holmes, "for mere authors only get one press notice a week. Only criminals, dramatists, and actors get them by the hundred."

"Then they may be actors."

"No, actors would come in a carriage."

"Can you tell me anything else about them."

"A great deal. From the mud on the boots of the tall one I perceive that he comes from South Norwood. The other is obviously a Scotch author."

"How can you tell that?"

"He is carrying in his pocket a book called (I clearly see) *Auld Licht* Something. Would anyone but the author be likely to carry about a book with such a title?"

I had to confess that this was improbable.

It was now evident that the two men (if such they can be called) were seeking our lodgings. I have said (often) that my friend Holmes seldom gave way to emotion of any kind, but he now turned livid with passion. Presently this gave place to a strange look of triumph.

"Watson," he said, "that big fellow has for years taken the credit for my most remarkable doings, but at last I have him---at last!"

Up I went to the ceiling, and when I returned the strangers were in the room.

"I perceive, gentlemen," said Mr. Sherlock Holmes, "that you are at present afflicted by an extraordinary novelty."

The handsomer of our visitors asked in amazement how he knew this, but the big one only scowled.

"You forget that you wear a ring on your fourth finger," replied Mr. Holmes calmly.

I was about to jump to the ceiling when the big brute interposed.

"That tommy-rot is all very well for the public, Holmes," said he, "but you can drop it before me. And, Watson, if you go up to the ceiling again, I shall make you stay there."

Here I observed a curious phenomenon. My friend, Sherlock Holmes *shrank*. He became small before my eyes. I looked longingly at the ceiling but dared not.

"Let us cut the first four pages," said the big man, "and proceed to

244

business. I want to know why---"

"Allow me," said Mr. Holmes, with some of his old courage. "You want to know why the public does not go to your opera."

"Exactly," said the other ironically, "as you perceive by my shirt stud."

He added more gravely, "And as you can only find out in one way I must insist on your witnessing an entire performance of the piece."

It was an anxious moment for me. I shuddered, for I knew that if Holmes went I should have to go with him. But my friend had a heart of gold.

"Never," he cried fiercely. "I will do anything save that."

"Your continued existence depends on it," said the big man menacingly.

"I would rather melt into air," replied Holmes, proudly taking another chair. "But I can tell you why the public don't go to your piece without sitting the thing out myself."

"Why?"

"Because," replied Holmes calmly, "they prefer to stay away."

A dead silence followed that extraordinary remark. For a moment the two intruders gazed with awe upon the man who had unraveled their mystery so wonderfully. Then drawing their knives---

Holmes grew less and less, until nothing was left save a ring of smoke which slowly circled to the ceiling.

The last words of men are often noteworthy. These were the last words of Sherlock Holmes: "Fool, fool! I have kept you in luxury for years. By my help you have ridden extensively in cabs, where no author was ever seen before.

"Henceforth you will ride in buses!"

The brute sunk into a chair aghast.

The other author did not turn a hair.

Meet the Mrs. (*Irene?*)

Anonymous

Tit Bits was the sister magazine of **The Strand.** *One suspects that its editor was part of the campaign to encourage Conan Doyle to bring back Sherlock Holmes from the Other Side---by keeping Sherlock fresh in the public mind. By my count, **Tit Bits** published at least half a dozen pieces about The Great Detective while Sherlock was thought to be lying peaceably oblivious to this world in the pool at the base of the Reichenbach Falls.*

The title of this piece tells it all, "Mrs., Dr. Sherlock Holomes." If you don't have Sherlock Holmes to kickaround, you have to find an alternative, and this is one of several parodies to reach the same inspired notion, that Sherlock must have had a Mrs., the result of a secret marriage to Irene Adler or one of the Violets, an event that Conan Doyle must have felt it wise to suppress.

It appeared February 9, 1895.

****

All of a sudden she turned to the man in the tramcar on the left and said: "You were putting down an ingrain carpet at your house this morning. Don't attempt to deny it, for I have most conclusive evidence."

"How do you know?" he stammered, in surprise.

"There is lint on your knees, sir, showing the kind of carpet, and your thumb is done up in a rag to prove that you hit it with a hammer. You have a bunion on your left foot. Deny it at your peril."

"Yes, I have a bunion, but---"

"I knew it, because you can't keep that foot still, while now and then you utter a cuss word under your breath. You are living with your second wife. Admit the truth of what I say, or take the consequence."

"How on earth can you tell that?" he asked, as he began to turn pale around the mouth.

"By the hairs and dandruff on your coat. Your first wife always brushed you before you went out. Now sir, you have a small child at home."

"Yes, a boy three years old; but---"

"I knew it because he shoved that jumping-jack into your pocket while you were playing with him just before you came out. You are also an absent-minded man. Denial will be useless, and may get you into serious trouble."

"I---I---"

"If you were not an absent-minded man you would not have pocketed that table-napkin for a handkerchief, nor come out with your old hat on. While your first wife has been dead for several years, you have not yet placed a tombstone on her grave. Don't try to bluff me, sir!"

"You are right, but---"

"Of course I am. When we passed that marble shop you gave one look at the tombstones and placed your hand on your wallet. Your present wife is not domestic."

"No, she is not, but how on earth can you tell?"

"The moths have eaten your coat, there are two buttons off your vest, and from the way you wriggle that right foot I'm sure you have holes in your stockings. Think not to deceive me."

"Great lands, woman!" he gasped as the perspiration stood out on his forehead, "but you must be---"

"Mrs. Dr. Sherlock Holmes, sir," she finished. "I have to get out here to solve a mystery in a butcher's shop. Blood has been found on a cleaver, the butcher's wife has got a new seal skin jacket, and the errand-boy has a boil on his leg. Sdeath! I will unravel the whole affair in five minutes, and spot the murderer! Good day, old man."

The Worm That Turned

J. W. Courtney

Dr. J. W. Courtney, M. D., was a distinguished Boston physician and medical researcher. While the internet lists a number of his medical writings, it gives few personal details.

*Jon Lellenberg described this parody appropriately as „A Doctor's Revenge." One would anticipate the editors of **The Boston Medical and Surgical Journal**chuckled and rubbed their hands as they accepted this piece for their May 1904 issue. Its full title was "Dr. Watson and Mr. Holmes, or The Worm that Turned."*

Dr. Watson over the years marveled at the deductive powers of Sherlock Holmes. It is only fair, at last, turnabout becomes fair play. And why shouldn't a doctor give Holmes some of his own back. After all, a physician, Dr. Joseph Bell, Conan Doyle's' mentor in medical school, taught Conan Doyle the trick of making deductions about a person's occupation and other details. Only later did Conan Doyle pass all this along to Sherlock Holmes.

Another from Shaw.

Dr. Watson begins his diagnosis, as doctors will, on the state of Sherlock Holmes's health.

****

"Ah, good morning, Holmes," said Dr. Watson, without even raising his eyes from the paper which lay before him on the table, at his clinic for diseases of the nervous system. "Somewhat surprised, I see, that I should know who it was," he continued, as he went on reading.

"It's very simple, as you are wont to say." He pushed back his chair, looked up and extended his hand. "In the first place, I had just looked at my watch and seen that it was a quarter after eleven. Now under no circumstances is a patient admitted after eleven; and when I looked over the assembly on the benches some ten minutes ago, there wasn't a soul there that didn't have some defect in his gait. My assistants and the hospital attendants are trained not to enter without knocking. What's more, there came to my nostrils, above the stuffy odor of the clinic, the smell of that awful Red Herring brand of cigarettes, which you alone of all my extensive acquaintance are able to smoke."

"Now, my dear fellow, as to your being surprised. You can't deny that since your awful experience with our late friend, Moriarty, your nerves have got the faintest bit on edge. As I read, your legs from the knees up fell just in range of vision from the tail of my eye, and I was able to see that my salutation produced the faintest upward twitch of your trousers through an involuntary contraction of the thigh muscles.

"'Pon my word, though, you are the most unsatisfactory fellow! I've been begging you to come here for years to see the only really interesting phase of human morbidity, and you have persistently denied yourself this intellectual treat. And now you drop in on me from the clouds, when I haven't a bally thing on hand that's worthwhile."

During this outburst, so astonishingly longwinded for the erstwhile shrinking and self-effacing Watson, Sherlock the magnificent stood gazing at him with the well-known look of amused superiority which he invariably kept on tap for his mix-ups with the upstart Lestrade. Not a muscle of his long, keen face relaxed, but his pallor deepened, until Watson, who watched him, naturally considered if he really did have pernicious anemia, or if his lemon-yellow complexion were merely the result of the excessive use of breakfast food subcu, coupled with the inhalation of fumes of Red Herring cigarettes. He knew that his quondam mentor was recentering the tigroid bodies of his higher cortical cells in the act of thinking, but just what was at the bottom of the obvious mental gymnastics eluded his penetration.

For the benefit of our readers, we will explain, Holmes was miffed, for it was now disagreeably obvious to this twentieth century prodigy that during his long demise, his microcephalic ex-serf, the doctor, (either by the excessive use of that minute portion of his anatomy which lay under his thatch, or by the vicarious function of some other organ), had developed his rudimentary faculty of thought. In Holmes' wildest flights of cocainized fancy, no such thing as a rival had ever taken shape. And now suddenly to bump into the possibility, so to speak, in tangible form, and that, too, in the form of this low-grade idiot of a Watson, made him feel like a four-ply Rip Van Winkle.

During this prolonged fit of abstraction Holmes had made up his mind on at least one point: Watson must be squelched, once and for all.

"You're right, my dear Watson," he said finally, with assumed cordiality. "I ought to have come round before, but you know how many really important things I have to disentangle, and how little time I have to waste on the obvious, but I've made up my mind to devote a morning to you, and if you name the day."

252

"Any day will suit me," said Watson, politely refusing a proffered Red Herring cigarette. "I'll go along with you now and we'll decide as we walk."

Watson rang the bell for an assistant, left the remaining patients in his charge, and started from the hospital with Holmes, arm in arm.

It was Monday and the throng about the doors was of the usual large proportions after the Sunday inactivity of the out-patient departments. At the exit from the lodge the way was temporarily blocked to Holmes and his *fidus Achates* by a burly fellow on crutches, who seemed to handle the one under his right arm with peculiar difficulty for a man of his powerful build.

As they went along Holmes turned to Watson and said with a tinge of malice, "Why can't the duffers of surgeons give these poor devils proper crutches? It's bad enough to think of that chap's family being without his support for a long time on account of his foot, but an extra two months' loaf with a crutch-maimed arm is an outrage. There are an awful lot of incompetents in your profession, Watson."

"I think you're entirely wrong in your conclusions, my friend," was his only reply. Then as the object of their remarks came along, he stopped him and said, "You'd have been better off without the liquor, wouldn't you my good man?" Watson's question was accompanied by a significant glance in the direction of the big fellow's right hand.

The lout, with the instinct of his class, at once recognized the professional calling of his questioner, hung his head sheepishly and replied, "I guess it was the booze that did me up all right for I was doing fine with the foot till I got out with a crowd of my friends Saturday night. Nothing would do them but they must stand treat to celebrate the getting better with the foot. I was loaded when I got home, but the hand

253

seemed all right then. Yesterday morning, though, when I woke up, it was all numb and deadlike, and it ain't been no use to me since."

During this reply, Holmes appeared restless and uneasy, and at the conclusion he took Watson by the arm and said, "I'm in quite a hurry, old man, and if you're coming along with me, you'll have to come at once."

Watson hastily directed the man to come to his clinic the next day and started along with Holmes.

Holmes was consumed with inward rage; he knew that Watson would rough him at the earliest opportunity, and decided to give him no opening. He immediately started in and talked a blue streak on the probable cost of the midnight oil consumed by Homer while writing the *Iliad*. He figured it out by a secret process of calculation, which he knew would excite Watson's envy, and this in itself brought a certain amount of balm to his wounded feelings.

Watson let him rattle on until they were near Holmes' lodgings, and then butted in with, "I say, old chap, do you still hold the views on surgical incompetency that you expressed a while ago, and do you still feel that you should not waste your time on the obvious?"

Holmes grunted and quickened his pace.

"Because if you do," went on the imperturbable doctor, "I think a morning at my clinic will prove a strong mental corrective. By the way, I must make a note to send you a reprint of my lecture on fallaciousness of the apparently obvious in clinical diagnosis. This case we just saw exemplifies my teachings beautifully, and you must confess, my dear Sherlock, that you did not give consideration to all the factors entering into it. Had you noticed the soiled condition of the padding on the tops of the crutches, it would have been obvious to you that the padding had been put there at the time the crutches were given."

"This fact in itself demonstrates that the surgeon was cautious, and precludes to a large extent the possibility of crutch paralysis; now this is Monday, and the day on which we usually get a crop of Saturday night paralysis, that is to say, paralysis of the radial nerve caused by a drunk's sleeping on his arm; but enough of this. You come around on Friday and I'll try to show you something interesting."

On Friday morning Watson left the place that most people call home, but which with him was merely a place to stay when he wasn't needed by Holmes. He proceeded to the latter's lodgings in Baker Street, and the two went on together to the hospital. Arrived there, Watson cast a searching glance over the benches and ushered Holmes into the consulting room. Then he rang the bell and ordered the externe to show in first the musician on the front seat.

"I'm sorry, sir," said the externe, "but I haven't had time to take any histories, and I don't know who you mean."

Watson walked to the door, threw it open, and beckoned to a man sitting on the front seat. The patient entered and sat down before Watson's table.

"Musician, did you say?"asked Holmes apathetically.

"Yes, musician, and I should add the player of a wind instrument."

Holmes examined the man's buccinators in their normal condition and then got him to puff out his cheeks. He appeared satisfied with his examination, and when Watson asked him if he had made up his mind as to how he, Watson, had arrived at his conclusion as to the man's occupation, he answered in a tired way, "why certainly, you have only to look at the muscles of his lips and cheeks; they tell the story."

"Wrong," said Watson; "it's much simpler than that. Just observe the little goatee he wears. I venture to say he believes the loss of that would prevent his playing for a week. Am I right?" he asked, turning to the man.

"Oh, yes sir. I wouldn't cut that off for the world; it's strengthening to the lip, and I shouldn't be able to play till it grew again."

Watson soon got at the facts of the case, examined and disposed of it.

During this time Holmes looked absently out the window.

The next patient was ushered in, and without speaking, presented a note to Watson. The latter, without looking at the note, exclaimed, "Ah a teamster, I see."

"That observation was superfluous," broke in Holmes superciliously. "I knew he was a teamster the moment I saw him. He has the complexion of a man much exposed to the weather and wears the sort of clothes common to people of that class."

"That may all be true, but it would apply equally as well to a cabman; and it is dangerous to draw conclusions on such general grounds. Perhaps you did not notice that this man took the note he brought me out of his hat---a typical teamster trick."

Holmes made no reply, but bit his lips furiously while Watson read the note. Watson turned the case over to his assistant and called for the next patient. It proved to be a man with a marked tremor of the right hand. Without a word, Watson took hold of the trembling hand and observed it closely for a few moments, Then he said quietly, "Here, my dear Holmes, is an interesting tremor in a left-handed plasterer, who has

256

done no work for some time. Am I right, my man?"

"Quite right, sir," was the answer, "I'm left-handed and I'm a plasterer by trade, but this cursed shaking has laid me up for nearly six months now."

At this point Holmes was about to say something but hesitated and looked the man over in silence. Watson sat quietly back in his chair and observed his friend's scrutiny of the patient with an amused twinkle in his eye.

Holmes' face was a study. It had grown several shades yellower than usual, and again made Watson think of pernicious anemia. The powerful magnifying lens was now brought into play and the man's nails, ears, and eyebrows thoroughly examined by its aid. Obviously Holmes was stumped. By this time he was breathing hard and mopping his brow.

After a time Watson broke in with: "Well, my dear Holmes, what do you say?"

"Nothing, except that it's beastly stuffy in this room," growled Sherlock, the peerless.

"Well, let's have a window open, and then, perhaps, I can show you a thing of interest about the man that you may have overlooked with your glass, You will first observe that the tremor involves the right hand. On looking at this hand closely, you will see a half softened callus over each joint of the thumb, and similar ones over the root joint and the one next to the forefinger. You see none over any other joints. This shows that these particular joints mentioned most habitually come in contact with a hard surface. Now, from my study of artisan's hands, I know that this condition is peculiar to a plasterer, and it is brought about by the contact of the mortar board. In this case it is the right hand that shows the condition, so the man must do the actual plastering with the left. I hardly need mention that the somewhat softened condition of the calluses indicates this man's abstinence from work for some time."

While Watson was engaged in demonstrating the reasons for his conclusions, Holmes paced rapidly up and down the room, apparently paying not the slightest attention. Finally he whipped out his watch, looked at it, and said, "By Jove, Watson, I must go. I've got an important engagement that I had almost forgotten."

"Oh, don't be in such an infernal rush," replied the doctor. "I've got to get away early myself. I'll tell you what I'll do. I'll just turn this man over to my assistant, see the next case or two hurriedly, and then go along with you."

At Watson's order the next case was led in. "This man," said the externe, "is a rubber-cutter, and his complaint is of headache and dizziness."

"Now, Holmes," said the doctor, "won't you just look at this fellow's gums with your glass and see if you don't see a dark line at the junction of the gums and teeth. You do---thank you. It's a clear case of lead poisoning, just as I thought. Now, my man, let me look at your tongue."

A sudden exclamation from Holmes caused Watson to look at him. As he did so he noticed that his friend's face had suddenly taken on an expression very like what one might expect to see in a mummy that had been spoiled in the making. "Did you speak?" he asked, somewhat maliciously.

"No," growled Holmes between his clenched teeth, "but the diagnosis in this case is too absurdly clear. This man has either been doing some painting at home, or else he uses hair wash containing lead.

Isn't that so, my good fellow?" asked Sherlock, addressing the patient.

"Aw, I never washes me hair," was the reply; "and I have enough to do in the shop without bothering with no painting at home. It ain't in my line."

Holmes collapsed in his chair.

"Perhaps he will tell us just what his functions as a rubber-cutter are, it will help you to arrive at a correct solution of the problem," put in the doctor dryly. "Exactly what is your work, my man?"

"I just put the patterns down on the sheet rubber and cuts around them with a knife, was the answer."

"Does that help you, Holmes?" asked Watson.

The great detective sat dejectedly and made no reply.

"Well, we won't waste any more time on it," rattled on Watson, "but the situation is just this. From your extensive reading and observations, you must know that in the preparation of rubber, there is used a considerable amount of litharge, or red oxide of lead. Now you don't have to examine the fellow's hands very closely to conclude that soap is not a large factor in his items of expenditure. My glance at his tongue showed me he is an habitual tobacco chewer. On the basis of these two observations, I concluded that the transference of really considerable amounts of the lead from fingers to mouth was a daily occurrence."

"And now I'm about ready to toddle along with you. From certain sounds I have heard in the last four minutes, I think there's a deaf man with general paralysis in the further room. I'll just run and look at him, and then I'm at your service."

259

Watson rose from his chair and went toward the door. As he was about to turn the knob, he heard a low moan followed by a thud, and looking round, he saw that Holmes had fallen apparently lifeless on the floor.

Another Tale of Sweet Revenge

Charles Battell Loomis

The author is American humorist Charles Battell Loomis (1861-1911). This parody, titled as "The Adventure of the Child's Perambulator" appeared on April 10, 1895, two months after his first parody and was also published in **Puck.**

For Sherlockians: There's a whiff of the Bohemian scandal, thatcase about the League of Red Heads, and The Six Napoleons. Another discovery in the Shaw collection.

****

I had not heard from Sherlock Holmes for some time, when one day I received a post card, with no date or signature, bearing the single word, "Come!"

I knew that I was wanted on a dangerous and delicate mission, so I put an American bowie knife, a dark lantern, a brace of revolvers, a bottle of smelling salts, and a ham sandwich in my grip. Then I kissed my wife good-by telling her I might be back in a six-month, next day or never, and bidding her to tell my patients to keep stout hearts and to continue to take whatever I had ordered until I returned. I hurried off to the station, and in two hours had reached the lodgings of Sherlock Holmes, in Baker Street, and knocked on the door which he at once opened.

"Ha! Watson, you've come," said he. I couldn't deny the fact

261

although I did not know by what subtle processes he had arrived at the conclusion.

"Well," said I, "what's in the wind today?"

"Do you value your life?"

"Not a ha'porth," said I.

"Good, neither do I. I have got a murder mystery on my hands besides which that of the Boscombe Valley sinks into insignificance. But, hark! what is that? I hear a footstep. Ten to one, it's Lestrade of Scotland Yard. I never mistake the cocksure gait of his. He's coming to consult with me."

I went to the window and looked out. For once, Holmes was mistaken. The noise he had heard was caused by a tally-ho and six that dashed by at a furious rate. Not a soul was in sight. The tally-ho stopped at the corner and a man alighted. The next minute he was knocking at our door, and a voice shouted: "Phair the divvle does Sherlock Holmes keep himself?"

"Walk in," said the great unraveler, and a red-headed man in a smock and overalls entered the room.

"You are an English gentleman, are you not?" asked Holmes.

"Phwat make ye think so?"

"Your disguise and accent."

"Can your frind be trusted?"

"Certainly, he is my colleague, Dr. Watso."

"Then behold me, Sir Edward Percyvale Vere Bermondsey-on-Trent Boggs," and with that he shed his smock and overalls, pulled off his wig and beard, and stood revealed as a slim, aristocratic looking fellow, whose ancestors, according to Burke's peerage, which Holmes at once consulted, turned up their noses at William the Conqueror.

"Sir Edward, take a sofa. We are at work at a little murder mystery, but we can let it stand for awhile. Please give me the smallest particulars of the mystery you want unraveled."

Sir Edward spread himself over the sofa, and, taking out a copy of the *Times*, said: "Yesterday's *Times* contains the following advertisement: 'If the finder of the child's perambulator that was mislaid somewhere between Charing Cross and Seven Dials will return same to Edward Percyvale Vere Bermondsey-on-Trent Boggs, 27 Henrietta Street, third bell, he will be handsomely rewarded, as the perambulator contained nothing save a child, of no value to any one save the owners.'"

"My wife is lying ill at my house in Henrietta Street, and the doctor has prescribed absolute quiet; but since early dawn yesterday the street has been filled with perambulators, containing all sorts and conditions of noisy children, and the bell has not ceased ringing. My wife and I are perfectly childless, and I am at a loss to conceive who could have put us to this great annoyance. This morning my wife's illness has taken a turn for the worse, in consequence of the ceaseless clamor, and if you can help me to find the man who inserted the advertisement, I promise you that I will furnish a murder with no element of mystery in it."

"This is a very lucid account of which promises to be the most interesting case I ever undertook. Pardon me if I ask a few questions that may appear to be trivial, but which nevertheless, may have a direct bearing on the subject.

"Was your wife ever married before?"

"She was not."

"Ha! That is very important, and now may I ask whether you have had in your employ a Pole at any time in the last six years?"

"No sir, I employ none but English."

"And quite right. Now one more question. What was the maiden name of your wife's mother?"

"Saunders."

"Enough, come here to-morrow at this time, and I will show you the busy-body who inserted the advertisement, or my name is not Sherlock Holmes."

During the whole interview, Sir Edward was smiling in a very peculiar way, and he now took his departure still smiling.

When he had gone, Holmes said, "It will not take long to clear up that mystery, though it is a very pretty one. Then we will make up for lost time on the murder case. In the meantime, let us forget that such things as mysteries that need ferreting. Hand me my violin, and I will play you seven variations of 'After the Ball,' by Grieg." For the next half hour he played for me in a manner to make the great Sarasate himself blush, and then he said, "Come we have idled enough. I will disguise myself, and you take this business directory and hunt up all the firms engaged in the manufacture of perambulators."

In a few minutes I had prepared a list of the perambulator manufacturers in the United Kingdom. Before I had finished, however, Holmes had stepped out of his bedroom, disguised as an unmarried

Baptist preacher of Pennsylvania, U. S. of A. Not a person could have guessed what he represented, so cleverly was he made up. I, who am comparatively unknown, did not need a disguise; but Holmes suggested I carry my revolvers, as he might have to place me in a dangerous position.

On leaving the house we jumped into a cab, and, after giving directions to the cabman to take us to Hogg & Chichester's, the leading manufacturers of perambulators, Holmes dismissed all thoughts of business from his mind, and, taking out a jews-harp, played the Spanish Rhapsody in a manner that I have rarely heard equaled.

Arriving at the warehouse, Holmes asked to see the foreman, and that worthy soon came into the room.

"Have you among your workman a Pole?"

"No sir, we have not a Pole."

"Quite so. Kindly let me see the man who is not a Pole."

"A young man with auburn hair and a pug nose, came to us in a minute.

"Are you the young man who is not a Pole?"

"I am."

"Is your name Saunders?"

"It is not."

"Do you ever see the *Times*."

"No, sir, the pink 'un is the only paper I ever read."

"What do you think of this affair."

"Nothing. Didn't even know there was an affair."

"Just so; that is all."

When we had regained the street, Holmes said; "This mystery is prettier than I first gave it credit for, still I have a clue. I consider it very auspicious that that young man is not a Pole. If he is not the man who inserted the advertisement, then we must go to the Isle of Wight for him."

"Why the Isle of Wight?" asked I.

"Wait," said he oracularly.

Just then we passed a restaurant. "How long since you ate?" asked he.

"Breakfast was my last meal," I replied.

"Do you know I haven't thought to eat for the last five or six days. Suppose we go in."

When we were seated, he ordered six hot, hard-boiled eggs, which when brought, he ate, shells and all. "I need the lime," he said. I looked with admiration at this remarkable man, who had the stomach of a camel and a Vidocq combined.

Suddenly the door of the restaurant was opened by no less a person than Sir Edward Etcetera Boggs.

"Ha!" said Holmes. "You are the very man I wanted to see. Have an egg."

Sir Edward, with the smile of the morning still lingering upon his face, declined the delicacy, but seated himself at our table, where he ordered a b. & s. and a cup of tea.

"Sir Edward, have you relatives in the Isle of Wight?"

"I have not."

"Do they spend the summer there?"

"They do not."

"H'm. Have you ever happened to drop a hint that your wife hated to have people answering advertisements for lost perambulators when she was sick?"

"No, I didn't know she did hate it until yesterday. Now let me ask you a few questions: Aren't you almost omnipotent?"

"Almost."

"Well, do you know yet who inserted the advertisement?"

"No."

"Isn't all this Isle of Wight business a bluff to give you time to chance on a clue?"

"Yes."

"Well then, I've won my bet with Watson. I inserted the

267

advertisement myself, and bet him that you couldn't find out who did it before we met again."

"You bet with Dr. Watson?---Who the devil are you?"

To the everlasting discomfiture of Know-it-all Holmes, Sir Edward pulled off the whole top of his smiling face and disclosed inside of the papier mache head

The well-known features of Lestrade, the Scotland Yard detective!

Brotherly Love

Charlton Andrews

*Charlton Andrews(1878-1939) was Indiana born, lived in New York city, and was a writer of articles, plays, and novels and adapted a number of foreign plays for the American stage. He wrote **The Drama Today** (1913) among other books. Andrews wound up his career in the 1920s and 1930s, writing mystery novels.*

His three pieces featuring Mycroft Holmes, are the first parodies involving a character in the stories, other than Sherlock Holmes and Watson. The descriptions of the historical parodies Mycroft solves seemed to me not quite as lively as Mycroft's comments about his brother, Sherlock.

*The three parodies about Mycroft were published in **The Bookman** in June, 1902, two months after the Conan Doyle story "The Empty House"appeared proclaiming the triumphant return of Sherlock Holmes. They were later rescued by Tom and Enid Schantz and published by their Aspen Press of Denver as **The Resources of Mycroft Holmes.***

****

Rushem, the Editor of*The Daily Saffron*, had sent for and employedme within twenty minutes after he received the following message, wireless from his London correspondent:

"Reason to believe interview could be had with Mycroft Holmes."

When I had been shown the Marconi-gram, Rushem asked, "You are still disposed to desert the chair of history in your university to become as journalist, Professor Mustie?"

I answered in the affirmative.

"You know who Mycroft Holmes is?"

I replied that he was the tall, corpulent, seven-year-older, and more nicely observing brother of Sherlock Holmes, who had first attained worldwide fame through Dr. Watson's account of his (Mycroft's) connection with 'The Affair of the Greek Interpreter," who was a member of the singularly unsociable Diogenes Club, London, and who applied his extraordinary faculty for figures in auditing books in certain government departments, Whitehall.

Rushem was pleased, as I had fully intended he should be, by my *multum in parva* mode of expression. I think he impulsively added a ten to the salary he was about to propose and I was employed on the spot.

Behold me, therefore, seven days later, in the Strangers' Room of the Diogenes Club, Pall Mall, seated opposite Mycroft Holmes, in the gentle art of interviewing him.

"Briefly, Mr. Holmes," said I, for the twentieth time mentally sizing him up to my combined satisfaction and mystification, "what my paper's readers want is to know whether there is any truth in the widespread rumors that you are setting up in competition with your brother, lately reappeared?"

Mycroft Holmes looked up sharply from his cigar-ash, in evident surprise and disappointment. "Softly, softly, my dear fellow," he expostulated at once; "this is scarcely the proper beginning if I remember---if I know myself. It is for me to speak first, I believe, and so we shall commence over."

He drew his ponderous weight higher up in his arm-chair and fixed his narrow eyes on mine in a manner well calculated to be impressive.

"In the first place," he continued at once, "it must be a source of some satisfaction to you, even though you are a citizen of a republic, to be aware that you are descended in an almost direct line from a king of France, that another of your forbears was for months the companion of a monarch of England, and that two other progenitors of yours fell at Waterloo, fighting on opposite sides."

"Indeed it is," I acknowledged before I thought; and then, I frankly confess, I sprang up in the most intense amazement; I had come fully prepared for the usual demonstration of keen powers of observation and deduction, but I had certainly expected them to be applied to matters of the present or, at least, recent. So I did exactly what I had previously resolved not to do: I exclaimed in accents of extreme astonishment, "Mr. Holmes, this is marvelous! How on earth do you do it?"

Mycroft Holmes smiled contentedly, "I shall tell you," he said, "presently. Now, we shall return to the interview. It is desirable to know whether I shall set up in competition with my brother, Sherlock: briefly, I shall not."

He paused, evidently to gather his forces, a frown coming over his low forehead, and continued, "Sherlock Holmes is---" in such a tone that I could not repress an involuntary, "Yes?" of expectancy and suspense.

"Sherlock Holmes is a vain coxcomb and an errant charlatan," went on Mycroft explosively. "The strain he exhibits comes into our line in the middle of the eighteenth century; there was a fellow married a Holmes, a certain would-be detective named Quiller, who rejoiced in the

271

sobriquet of---"

"Foxy!" I cried, exultation mingling with my surprise.

"Foxy," repeated Mycroft, nodding and pausing to interject, "Very clever in you, my dear Mustie!"

Then, "Look at my brother's career," he cried sharply, "full of egregious conceit and inordinate self-advertisement, as it is! Why, it has been an eyesore and a nuisance to me for years, and, now that he has accomplished this supreme spectacularity of coming back from the dead, I can no longer endure the thought of it!"

"Learn, then, young man, and report my words accurately,---that I am not to be in competition with my brother and that, ever since that morning when I drove his absurd Boswell to Victoria Station---the morning Sherlock left for his notorious interview with Moriarty in Switzerland---in utter disgust I have completely abandoned all effort and interest in the modern business of detection. No I am no longer auditing for the government. Yes, I am devoting myself, body and soul, to a new pursuit. (You see, I anticipate your questions.) What is my business? I am for the remainder of my natural life, Mycroft Holmes Esquire, Solver of Historical Mysteries."

It was very natural that I should bow profoundly here, as he slightly nodded his head. "But if you please," I said, "condescend to solve for me the present *mystery* of the words you have just uttered."

"Readily! My income is sufficient for my needs. My sole object in life is to redeem the name---my name---my brother has succeeded in bringing so low. It is a difficult task to restore lost dignity: but I shall do it. Briefly, my business is not to waste my moments in the trite processes of unraveling tangles of today, tangles whereof the beginnings, ends, and entire lengths of every thread are capable of being rendered visible: my business lies with the solution of those Gordian knots of long ago, nine-tenths of whose component skeins are forever hid in the black fastnesses of the past."

I was enraptured, and I let him see it. He was by no means chagrined. After a time I exclaimed, "And so you can finally answer all those perplexing old questions, like Who wrote Shakespeare? and the Letters of Junius? and Who was the man in the Iron Mask?"

Mycroft Holmes shrugged his massive shoulders. "My dear Mustie," he said, with a smile, "you underestimate me. I assure you I have done nothing with these matters which are the common property of every amateur investigator. What I have done is to ascertain whose step-aunt married the seventh Earl of Willingham, how Giles Harcourt bought the broken corkscrew from the blind Crusader, how the centurion Alertius overcame the Pompeianlector---"

"But my dear Mycroft," I interrupted (I might as well be familiar, too), "these are matters of the slightest interest to the public, compared with the mysteries, I have mentioned. Come get to work on something everybody knows about, and I will be your Boswell, your Watson!"

I could see the suggestion pleased him immensely, though he tried hard not to show it. "Very well," he said after a moment, "be it as you say."

Sherlock Holmes vs Conan Doyle

Anonymous

The Adventures of Sherlock Holmes *had just been published as a runaway best seller. And so, in the October 29, 1892 issue of **The National Observer,** an anonymous journalist seeks out Sherlock Holmes for his reactions. Its original title was "The Real Sherlock Holmes."*

It ends with a mystery for us readers to puzzle out for ourselves, though the answer may be yellow or perhaps that amalgam of yellow and blue. We leave it to bibliographers to reveal the correct answer.

****

In view of the recent publication of Mr. Sherlock Holmes's more celebrated cases (writes our representative) I called upon the famous scientific detective for the purpose of elucidating if possible some of his more eventful and thrilling episodes in his adventures.

I found the celebrated sleuth-hound, whose fame is now European, seated before a comfortable fire in his cosily furnished rooms in Baker Street. His chin was sunk upon his chest, and his lynx eyes were fixed upon the ceiling with that hawk-like expression which his portraits have rendered so familiar to us.

"Good evening," he said, without turning his head or altering his gaze, as I entered. "You could not have come at a better time. I was just off to bed. You wish to interview me," he added, as his eyes literally pierced me through and through.

"You wear a high hat on Sundays, you are fond of cream tarts, Mr. William Watson is your favourite author, and seventeen years and six months ago you had a cousin who died."

"Really, Mr. Holmes," I stammered in amazement. "It is quite true, though how on earth you know – "

"It is very simple," he said, smiling. "Moreover, it saves me from *ennui*- it and cocaine. Life, my dear sir, (your name, by the way, begins with a D, as I see from your handkerchief) is only interesting because it is mysterious. What is ordinary is merely that which is not remarkable, and if you could open all the windows and sail over this vast city, you would behold strange secrets. I do not seem to be able to persuade you of the importance of the improbable," he said reflectively.

"I have come, Mr. Holmes," I began hastily, knowing from Dr. Conan Doyle's account of his weakness for this vein of reflection, and fearing to be taken beyond my depths; "I have come to ask you about the book – "

"You mean," he interrupted, "my treatise on the 742 ways of saying the word 'damn!"

"No, I refer to Dr. Doyle's collection of your adventures."

"I have heard of the man," said Mr. Holmes. "It is my business to know about all kinds of people. But I've never met him. If you will look in my Index, under the heading Plagiarists"

"But," I objected, "Dr. Doyle is a novelist."

275

"True, but he is also a plagiarist - the very worst kind of plagiarist, seeing that he steals from life. Oddly enough, as there was no classical concert this evening, I was just dipping into the very book to which you refer."

He waved his hand towards the table, and leaned back in his chair with a little soft laugh. As he put his fingertips together and, closing his eyes, assumed a languid expression of weariness. I guessed what was coming, and so seized my opportunity and my note book.

"It is perhaps," Mr. Holmes resumed, "just as well, my good man, that people will not stick to the truth, otherwise my occupation - and it is a pleasant way of passing the time - would be gone. This man, (who is a stranger to me) has compiled a book purporting to be my adventures. It is, in fact, a garbled version of some very inferior incidents in my professional career; but where or how he got hold of them, I cannot say, although my mind is already made up.

"You see Watson could never keep his tongue quiet, and he was the densest of men I ever saw, as you may have perceived. If a man wore a muddy coat, he would wonder how I knew he had been splashed. And then Scotland Yard has always been jealous of me. They may have given me away.

"But in any case, it is of no consequence. Dr. Doyle, by the way, I am in a position to state, has written eight other books; and this one appeared originally in the columns of a magazine, where it ran for twelve months. Am I not right?"

"Certainly, but how – "

"It is merely the faculty of observation, he replied. "By examining the book, I find out all that. Obviously, too, he is a man of few scruples and no respect for the truth. He is an unfair man, striving, like all in his class, to make 'copy' where he can.

"I have been grossly misrepresented by him. Do you really think I made that blunder in 'A Scandal in Bohemia?' Do you imagine I had as little a finger in 'The Engineer's Thumb' or 'The Copper Beeches' as he makes out? And do you suppose I interfered as ineffectually in the 'Five Pips' as he represents?"

"What do you suppose was his object, Mr. Holmes?"

The famous detective looked me full in the face.

"Gain," said he simply.

I started back in astonishment.

"Yes," he resumed; "it is all easy when you see the explanation. You see the book is large and expensively brought out; moreover it is issued by a publisher who caters to the million. Hence it is clear a very large sale is anticipated. Why? Because the book is supposed to contain a popular element, and that popular element is myself."

"Now, it follows that Dr. Doyle must have heard of me, through Watson or the police; that he saw I should suit his game (which was money); having invented spurious stories about me that he hit upon a publisher similarly unscrupulous. With my name and a fairly accurate account of those interesting cases of mine, 'The Blue Carbuncle' and 'The Speckled Band', he made a good start; and after that anything would sell, even stuff like 'The Engineer's Thumb' or 'The Noble Husband'. It is a case of moral degeneration."

"What else do you gather of Dr. Doyle?" I asked.

Mr. Holmes yawned.

"He is evidently a smoker; for your smoker always attributes the odious vice to his hero (I need hardly say I never touch tobacco). It is clear too he is not a teetotaler."

"One word more, and I have done, Should you say Dr. Doyle was young or old?"Mr. Holmes got up and stretched himself. "I need only refer you to the colour of the book."

FROM LITERATURE AND LIFE

The Naked Lady and The Snake

Louis Baury

All I could find out about Louis Barry is that he published this clever parody, titled, "As They Would Have Told It: After Conan Doyle," in **The Smart Set** *in July 1909. A Shaw discovery.*

****

My friend Sherlock Holmes had been idle for a week, and the strain was beginning to tell on him. For the last three days he had done nothing but smoke his pipe and inject cocaine in his arm with my bicycle pump, and I was worried. But tonight his eyes held the old gleam of interest as he tossed a telegram into my lap.

"I received this today, Watson," he said carelessly, "and I think it promises a very pretty tangle."

A knock at the door interrupted him.

"Ah, if I mistake not, here is our client now. Come in!" he added.

In answer to Holmes's summons, a tall, stately girl, with agitated mien, entered.

"My dear Madam," said he without turning around, "I perceive you

279

left home in considerable hurry."

The woman started perceptively.

"How do you know?" she asked.

"You have nothing on," replied he, with customary delicacy.

"But how could you know, your back was turned?"

"Precisely. I saw it in the mirror."

All of Holmes's deductions were so simple when explained.

"But about your story, madam, you may speak with perfect freedom before my friend, Dr. Watson. He is perfectly harmless and will do nothing but make copy out of you."

"My name," she said proudly "is Eve. I have been wronged, Mr. Holmes, horribly wronged. All the world says it was I who gave that fatal apple to Adam, and it was not so, Mr. Holmes. I have come to you to see if you can help to establish my innocence."

"I will try, madam," replied Sherlock Holmes. "I have heard the usually accepted version of your story, and I will do my best."

For three days Holmes neither slept or ate, and I saw but little of him. When he entered the Baker Street apartment on the fourth day, however, I knew something had happened.

"Well?" I inquired.

"It is done, Watson," he cried, sinking into a chair. "The case is solved."

"My dear Holmes," said I, "how did you do it?"

"It was very simple," replied he. "I went down to Eden and worked the whole ground over carefully with a microscope and pair of tweezers. Near the large apple tree in the centre of the garden I found what Lynx, of Eden Yard, who started on the case, failed to discover---a long thin track, resembling the imprint of an automobile tire. But remember, Watson, automobiles had not yet been invented."

How often I was impressed with his wonderful knowledge!

"At this date, the track could only have been made by one thing---a snake. There I had a start."

"I cast about for further evidence of a snake, and sure enough, clinging to the trunk of a tree I found three rattles. Adam and Eve had no children and children and snakes are the only creatures who use rattles. Thus the snake theory was established beyond doubt."

"I had only to find a snake with three rattles missing. But for as while that blocked me. The nearest I could come to what I wanted was one with four missing. That left one rattle still to be accounted for. Then I thought of Adam."

"You know, Watson, I am something of a boxer. I struck Adam several sharp blows in the jaw, until his teeth rattled. Then the fourth rattle was accounted for. Adam ate the apple and had the fourth rattle; the other three rattles were found under the tree with the track of the snake."

"The chain of evidence was undeniable. Is there anything you do not understand?"

"Nothing, my dear Holmes. You are wonderful."

"No, Watson, logical. I am glad the young lady is vindicated," he added, as he reached for the bicycle pump.

M. Dupin Calls On Sherlock Holmes

Arthur Chapman

Conan Doyle could never convince some Americans that Sherlock Holmes's view of Edgar Allen Poe's detective, M. C. Auguste Dupin, was not his own.

On December 14, 1912, **Life** *published a longish poem by an American critic, Arthur Guiterman, which is here quoted only in part. It was titled,* **Letters to the Literati: To Sir Arthur Conan Doyle.**

Faith! As a teller of tales you've the trick with you!
Still there's a bone I've been longing to pick with you:
Holmes is your hero of drama and serial;
All of us know where you dug your material
Whence he was molded---'tis almost a platitude;
Yet your detective, in shameless ingratitude---
Sherlock your sleuthhound, with motives ulterior,
Sneers at Poe's 'Dupin' as 'very inferior,'
Labels Gaboriau's clever 'Lecoq' indeed,
Merely 'a bungler,' a creature to mock, indeed!
This, when your plots and your methods in story owe
Clearly a trifle to Poe and Gaboriau,
Sets all the Muses of Helicon sorrowing.
Borrow Sir Knight, but be candid in borrowing!

A somewhat touchy Conan Doyle had his response out in two weeks. His own poem was tactfully titled, **To An Undiscerning Critic**, *published*

283

*on December 28, 1912 in **London Opinion.** Here's the gist.*

Sure there are times when one cries with acidity,
"Where are the limits of human stupidity?"
Have you not learned, my esteemed commentator,
That the created is not the creator?

*The American poet and critic, Arthur Chapman, (1873-1935) placed the blame where Conan Doyle no doubt felt it should more appropriately be placed. The writer has M. C. Auguste Dupin escape from one of Edgar Allen Poe's tales of mystery and confront his critic, Sherlock Holmes, but still also take a few nasty swipes at Conan Doyle as well. It appeared on February 1905 in **The Critic and Literary World** as "The Unmasking of Sherlock Holmes.*

****

In all my career as Boswell to the Johnson of Sherlock Holmes, I have seen the great detective agitated only once. We had been quietly smoking and talking over the theory of thumbprints, when the landlady brought in a little square of pasteboard at which Holmes glanced casually and then let drop on the floor. I picked up the card and as I did so I saw that Holmes was trembling, evidently too agitated to tell the landlady to show the visitor in or to send him away. On the card I read the name:

Monsieur C. Auguste Dupin,

Paris

While I was wondering what there could be in that name to strike terror to the heart of Sherlock Holmes, M. Dupin himself entered the room. He was a young man, slight of build, and unmistakably French of feature. He bowed as he stood in the doorway, but I observed that Sherlock Holmes was too amazed or too frightened to return the bow.

My idol stood in the middle of the room, looking at the little Frenchman on the threshold as if M. Dupin had been a ghost. Finally, pulling himself together with an effort, Sherlock Holmes motioned the visitor to a seat, and, as M. Dupin sunk into the chair, my friend tumbled into another and wiped his brow feverishly.

"Pardon my unceremonious entrance, Mr. Holmes," said the visitor, drawing out his meerschaum pipe, filling it, and then smoking in long, deliberate puffs. "I am afraid, however, that you would not care to see me, so I came in before you had an opportunity of telling your landlady to send me away."

To my surprise Sherlock Holmes did not annihilate the man with one of those keen, searching glances for which he has become famous in literature and the drama. Instead he continued to mop his brow and finally mumbled weakly:

"But---but--I thought y-y-you were dead, M. Dupin."

"And people thought you were dead, too, Mr. Sherlock Holmes," said the visitor in his high deliberate voice. "But if you can be brought to life after being hurled from a cliff in the Alps, why can't I come out of a respectable grave just to have a chat with you? You know my originator, Mr. Edgar Allan Poe, was very fond of bringing people out of their graves."

"Yes, yes, I'll admit I've read that fellow, Poe," said Sherlock Holmes testily. "Clever writer in some things. Some of his detective stories about you are not half bad, either."

"No, not half bad," said M. Dupin, rather sarcastically, I thought. "Do you remember the little story of 'The Purloined Letter' for instance? What a little gem of a story that is! When I get to reading it over I forget

285

all about you and your feeble imitations. There is nothing forced there. Everything is as sure as fate itself---not a false note---not a thing dragged in by the heels. And the solution of it all is so simple that it makes most of your artifices seem clumsy in comparison."

"But if Poe had such a good thing in you, M. Dupin, why didn't he make more of you?" snapped Sherlock Holmes.

"Ah, that's where Mr. Poe proved himself a real literary artist, said M. Dupin," puffing away at his eternal meerschaum. "When he had a good thing, he knew enough not to ruin his reputation by running it into the ground. Suppose, after writing 'The Murders of the Rue Morgue' around me as the central character, he had written two or three books of short stories in which I figured. Then suppose he had let them dramatize me and further parade me before the public. Likewise suppose, after he had decently killed me off and announced he would write no more detective stories, he had yielded to the blandishments of the publishers and had brought out another interminable lot of tales about me?"

"Why, naturally, most of the stuff would have been worse than mediocre, and people would have forgotten all about that masterpiece, 'The Murders of the Rue Morgue,' and also about 'The Purloined Letter,' so covered would those gems be in a mass of trash."

"Oh, I'll admit that my string has been overplayed," sighed Sherlock Holmes moodily, reaching for the hypodermic syringe, which I slid out of his reach. "But maybe Poe would have overplayed you if he could have drawn down a dollar a word for all he could write about you."

"Poor Edgar---poor misunderstood Edgar!---maybe he would," said Dupin thoughtfully. "Few enough dollars he had in his stormy life. But at the same time, no matter what his rewards, I think he was a versatile genius enough to have found something new at the right time. At any rate he would not have filched the product of another's brain and palmed it off as his own."

"But great Scot, man!" cried Sherlock Holmes, "you don't mean to say that no one else but Poe has a right to utilize the theory of analysis in a detective story, do you?"

"No, but see how closely you follow in all other particulars. I am out of sorts with fortune and so are you. I am always smoking when thinking out my plans of attack, and so are you. I have an admiring friend to set down everything I say or do, and so have you. I am always dazzling the chief of police with much better theories than he can ever work out, and so are you."

"I know, I know, said Sherlock Holmes," beginning to mop his forehead again. "It looks like a bad case against me. I've drawn pretty freely on you, M. Dupin, and the quotation marks haven't always been used as they should have been where credit was due. But after all, I am not the most slavish imitation my author has produced. Have you ever read his book, **The White Company** and compared it with **The Cloister and the Hearth**? No, well do so if you want to get what might be termed 'transplanted atmosphere.'"

"Well it seems to be a great age for the piratical appropriating of other men's ideas," said M. Dupin, resignedly. "As for myself I don't care a rap about your stealing my thunder, Sherlock Holmes. In fact, you're a pretty decent sort of chap, even though you are trying my patience with your continual refusal to retire; and besides you only make me shine the brighter in comparison. I don't even hold that 'Dancing Men' story against you, to which you made use of a cryptogram that instantly brought up thoughts of 'The Gold Bug.'"

"But you did not figure in 'The Gold Bug'" said Sherlock Holmes with the air of one who had won a point.

"No, and that merely emphasizes what I have been telling you---that people admire Poe as a literary artist owing to the fact that he did not overwork any of his creations. Bear that in mind, my boy, and remember, when you make your next farewell, to see that it is not one of the Patti kind, with a string to it. The patience of even the American reading public is not exhaustless, and you cannot always be among the 'six best-selling books' of the day."

And with these words, M. Dupin, pipe and all, vanished in the tobacco-laden atmosphere of the room, leaving the great detective, Sherlock Holmes, looking at me as shamefacedly as a schoolboy who had been caught with stolen apples in his possession.

Sherlock Holmes Meets Edwin Drood

Andrew Lang

During Conan Doyle's life, four Sherlockian parodies appeared having Sherlock Holmes trying to solve the mystery of Dickens's novel about Edwin Drood. Andrew Lang (1844-1912) wrote two of them. This one, the first, **Longman's Magazine** *published in their September 1895 issue titled "At the Sign of the Ship."*

.

Conan Doyle himself managed to get a medium to bring back Charles Dickens and he reports the two of them also discussed the ins and outs of the famous unfinished case. Conan Doyle says Dickens told him that Drood was hiding out with Rev. Crisparkle.

But if you want to wrestle with the questions of whether Drood survived and who was Datchery, you will be disappointed because I cut all that part out. But you may nevertheless enjoy what remains from the way Watson leads Holmes into it.

For the curious---Lang has Sherlock adopt what is called the Richard A. Proctor hypothesis; students call it one of the survivalist theories. Drood, they argue, was not murdered. In Lang's parody/pastiche, he comes back as Datchery, the detective, thus able to keep an eye on his wicked uncle.

Andrew Lang wrote five books of poetry and two novels, but his main reputation was as an influential literary critic. In his time he gave what he thought of as loads of useful advice to A. Conan Doyle. There's no record of how much Conan Doyle profited from it.

****

One day, says Dr. Watson, when business was slack at Baker Street, I ventured to ask Sherlock, "Did you ever apply your astonishing powers of analysis, to any of the unsolved mysteries of the historic past?"

"Such as who killed Cock Robin," replied my friend sardonically.

Accustomed to the superiority of my friend's manner, which veils his real humility, I winced, but answered, "No, in that case we have the confession of the criminal."

"Of the sparrow? Confessions, of all evidence, are the least trustworthy."

"But I meant questions such as, 'Who was the man in the Iron Mask?'"

"No," said Sherlock, "I never touch them. There is no money in them, and the evidence is never complete."

"But, have you ever considered *The Mystery of Edwin Drood*?"

"Never heard of it," said Sherlock, who as I have often remarked, is not a man of wide general reading.

"Then try this, I said, and handed him---"

and so forth

Ratty and The Wind in the Willows

Kenneth Grahame

*Kenneth Grahame, (1859-1932) wrote several children's books as well as the charming children's classic, **The Wind in the Willows** (1908). He included an episode that owes some to the Great Sherlock.*

On his day job, Grahame was a secretary for the Bank of England.

Ratty and Mole are lost in a snowstorm and then it gets worse, Mole cuts his foot on something or other.

Sherlockian David Skene Martin unearthed this gem, hidden right there for all of us to see,right there in plain view.

****

"What's up, Ratty," asked the Mole.

"*Snow* is up," replied the Rat briefly; "or rather *down*. It's snowing hard."

The Mole came and crouched beside him, and looking out, saw the wood that had been so dreadful to him in a quite changed aspect. Holes, hollows, pools, pitfalls, and other black menaces to the wayfarer were vanishing fast, and a gleaming carpet of faery was springing up everywhere, that looked too delicate to be trodden upon by rough feet. A fine powder filled the air and caressed the cheek with a tingle in its touch, and the black boles of the trees showed up in a light that seemed to come from below.

"Well, well, it can't be helped," said the Rat after pondering. "We must make a start, and take our chance, I suppose. The worst of it is, I don't exactly know where we are. And now this snow makes everything look so different."

It did indeed. The Mole would not have known that it was the same wood. However, they set out bravely, and took the line that seemed most promising, holding on each other and pretending with invincible cheerfulness that they recognized an old friend in every fresh tree that grimly and silently greeted them, or saw openings, gaps, or paths with a familiar turn in them, in the monotony of white space and black tree trunks that refused to vary.

An hour or two later---they had lost all count of time---they pulled up, dispirited, weary, and hopelessly at sea, and sat down on a fallen tree-trunk to recover their breath and consider what was to be done. They were aching with fatigue and bruised with tumbles; they had fallen into several holes and got wet through; the snow was getting so deep that they could hardly drag their little legs through it, and the trees were thicker and more like each other than ever. There seemed to be no end to this wood, and no beginning, and no difference in it, and, worst of all, no way out.

"We can't sit here very long," said the Rat. "We shall have to make another push for it, and do something or other. The cold is too awful for anything, and the snow will soon be too deep for us to wade through." He peered about him and considered. "Look here," he went on, "this is what occurs to me. There's a sort of dell down there in front of us, where the ground seems all hilly and humpy and hummocky. We'll make our way down into that, and try to find some sort of shelter, a cave or a hole with a dry floor in it, out of the snow and wind, and there we'll have a good rest before we try again, for we're both of us pretty dead beat. Besides, the snow may leave off, or something may turn up."

So once more they got on their feet, and struggled down into the dell, where they hunted about for a cave or some corner that was dry and a protection from the keen wind and the whirling snow. They were investigating one of the hummocky bits the Rat had spoken of, when suddenly the Mole tripped up and fell forward on his face with a squeal.

"O, my leg!" he cried. "O, my poor shin!" and he sat up in the snow and nursed his leg in both his front paws.

"Poor old Mole!" said Rat kindly. "You don't seem to be having much luck to-day, do you? Let's have a look at the leg. Yes," he went on, going down on his knees to look, "you've cut your shin, sure enough. Wait till I get my handkerchief, and I'll tie it up for you."

"I must have tripped over a hidden branch or stump," said the Mole miserably. "O my! O my!"

"It's a very clear cut," said the Rat, examining it again attentively. "That was never done by a branch or stump. Looks as if it were made by a sharp edge of something in metal. Funny!" He pondered awhile and examined the humps and slopes that surrounded them.

"Well, never mind what done it," said the Mole, forgetting his grammar in his pain. "It hurts just the same whatever done it."

But the Rat, after carefully tying up the leg with his handkerchief, had left him and was busy scraping in the snow. He scratched and shoveled and explored, all four legs working busily, while the Mole

293

waited impatiently remarking at intervals, "O, come on, Rat!"

Suddenly the Rat cried, "Hooray!" and then "Hooray-oo-ray-oo-ray-oo-ray!" and fell to executing a feeble jig in the snow.

"What have you found, Ratty?" asked the Mole, still nursing his leg.

"Come and see!" said the delighted Rat, as he jigged on.

The Mole hobbled up to the spot and had a good look.

"Well," he said at last, slowly, "I see it right enough. Seen the same sort of thing before, lots of times. Familiar object I call it. A door scraper! Well, what of it? Why dance a jig around a door scraper?"

"But don't you see what it *means,* you---you dull-witted animal?" cried the Rat impatiently.

"Of course I see what it means," replied the Mole. "It simply means that some very careless and forgetful person has left his door-scraper lying about in the middle of the Wild Wood, *just* where it's sure to trip somebody up. Very thoughtful of him, I call it. When I get home I shall go and complain about it to---to somebody or other, see if I don't."

"O dear! O dear!" cried the Rat, in despair at his obtuseness. "Here stop arguing and come and scrape!" And he set to work again and made the snow fly in all directions around him.

After some further toil his efforts were rewarded, and a very shabby door-mat lay exposed to view.

"There, what did I tell you?" exclaimed the Rat, in great triumph.

"Absolutely nothing whatever," replied the Mole, with perfect truthfulness. "Well now," he went on, "you seem to have found another piece of domestic litter, done for and thrown away, and I suppose you're perfectly happy. Better go ahead and dance your jig round that if you've got to and get it over, and then perhaps we can go on and not waste any more time over rubbish-heaps. Can we eat a door-[mat? Or sleep under the door-mat? Or sit on a door-mat and sledge home over the snow on it, you exasperating rodent."

"Do---you---mean---to---say," cried the excited Rat, "that this door-mat doesn't tell you anything?"

"Really, Rat," said the Mole quite pettishly, "I think we've had enough of this folly. Who ever heard of a door-mat telling anyone anything? They simply don't do it. They are not that sort at all. Door-mats know their place."

"Now look here, you---you thick-headed beast," replied the Rat, really angry, "this must stop. Not another word, but scrape---scrape and scratch and dig and hunt around, especially on the sides of the hummocks, if you want to sleep dry and warm to-night, for it's our last chance!"

The Rat attacked a snow-bank beside them with ardour, probing with his cudgel everywhere and then digging with fury; and the Mole scraped busily too, more to oblige the Rat than for any reason, for his opinion was that his friend was getting light-headed.

Some ten minutes' hard work, and the point of the Rat's cudgel struck something that sounded hollow. He worked till he could get a paw through and feel; then called the Mole to come and help him. Hard at it went the two animals, till at last the result of their labours stood full in view of the astonished and hitherto incredulous Mole.

In the side of what seemed to be a snow-bank stood a solid looking little door, painted a dark green. An iron bell-pull hung by the side, and below it, on a small brass plate, neatly engraved in square capital letters, they could read by the aid of moonlight---

Mr. Badger

The Mole fell backwards on the snow from sheer surprise and delight. "Rat!" he cried in penitence, "you're a wonder, that's what you are. I see it all now! You argued it out, step by step, in that wise head of yours, from the very moment I fell and cut my shin, and you looked at the cut, and at once your majestic mind said to itself, 'Door-scraper!' and then you turned to and found the very door-scraper that done it. Did you stop there? No. Some people would have been quite satisfied, but not you. Your intellect went on working. 'Let me only just find a door-mat,' says you to yourself, and my theory is proved!' And, of course you found your door-mat. You're so clever. I think you could find anything you liked. Now, says you, 'that door exists, as plain as if I saw it. There's nothing else remains to be done but to find it!'

"Well, I've read about that sort of thing in books, but I've never come across it before in real life. You ought to go where you'll be properly appreciated. You're simply wasted here, among us fellows. If I only had yourhead, Ratty---"

"But as you haven't," interrupted the Rat rather unkindly. "I suppose you're going to sit on the snow all night and *talk*?Get upat once and hang on to that bell-pull you see there, and ring hard, as hard as you can, while I hammer!"

While the Rat attacked the door with his stick, the Mole sprang up at the bell-pull, clutched it and swung there, both feet well off the ground, and from quite a long way off they could faintly hear a deep-toned bell respond.

Rescuing Elsa

A Long-Suffering Damsel in Distress

John Kendrick Bangs

The author claims an enchanted typewriter he found in his attic began typing out messages from someone called Jim (more formally James) last name, Boswell, now in Hades. Jim sends along some stories that Sherlock Holmes had written.

Sherlock's stories tell of his adventures after that unfortunate incident at the Reichenbach Falls. According to Boswell, Sherlock first wrote up an adventure that involved Queen Victoria's Diamond Jubilee. His second adventure may especially appeal to those who share Sherlock's musical tastes, and so I have chosen it.

Writers of Sherlockian parodies seldom vary their output---but not so the prolific John Kendrick Bangs. He has Sherlock Holmes arriving in Hades solving a mystery involving Captain Kidd, involved in every day mysteries as both Shylock and Sherlock Holmes, and even has a series with the combination Raffles Holmes.

John Kendrick Bangs (1862-1922) was a journalist and professional humorist who produced 65 books. He was also one of the most prolific American writers of Sherlock Holmes parodies. The total of individual pieces is somewhere in the twenties.

*Most were published in the **New York Herald** or serialized in **Harper's Weekly,** both of which he edited at one time or another. This parody appeared September 2, 1899 in **Harper's Weekly as "Sherlock Holmes Again,"** and then in **The Enchanted Type-Writer** (1899).*

When Arthur Conan Doyle visited America in 1894, he stayed with Bangs and they became close friends. Bangs dedicated his first Sherlockian book, which was the first long Sherlockian parody, to Arthur Conan Doyle.

*Francis Hyde Bangs, his son, wrote, **John Kendrick Bangs: Humorist of the Nineties. The Story of an American Editor-Author-Lecturer and His Associations.***

A topical note: America had recently gone through an election campaign pitting the Free Silverites of William Jennings Bryan against the Gold Bugs of William McKinley. Some citizens compromised by being Bimetalists.

****

The door opened and a beautiful woman stood before me clad in most regal garments, robust of figure, yet extremely pale. It seemed to me I had seen her somewhere before, yet for a time I could not place her.

"Mr. Sherlock Holmes?" said she in deliciously musical tones, which singular to relate, she emitted in a fashion suggestive of a recitative passage in an opera.

"The same," said I, bowing with my accustomed courtesy.

"The ferret?" she sang, in staccato tones which were ravishing to my

298

musical soul.

I laughed. "That term has been applied to me, Madame," said I chanting my answer as best I could. "For myself, however, I prefer to assume the more modest title of detective. I can work with or without clues, and have never yet been baffled. I know who wrote the Junius letters, and upon occasion have been known to see through a stone wall with my naked eye. What can I do for you?"

"Tell me who I am!" she cried, tragically, taking the centre of the room and gesticulating wildly.

"Well --- really, Madame," I replied. "You didn't send up a card---"

"Ah!" she sneered. "This is what your vaunted prowess amounts to, eh? Ha! Do you suppose if I had a card with my name on it I'd have come to you to inquire who I am? I can read a card as well as you can, Mr. Sherlock Holmes."

"Then as I understand it, Madame," I put in, "you have suddenly forgotten your identity and wish me to---"

"Nothing of the sort. I have forgotten nothing. I never knew for certain who I am. I have an impression, but it is based on only hearsay evidence," she interrupted.

For the moment I was fairly puzzled. Still I did not wish to let her know this, and so going behind my screen and taking a capsule full of cocaine to steady my nerves, gained a moment to think. Returning, I said:

"This really is child's play for me, Madame. It won't take more than a week to find out who you are, and possibly, if you have any clews at all to your identity, I may be able to solve this mystery in a day."

299

"I have only three," she answered, and taking a piece of swan's down, a lock of golden hair, and a pair of silver-tinsel tights from her portmanteau she handed them over to me.

My first impulse was to ask the lady if she remembered the name of the asylum from which she had escaped, but I fortunately refrained from doing so, and she shortly left me, promising to return at the end of the week.

For three days I puzzled over the clews, swans down, yellow hair, and a pair of silver-tinsel tights, while very interesting no doubt at times, do not form a very sound basis for a theory establishing the identity of so regal a person as my visitor. My first impression was that she was a vaudeville artist, and that the exhibits she had left me were a part of their make-up. This I was forced to abandon shortly, because no woman with the voice of my visitor would sing in vaudeville. The more ambitious stage was her legitimate field, if not grand opera itself.

At this point she returned to my office, and I, of course, reported progress. That is most valuable things I learned while on earth---when you have done nothing, report progress.

"I haven't quite succeeded as yet," said I, "but I am getting at it slowly. I do not, however, think it wise to acquaint you with my present notions until they are verified beyond peradventure. It might help me somewhat if you were to tell me who it is you think you are. I could work either forward or backward on that hypothesis, as seemed best, and so arrive at a hypothetical truth anyhow."

"That just what I don't want to do," said she. "That information might bias your final judgment. If, however, acting on the clews which you have, you confirm my impression that I am such and such a person, as well as the views which other people have, than will my status be well

300

defined and I can institute my suit against my husband for a judicial separation, with back alimony, with some assurance of a successful issue."

I was more puzzled than ever.

"Well," said I slowly, "I, of course, can see how a small bit of swan's-down and a lack of yellow hair backed up by a pair of tinsel tights might constitute reasonable evidence in a suit for separation, but wouldn't it---er---be more to your purpose if I should use these data as establishing the identity of---somebody else?"

"How very dense you are," she replied, impatiently. "That's precisely what I want you to do."

"But you told me it was your identity you wished proven," I put in, irritably.

"Precisely," she said.

"Then these bits of evidence are---yours?" I asked, hesitantly. One does not like to accuse a lady of an undue liking of tinsel.

"They are all I have left of my husband," she answered with a sob.

"Hum!" said I, my perplexity increasing. "Was the---ah---the gentleman blown up by dynamite?"

"Excuse me, Mr. Holmes," she retorted, rising and running the scales. "I think, after all, I have come to the wrong shop.. Have you Hawkshaw's address handy? You are too obtuse for a detective."

My reputation was at stake, so I said significantly:

"Good! Good! I was merely trying one of my disguises on you, Madame, and you were completely taken in. Of course, no one would ever know me for Sherlock Holmes if I manifested such dullness."

"Ah!" she said, her face lightening up. "You were merely deceiving me by appearing to be obtuse."

"Of course," said I. "I see the whole thing in a nutshell. You married an adventurer; he told you who he was, but you've never been able to prove it; and suddenly you are deserted by him, and on going over his wardrobe you find he has left nothing but these articles: and now you wish to sue him for a separation on the grounds of desertion, and secure alimony if possible."

It was a magnificent guess.

"That is it precisely," said the lady. "Except as to the extent of his 'leavings.' In addition to the things you have he gave my small brother a brass bugle and a tin sword."

"We may need to see those later," said I. "At present I will do all I can do for you on the evidence in hand. I have got my eye on a gentleman who wears silver tinsel tights now, but I am afraid he is not the man we are after because his hair is black, and, as far as I have been able to learn from his valet, he is utterly unacquainted with swans-down."

We separated again and I went to the club to think. Never in my life before had I had so baffling a case. As I sat in the café sipping a cocaine cobbler, who should walk in but Hamlet, strangely enough picking particles of swan's-down from his black doublet, which was literally covered with it.

"Hello Sherlock!" he said, drawing up a chair and sitting down beside me. "What you up to?"

"Trying to make out where you have been," I replied. "I judge from the swan's-down on your doublet that you have been escorting Ophelia to the opera in the regulation cloak."

"You're mistaken for once," he laughed. "I've been with Lohengrin. He's got a pair of swans that can do a mile in 2.10---but it makes them moult like the devil."

"Pair of what?" I cried.

"Swans," said Hamlet. "He's an eccentric sort of duffer, that Lohengrin. Afraid of horses, I fancy."

"And so he drives swans instead?" said I, incredulously.

"The same," replied Hamlet. "Do I look as if he drove squab?"

"He must be queer," said I. "I'd like to meet him. He'd make quite an addition to my collection of freaks."

"Very well," observed Hamlet. "He'll be here tomorrow to take luncheon with me, and if you come, too, you'll be most welcome. He's collecting freaks, too, and I haven't a doubt would be pleased to know you."

We parted and I sauntered homeward, cogitating over my strange client, and now and then laughing over the idiosyncrasies of Hamlet's friend the swan-driver. It never occurred to me at the moment, however to connect the two, in spite of the link of swans-down. I regarded it merely as a coincidence.

The next day, however, on going to the club and meeting Hamlet's strange guest, I was struck by the further coincidence that his hair was of precisely the same shade of yellow as that in my possession. It was of a hue that I had never seen before except at performances of grand opera, or on the heads of fool detectives in musical burlesques. Here, however, was the real thing growing luxuriantly from the man's head.

"Ho-ho!" thought I to myself. "Here is a fortunate encounter; there may be something in it," and then I tried to lead him on.

"I understand, Mr. Lohengrin, that you have a fine span of swans."

"Yes," he said, and I was astonished to note that he like my client, spoke in musical numbers. "Very. They're much finer than horses, in my opinion. More peaceful, quite as rapid, and amphibious. If I go out for a drive and come to a lake they trot quite as well across its surface as on the highways."

"How interesting," said I. "And so gentle, the swan. Your wife, I presume"

Hamlet kicked my shins under the table.

"I think it will rain tomorrow," he said, giving me a glance which if it said anything said shut up.

"I think so, too," said Lohengrin, a lowering look on his face. "If it doesn't, it will either snow or hail, or be clear." And he gazed abstractedly out of the window.

The kick and the man's confusion were sufficient proof. I was on the right track at last. Yet the evidence was unsatisfactory because merely circumstantial. My piece of down might have come from an opera cloak and not from a well broken swan, the hair might equally clearly have come from some other head than Lohengrin's, and other men have had trouble with their wives.

The circumstantial evidence lying in the coincidences was strong but not conclusive, so I resolved to pursue the matter and invite the strange individual to luncheon with me, at which I proposed to wear the tinsel tights. Seeing them he might be forced into betraying himself.

This I did, and while my impressions were confirmed by his demeanor, no positive evidence grew out of it.

"I'm hungry as a bear!" he said, as I entered the club, clad in a long, heavy ulster, reaching from my shoulders to the ground, so that the tights were not visible.

"Good," said I. "I like a hearty eater," and I ordered a luncheon of ten courses before removing my overcoat; but not one morsel could the man eat, for on removing my coat his eye fell on my silver garments, and with a gasp he well nigh fainted. It was clear. He recognized them and was afraid, and in consequence lost his appetite. But he was game, and tried to laugh it off.

"Silver man, I see," he said nervously, smiling.

"No," said I, taking the lock of golden hair from my pocket and dangling it before him. "Bimetallist."

His jaw dropped in dismay, but recovering himself instantly he put up a fairly good fight.

"It is strange, Mr. Lohengrin," said I, "that in the three years I've never seen you before."

"I've been very quiet," he said. "Fact is, I have had my reasons, Mr. Holmes, for preferring the life of a hermit. A youthful indiscretion, sir, has made me fear to face the world. There was nothing wrong about it, save that it was a folly, and I have been anxious in these days of newspapers to avoid any possible revival of what might in some eyes seem scandalous."

I felt sorry for him, but my duty was clear. Here was my man---but how to gain direct proof was still beyond me. No further admissions would be got out of him, and we soon parted.

Two days later the lady called and again I reported progress.

"It needs but one thing, Madame, to convince me that I have found your husband," said I. "I have found a man who might be connected with swans-down, from whose luxuriant curls might have come this tow-coloured lock, and who might have worn the silver-tinsel tights---yet it is all *might* and no certainty."

"I will bring my small brother's bugle and the tin sword," said she. "The sword has certain properties which may induce him to confess. My brother tells me that if he simply shakes it at a cat the cat falls dead."

"Do so," said I, "and I will try it on him. If he recognizes the sword and remembers its properties when I attempt to brandish it at him, he'll be forced to confess, though it would be awkward if he is the wrong man and the sword should work on him as it does on the cat."

The next day I was in possession of the famous toy. It was not very long, and rather more suggestive of a pancake-turner than a sword, but it was a terror. I tested its qualities on a swarm of gnats in my room, and the moment I shook it at them they fluttered to the ground as dead as door-nails.

"I'll have to be careful of this weapon," I thought. "It would be terrible if I should brandish it at a motor-man trying to get one of the

306

Gehenna Traction Company's cable-cars to stop and he should drop dead at his post."

All was now ready for the demonstration. Fortunately the following Saturday night was club night at the Houseboat, and we were all expected to come in costume. For dramatic effect I wore a yellow wig, a helmet, the silver-tinsel tights, and a doublet to match, with the brass bugle and the tin sword properly slung about my person. I looked stunning, even if I do say it, and much to my surprise several people mistook me for the man I was after. Another link in the chain! *Even the public unconsciously recognized the value of my deductions. They called me Lohengrin!*

And of course it all happened as I expected. It always does. Lohengrin came into the assembly-room five minutes after I did and was visibly annoyed at my make-up.

"This is a great liberty," said he grasping the hilt of his sword; but I answered him by blowing the bugle at him, at which he turned livid and fell back. He had recognized its soft cadence. I then hauled the sword from my belt, shook it at a fly on the wall, which immediately died, and made as if to do the same with Lohengrin, whereupon he cried for mercy and fell upon his knees.

"Turn that infernal thing the other way!" he shrieked.

"Ah!" said I, lowering my arm. "Then you know its properties?"

"I do---I do," he cried. "It used to be mine---I confess it!"

"Then," said I, calmly putting the horrid bit of zinc back in my belt, "that's all I wanted to know. If you'll come up to my office some morning next week I'll introduce you to your wife," and I turned from him.

My mission accomplished, I returned to my quarters where my fair client was awaiting me.

"Well?" she said.

"It's all right, Mrs. Lohengrin," I said, and the lady cried aloud with joy at the name, for it was the very one she had hoped it would be.

"My man turns out to be your man," said I, "and I turn him over therefore to you, only deal gently with him. He's a pretty decent chap and sings like a bird."

Whereon I presented her with my bill for 5000 eboli, which she paid without a murmur, as was entirely proper that she should, for upon the evidence which I had secured for the fair plaintiff, in the suit for separation of Elsa vs. Lohengrin on the ground of desertion and non-support, obtained her decree, with back alimony of twenty-five per cent of Lohengrin's income for a trifle over fifteen hundred years.

How much that amounted to I really don't know, but that it was a large sum I am sure, since Lohengrin must have been very wealthy. He couldn't have afforded to dress in solid silver-tinsel tights if he had been otherwise.

The International Society of Infallible Detectives

Carolyn Wells

*Here Sherlock Holmes is the leader of a group of well known fictional detectives of the day. They are all on the track of a fugitive, each detective following his own methods. Carolyn Wells wrote three parodies featuring the Infallibles, this one titled "Sure Way to Catch Every Criminal. Ha! Ha!". Bill Blackbeard unearthed this one and published it in his **Sherlock Holmes in America.***

Carolyn Wells, (1870s-1942) wrote a great many popular mystery novels before and after World War I, a book on how to write mysteries, and several poems about Sherlock Holmes and Baker Street.

This parody was syndicated by Hearst on July 11, 1912.

****

The International Society of Infallible Detectives had assembled in their luxurious offices on Fakir Street, this time to hold an indignation meeting.

"Utterly absurd," declared President Sherlock Holmes, "the Bertillon system is sufficiently unnecessary, but this Portrait Parle is a thousand times worse."

"What is it?" asked the Thinking Machine, querulously, "what is a Portrait Parle?"

"Don't you know any French?" asked M. Lecocq, superciliously; "it is a---a portrait that tells."

"It's a speaking likeness," broke in Raffles, and Holmes exclaimed: "Speaking likeness! It's a screaming absurdity!"

"It's a roaring farce," contributed Arsene Lupin to the general opinion, and Luther Trant remarked thoughtfully: "It's a thundering shame!"

"But what is it?" whined the Thinking Machine, "do somebody tell me!"

"Well," said Raffles, who was ever polite to the pettish old man, "it's a way of describing criminals so you can always recognize 'em. It's a special description of each feature, a record of each measurement and a detailed account of any peculiarities the subject may possess."

"Perfectly absurd!" ranted Holmes, "as if those weren't the very things I deduce from abstract clews. The very deductions I have built my fame upon! Show me the clews, and I describe the Portrait Parle myself!"

"Marvelous, Holmes! Marvelous!" said Dr. Watson, but a trifle mechanically, as he was absorbed in an intricate testing experiment, and had his head in a rubber bag.

"I think it's a great thing," declared M. Lupin, "if I had had such a help in my younger days, I should now be even more celebrated than I am."

310

"Nonsense, Lupin," said Holmes, with a slight trace of saturninity in his tone, "only a defective detective needs such a help. To my mind this Portrait Parle takes away all my chance for spectacular exploits; it leaves me no room for marvelous deductions."

"And incidentally leaves me without an appropriate comment," said Watson, who had recovered his head.

"Detecting isn't what it used to be," complained M. Lecocq; "why even the climate has changed, and that 'light snow' rarely falls at the right moment."

"But one doesn't need footprints with finger and thumb prints," observed Luther Trant.

"No," grunted the Thinking Machine, "and with this new Portrait Parle one doesn't need a detective instinct at all."

"Of course not," assented Holmes, bitterly, "one might as well see the omelette and then deduce broken eggs."

"Marvelous, Holmes, marvelous," breathed Watson, sadly, half fearing he said the words for the last time.

At that juncture the telephone rang and the Chief of Police wished speech with the society.

Being nearest the instrument, Arsene Lupin answered.

"Here's luck, fellows," he said, after hearing the message. "The Chief wants us to hunt up a hidden criminal and he is sending us his Portrait Parle."

Various sniffs, sneers and snorts greeted this information, but with true detective taciturnity they awaited the arrival of the new labor-saving device. A messenger arrived with a box, which Watson placed on the table.

The members of the society gathered round and stood agape, agog and agley, while President Holmes lifted the cover.

They saw what seemed to be a collection of hastily gathered junk. There was an old lantern, a gimlet, an iron hook, and a hatchet. Then in a small box was a scarab, or Egyptian beetle. In another box was an apple and a carrot, wrapped in a sheet of butcher's paper was an uncooked mutton chop. In a caterer's box was a tempting looking pie.

Raffles looked at the pie appropriatively, but, after all, he was only a dilettante detective. The others, being the real thing, scorned to think of food, save for the Thinking Machine who greatly desired to munch the apple.

President Holmes folded his arms and put on a look that was saturnine to his very finger tips. "What do you hear the Portrait Parle say, gentlemen?" he asked.

M. Lupin thrust his hand among his frogged lapels and said, oracularly:"It is a great scheme. Behold we construct our man at once. He is an archeologist, we learn from the scarab."

"And a butcher, we learn from the cutlet," broke in M. Lecocq, who was ever the jealous rival of his compatriot.

"He is a pastry cook," suggested Raffles, still eyeing the pie, which was a meringue.

"A carpenter, more likely," said Arsene Lupin, "see the gimlet, the hatchet and the big iron hook."

"And the lantern?" asked Holmes, looking aquiline for a change, "That proves the farmer," whined the Thinking Machine, insistently.

"Not at all," said Holmes, "it proves we are to look for an honest man."

Watson declaimed a few well chosen words, and then Raffles said airily: "But we're to look for a criminal. The lantern merely means it's a light matter, after all."

Does the carrot imply we are donkeys?" demanded M. Lecocq, who was quick to catch an implication. But no one replied, for each was intent on puzzling out the meaning of the Portrait Parle.

"The hatchet indicates it is buried," mused Holmes, "and the lantern will be useful in digging."

"We don't have to dig at night," said Raffles. "I think the mutton chop and pie indicate dinner time."

"Well, anyway, we're to dig," persisted Holmes, and Lupin said solemnly, "Of course, why, that beetle is the clew as the Gold Bug was. It's a case of buried treasure. The Hook, of course, is a locality, a peninsula or rocky coast."

"And the apple, indicates the Garden of Eden, I suppose," jeered Arsene Lupin, "it's too far away, I won't go there."

"You're too literal, said the Thinking Machine, peevishly, "these things are merely imaginative suggestions. The apple is remindful of Paris and Helen, and so, l reason, the criminal we are in search of is a beautiful woman."

313

"Then let us *cherchez la femme* at once," cried Raffles, who was ever gallant.

"We'll never accomplish anything working together," said Holmes, at last. "All celebrated detectives must celebrate alone. Go your ways, my friends, remember the Portrait Parle, and return to-morrow night with the criminal it represents."

Glad to pursue their favorite and well known methods, the infallible detectives broke up the meeting and disappeared.

Back to Fakir Street rooms they trooped the next night, each triumphantly leading a criminal of his own selection, and each secure in a true detective complacency that his was the right man.

M. Lupin had arrested a prominent archeologist, the Thinking Machine brought a blustering, well-to-do farmer, and Raffles brought a dapper French pastry cook. Each had his quarry, and as the meeting convened President Holmes prepared to hear and pass judgment on the various claims from his own infallible viewpoint.

The telephone bell rang.

"Is this Mr. Holmes?" asked the Chief of Police.

"Yes, said Holmes," asininely---I mean aquilinely.

"Well, we have found the criminal we wanted, so you may call off your search."

"Indeed," said Holmes. "May I ask you to bring him over here and compare him with the Portrait Parle you sent me?"

314

"I will bring him at once," replied the urbane and obliging Chief.

The members of the International Society of Infallible Detectives sat in grim gloom until the Chief arrived, leading an abject looking criminal, whom they scanned with interest. He was assuredly not a scientific man, nor was he apparently a farmer; nor, yet, to all appearances, a carpenter or pastry cook.

"I fear," began President Holmes, in a sarcastic monotone, "we do not entirely understand the fluent language of your Portrait Parle."

"No," said the Chief of Police, in surprise; "why, my dear sir, you've only to look at this man to see he is perfectly photographed by the Portrait Parle I sent you. Observe his features!"

"Is he not lantern-jawed, beetle browed, gimlet-eyed, apple-cheeked and hatchet-faced? Has he not a hook nose, mutton chop whiskers, carroty hair and a pie mouth? Are you so dense you cannot understand such a speaking description?"

"Enough, Chief," said Holmes, with a wave of his long white hand, "enough, your Portrait Parle is a chatterbox!"

Those Bloody-Minded Mystery Writers

Edmund Lester Pearson

*In this parody, published July 12, 1928 in the humor magazine, **Life**,as "Help! Help! Sherlock!" Edmund Lester Pearson took on the most popular American mystery writer of the 1920s.*

S. S. Van Dine was the pseudonym of Willard Huntington Wright, (1889-1939) an art critic who had written scholarly art treatises that made him very little money. In the early twenties, he became seriously ill. His doctor ordered him to read nothing but light fiction He read mainly mysteries. He soon decided he could do better. Given his highbrow reputation, he insisted that the publishers must keep his authorship a tantalizing secret.

Pearson was one of those suspected of being S. S. Van Dine, a charge he seems to have bitterly resented, in part perhaps because Van Dyne filled his mysteries with a great deal of pretentious, esoteric, and irrelevant information, an insufferable detective, Philo Vance, and many corpses.

The poet Ogden Nash gave his opinion in rhyme:

Philo Vance, needs a kick in the pance.

*Edmund Lester Pearson (1880-1937) was a librarian. In 1906, he began a column titled, "The Librarian" in **The Boston Evening Transcript** which he continued until 1920. He filled it with literary discussions and odds and ends, including having Sherlock Holmes solve* *the Edwin Drood mystery. In 1909 Pearson had tried free lancing but couldn't make it. So in 1914 he joined the New York Public Library as editor of their publications. He remained until 1927.*

His first books were on library matters and collections of his literary essays. He also throughout his life wrote articles of general interest and book reviews. Then he began a series of studies in the true crime field with **Studies in Murder** *(1924) which was popular enough to allow him to quit his day job once more, this time with a series of successful books on famous true crimes, including one on Lizzie Borden.*

✳✳✳✳✳✳✳✳✳

It was in the summer of 1929 that I ran down to his home in Sussex, to see my old friend, Sherlock Holmes.

I found Holmes seated in the garden, near his beehives. His eyes were closed, and he sat without moving, a rug over his knees. Mrs. Hudson, his housekeeper, told me that he had been sorely afflicted with rheumatism, and could only hobble from his bed to his chair in the garden.

"Ah, Watson!" said he, without looking up, or even opening his eyes, "You bring the usual whiff of idioform with you."

"Holmes," I replied, "I have been talking by telephone with Creedon of the New York police. There has been a murder in the Browne family; in the old family mansion in 54th Street."

"Wonderful people," the Americans, murmured Holmes. "Their motto is: A murder a day keeps boredom away."

"Creedon says the situation is serious. It is now the custom in New York, it appears, for a murderer to establish himself in the household,

317

and work right through, from the second housemaid up to the head of the family."

Holmes opened one eye.

"One of the Browne family has been killed---or so I understand Creedon's phrase. 'Bumped off' was what he said. An amateur has been retained. He is the leading consultant in the States, the greatest criminal expert ever produced in America. His name, I understand, is Philo Vance."

Holmes sprang up, his eyes blazing.

"My God, Watson! Vance! Do you realize what happened when he handled the Greene murder case? And now the Browne family! They're all doomed, I tell you, every man jack of them!"

In a second the aged detective, his rheumatism cured as by a miracle, was dashing toward the house, shouting for Mrs. Hudson to pack our bags. He rushed to the telephone, and put through a call to the Government aerodrome. Two hours later, Holmes and I, seated in the cockpit of one of the swiftest planes, were far out over the Atlantic, bound for New York on our errand of rescue.

Holmes, with his old fore-and-aft cap pulled down over his hawklike face, gazed straight ahead. He spoke only once during the next twenty hours. This was to mutter: "Philo Vance retained! Poor devils!"

Next day, at noon, we stood in the library of the Browne mansion. There were present the District Attorney of New York, three detectives, and a large delegation of journalists. We had already viewed the body of young Jethro Browne. As we were talking with the officials, the policemen separated, and one of them announced in tones of very great respect:

318

"Mr. Philo Vance, sir!"

It was plain that they considered this a great moment: the meeting of the two famous detectives. We looked toward the door, where there appeared a young man, hastily fitting a monacle into his eye. It gave him much trouble, but at last he got it to stay in place, then he came forward and saluted Holmes.

"Mr. Holmes! Ah, most extraordin'ry! Simply rippin', I'm sure. Charmed to have you here."

Holmes bowed.

"Mr. Vance," said he, "perhaps you will outline your plans, we need not work at cross-purposes."

"Right-o!" said the American detective. "Awf'ly toppin' of you old bean. This is the way of it, d'ye see?"

"This afternoon I shall take all these police johnnies up to the Metropolitan Museum an' show 'em the old weapons in the Armor Room. Deliver a little talk, myself, what, what? All about the petronels, and arquebuses, an' so on. While we are there I expect Grandpa and Grandma Browne to be assassinated."

"Tomorrow, a little conference on modern music; I'll have the whole police force there and describe how Gershwin derives from Bildad, the Assyrian composer. Aunt Minnie, and the twins, will prob'ly be murdered while we are absent. At noon, my friend, the District Attorney and I will lunch at the Club, and settle the question of the difference between Eggs Benedict and Eggs Benedictine. Directly after lunch I expect to hear that Sister Susie, the butler, little Ned, and old Uncle Peter have been slain. That evening I'll compile a

319

bibliography of crime, while our friend the murderer is at work on Browne *pere*, the cook, and the rest of the girls. I may find a moment to enlighten old Markham on the work of the Viennese psychiatrists.

"Thursday, I'm going down to the Grosvenor to see a chap who has a collection of Japanese sword-guards, and when I come back I expect to hear that, except for little Eloise, they're all jolly well mopped up. What, what? Then I'll bring my powers to bear, and maybe drag dear, dear Eloise off to the dungeon. If they're all dead but Eloise it will be clear she's the murderess. Clever, what? *N'est-ce pas? Nicht wahr? Hoi polloi? Lambdsa,, mu, nu?*

"You are a linguist," Mr. Holmes?

"Not precisely," said Holmes. "It is very satisfactory to know your program, Mr. Vance, and I am sure we shall not conflict in any way. Also, to use your racy American phrase, it is quite clear to me now where the Browne family will get off. I will meet with you here, Thursday afternoon---in time for the arrest."

Holmes went to work with his usual energy, and on Thursday we were again in the library of Mr. Browne. In addition to the others, there were present a group of eight or nine ladies and gentlemen who were not at the other interview. Vance had not arrived; it was understood he had taken the traffic police up to see the paintings in the Hispanic Museum.

Finally he came in, polishing his monacle.

"Ah," said he. "Simply top-hole, eh what? Quite ready for the arrest? Where's little Eloise?"

"My daughter," said Mr. Browne, coming forward, "is here. But I do not think she will be arrested. You see, Mr. Vance, my family and myself have an aversion to being murdered. We wouldn't for the world interrupt your delightful *causeries* on art, but we observed how our neighbors, the Greenes, were slaughtered one by one, while you enlightened the American public on Venetian glass and German criminology. As a detective, if I may say so, you are a charming professor of aesthetics."

"Mr. Holmes, here, pursuing those methods which have made him celebrated, arrested my chauffeur two days ago. The chauffeur has confessed to killing my son, and planning to kill the rest of us. He is now in the Tombs, and I take pleasure in proffering Mr. Holmes this check."

"Oh, I say, y'know!" exclaimed the American detective.

"Mr. Vance," said Mr. Holmes, "had you any relatives in Scotland Yard?"

"I studied under Inspector Gregson," said Vance.

"Ah, I thought as much. I seemed to recognize the old Gregson touch. It has grown lighter, with the years. Dear old Gregson! How I loved him! How the murderers relied on him! Do let me present Dr. Watson---you have so much in common!"

Rescuing the Mr. Chips of Yale

G. S.

It's pleasant to include a parody in which a student honors a professor, in this case William Lyon Phelps, (1865-1943), for forty-one years a kind of Mr. Chips of Yale. In the late twenties and through the 1940s, he was one of the most popular and even beloved persons on the literary scene. He lectured widely, especially to women's clubs. His field was the classics of English literature, but he wrote that he also "relished detective stories" and was especially an admirer of the Conan Doyle tales. Phelps said his happy temperament came from appreciating the many things of this world, which happily included Sherlock Holmes.

But Phelps never expected to participate in a Sherlock Holmes mystery. A Yalee about to graduate here gives him that dubious honor as a commencement gift, as "The Commencement Mystery." Still the author can't resist adding in a few mild jibes, as students will. It appeared in **The Yale Record** *on June 1, 1927.*

The William Lyon Phelps Foundation still keeps fifty of the essays Phelps wrote available on the internet. And you will also find his best known quote,

"This is the first test of a gentleman, his respect for those who can be of no possible value to him."

Phelps did seem to see one of his missions in life as smoothing off the rough edges and introducing a little civility and culture into the lives of those Yale undergraduates.

322

"Watson, my dear fellow," said Holmes, "send down to P. Rings for some more cocaine; I am terribly bored with New Haven---Ah, good morning, Lestrade. Will you kindly explain your cablegram which has brought Watson and myself all the way from London to this wretched hole?"

"Why the fact is, Mr. Holmes," replied the Inspector, "there's been a bad business in these parts. Professor Phillips has disappeared on the eve of Commencement exercises, and we and the New Haven police can make nothing out of it. The President of the University himself requested that you be set upon the case immediately. The ladies of the Browning Club are on the verge of hysteria."

"Are there no clues, Lestrade?"

"One only, Mr. Holmes. The janitor of the building in which Mr. Phillips holds his classes, an elderly person who introduced himself as the Lampson Professor of Light and Heat, states he saw the unfortunate professor on the day of his disappearance. Mr. Phillips, he reports, seemed slightly perturbed and was muttering to himself, 'God's in his heaven, all's right with the world', as though by way of self-assurance. Beyond this we know nothing."

"Well, well," chuckled Holmes, rubbing his hands, "this is indeed a mystery worthy of our attention. Let us hasten forth, Watson."

As we were proceeding across the campus, an aged crone came limping up to us, propelling a large cart filled with laundry. Holmes nodded amiably to her, and she responded.

"Ah, God's blessin' on ye, sonny! Where do yer send yer laundry?"

323

"Don't mind her, Mr. Holmes," said Lestrade. "That's only God Bless You Mary."

Holmes, however, did not seem convinced.

"Watson," he whispered, his voice vibrating with excitement, "don't you recognize the steely glint of those eyes?---you don't? Well, never mind. We'll follow the old dame."

Our quest took us through some of the dingiest slums of New Haven. Finally we came out upon the harbour and observed our quarry making for the end of the docks, as though intending to wash her laundry there.

"Quick, Watson!" shouted Holmes. "There is no time to lose!" And with that he hastened up to the laundress and confronted her with his revolver.

"Lestrade," said he, "allow me to present to you Colonel Sebastian Moran, one of the most dangerous criminals in the world. And now, Watson, examine the laundry basket."

I did as he directed. What was my amazement to find beneath a pile of B. V. D.'s the unconscious form of Professor Phillips, with a chloroform sponge attached to his face. With the aid of Holmes' brandy flask we quickly revived him."

"We arrived not a moment too soon, Mr. Phillips," Holmes remarked. "In another minute you would have been at the bottom of the harbour. As it is, however, you have just time to get to your lecture at the Baptist Ladies' Union. Watson, I think I'll trouble you to get me that cocaine at P. Ring's."

Sherlock Holmes, Jr. Meets Santa Claus

Anonymous

*Sherlock, Jr. and the Watson boy discuss one of the great mysteries of childhood---Is there really a Santa Claus?   This parody greeted the readers of **The Chicago Sunday Tribune** on Christmas Day, December 25, 1904, on The Top of the Morning Humor page. It's not quite a "Yes, Virginia, there is etc.," but it has its points. It's a Shaw discovery.*

✱✱✱✱✱✱✱✱

The Watson boy enters the Sherlock Holmes woodshed and found Sherlock Holmes, Jr. busily engaged deducing the fact that there was a wood pile in front of him and he was expected to saw and split enough fuel to last a week.

"Sherl," said the Watson boy, "do you believe in Santa Claus?"

"Do I believe it? Cert. Why don't you know how I got on his trail last Christmas and ran him down."

"No. You didn't tell me about it. How was it?"

"Well, pa an' ma had been telling me all the time that I ought to be a good boy an' do all the chores as quick and well as I could, and go to bed early, an' all that sort of thing, an so I did just like pa does when he begins deducing."

The Watson boy sat down on the sawbuck and looked at Sherlock

325

Holmes, Jr. with undisguised admiration.

"What did you deduce?" he asked.

"In the first place I didn't deduce anything until Christmas day. The night before I hung up my stocking like I always do, an' then I went to bed an' kept one eye open."

"One eye open?"

"Yep, that's the way all good detectives sleep, you know."

"My! Wasn't you afraid something would drop in your eye?"

"No, of course not. So along about midnight I heard stealthy footsteps in the hall. Now I reasoned to myself, there can't be footsteps without feet to make them. And there can't be feet without they belong to someone---."

"There's three feet in a yard," argued the Watson boy.

"But they don't make footsteps," scornfully replied the Holmes boy. "They can't make footsteps, can they?"

The Watson boy was silenced and the other resumed.

"So I kept on listening and pretty soon the footsteps got right close to my room an' I hopped out of bed an ran to the door."
"What did you see? Did you see Santa Claus?"

"No, I saw pa there in his pajamas. He had his arms full of toys and things."

"So it was him that you heard?"

"No, I told him what I had been listening to an' how I had reasoned it all out an' he patted me on the head and said I'd make a great detective some day, an' that he had heard the same thing an' had come to the hall to investigate and there was Santa Claus sure as you live an' pa said he took the presents from Santa Claus an' was bringing them to me."

"But that don't prove there is a Santa Claus," said the Watson boy, from his place on the sawbuck.

"It don't? Look here, pa took me out in the yard the next morning an' showed me where Santa had slid around in the snow before he got into the house, an' went through a long string of talk just like he does to your pa when he is ferreting out some big mystery, an' by jinks, pa had it all dead to rights about Santa."

"But how did you deduce?"

"Easy. Pa's been busted ever since and ma didn't get a single thing she wanted, an pa got a smoking jacket that fits him like a baby's shirt would, an' don't look the least like the one Gillette wears, an' a pair of slippers built for steamboat awnings; so there must be a Santa Claus, because nobody else but a stranger would come around at night an' leave such a lot of misfits."

SHERLOCKIAN PARODY ELSEWHERE

Sherlock on Stage

Several Authors

On November 25, 1893, a one hour revue opened at the Royal Court theater, the first appearance of Sherlock Holmes on stage. **Under the Clock** *was a hit and ran for 92 performances, until March 3, 1894.*

Later some suggested to Seymour Hicks, co-author with Charles Brookfield, that they revive it, but he pointed out the revue was too topical, and he was right. It is based on the visit ofThe then notorious French novelist, Emile Zola making a widely advertised first trip to England.

The plot has Sherlock, played by Brookfield, greeting him and introducing him toWatson and the leading actors of the day---all played by Hicks. Hicks gave imitations of Beerbohm Tree, Henry Irving, Wilson Bancroft, and other well-knowns, while a Miss Lottie Venna, who appears as a lady detective, did Mrs. Patrick Campbell in **The Second Mrs. Tanqueray**, *and others.*

Under the Clock *was written by Charles H. E. Brookfield (1857-1913) and Seymour Hicks (1871-1949), with music by Edward Jones. Ironically Brookfield went on to become, in 1911, England's Examiner of Plays for The Lord Chamberlain's Office, the official who censored plays and later movies. Seymour Hicks remained an actor during his long life and was knighted in 1934. He wrote and starred in musical revues and music hall and performed for the troops in both World Wars.*

This is only one of an astonishing number of twenty Sherlockian parody revues and plays that appeared before World War I according to Holmesian Michael Pointer. Roger Johnson suggests that Conan Doyle probably did not give his permission for this production, and may not even been aware of it.

Unlike most stage performances, it is completely in rhyme.

The script was edited by Richard Lancelyn Green in 1981 in a pamphlet of 100 copies, titled **Under the Clock or SheerlockAn Extravaganza in One Act.** *Green provided an introduction. A rare item but part of the Shaw gift at the Minnesota Sherlock Holmes collection.*

****

When the Zola character arrives at the door:

Watson: *How shall we ascertain the stranger's nation?*

Holmes: *By ringing forth some sudden ejaculation.*

(Holmes places a book on the door)

This book shall fall on our incoming guest,
  He'll press the button, and we do the rest.
  Hush!

(The book falls on Nana's head)

Nana: *Sacre'nom d'un pipe! O, c'est immense!*
Watson: *An emissary from la belle France!*

William Gillette (1853-1937) at age 46, already an established actor and author of several plays, was given permission by Conan Doyle to write the play **Sherlock Holmes: A Play, Wherein Is Set Forth the Strange Case of Miss Alice Faulkner**. *Conan Doyle was given co-authorship. It opened October 23, 1899 with Gillette playing the lead. He performed the role over 1300 times during a thirty year period.*

With Conan Doyle's permission, Gillette fashioned a Holmes so out of character that one could argue the play could pass as Sherlockian parody. Here is its ending, and you decide.

****

Holmes:*(coming a step closer to her)*
Your faculty---of observation is---is somewhat remarkable, Miss Faulkner---and your deduction is quite correct! I suppose---indeed I <u>*know*</u>*---that I love you. I love you. But I know as well what I am--- and what you are---I know that no such person as I should ever dream of being a part of your sweet life! It would be a crime for me to think of such a thing! There is every reason why I should say goodbye and farewell! There is every reason---*

(Final Alice theme is heard as she rests her cheek against his manly bosom.)

CURTAIN

Too late!!

But Gillette's **Sherlock Holmes** *came in for parody.To keep interest high, Gillette had gone all out for melodrama and had centered his plot,* *as have many others, on the nefarious Professor Moriarty.*

T. Malcolm Watson and Edward La Serre (Edward F. Spence), wrote a one hour parody play, **Why D'Gillette Him Off?** *whichappeared from October 29, 1901 to February 1, 1902, while the Gillette play was running in London. Gillette bitterly resented their effort. Still their jabs forced him to cut or alter some pieces of business in his play.*

Sheerlock Jones, A Dramatic Criticism in Four Paragraphs and as Many Headlines, *was edited by Richard Lancelyn Green with an introduction,* London: Peter Schoffer, 1982. *The pamphlet gives the full text, contains a forward that Edward F. Spence wrote as part of his autobiography published in 1930, Watson and Spence's reviews of Gillette's play, and a review of their parody.*

The play is full of funny lines and situations and here is only a taste.

This excerpt opens with the usual failure of Sheerluck to make correct deductions. I especially like Sheerluck's confident response to criticism:

Sheerlock: ***Excellent, but you mustn't be offended if I persist in preferring my deductions to your facts.***

One of the big scenes in the Gillette play was the melodrama in:

The Gas Chamber at Stepney!

The Moriarty figure is known as MacGillicuddy. He wants to have Sheerluck Jones murdered elegantly and artisticly in agas bath while his gang members just want to bash him over the head or cut his throat. At that point:

(Enter Gas Collector with a bag of tools)

331

MacGillicuddy: *Who are you?*

Gas Collector: *It's all right, Governor, I've come to cut off the gas.*

Omnes (aghast): *Cut off the gas!*

Gas Collector: *Yes, it's a biggish bill, you're used a rare lot this quarter, and you've had your notices right enough.*

MacGillicuddy: *Can't you call tomorrow, we're very busy today?*

Gas Collector: *No, business is business.*

Pinch: *He'll ruin our skame. (Loud aside) Let's bash him and finish him off.*

MacGillicuddy: *No, no Pinch, honour among thieves. He belongs to the gas company.*

****

*Gillette, himself, wrote a Sherlockian parody for the stage in which he performed the title role. He played it once in America and later briefly as a twenty-minute curtain raiser to a play that soon failed.. Its title was, **The Predicament of Sherlock Holmes, A Fantasy in One Act.***

Holmes is seated on the floor before the fire smoking. The doorbell rings loudly and impatiently. A woman is heard, screaming at the page, Billy, that she must see Holmes on a matter of life and death. Gwendolyn Cobb pushes past Billy and enters 221B and finds Holmes in dressing gown, now having moved to a chair. He motions her to sit. She is soon wandering around the room, all the while talking without letup.

Where's the tobacco? (looking on the mantel, takes jar) Here!

(smells)   Is it true you smoke that terrible shag tobacco?   What is it like? (drops jar)   Oh, I'm sorry! (steps back and breaks violin) Oh! Isn't that too bad! (stamps about on violin trying to extricate herself. Continues talking and apologizing all the while.   Suddenly sits on lounge to get loose from the violin and breaks the bow which lies across the arm of the lounge)Oh, dear me! I'm so sorry! Mercy what was that? (takes out broken violin bow)

I'm afraid you won't want me to come again—if I go on like this! Oh! (springs to her feet)   What have you there cooking over that lamp—I would like a cup of tea! (goes up to retort)

But I suppose—(smells of things)   No—it isn't tea!   What a funny thing you're boiling in it! It looks like a soap bubble with a handle! I'm going to see what—(takes up retort and instantly drops it on the floor) Oh! it was hot! Why didn't you tell me it was hot? (gesturing excitedly) How could I know—I've never been here before—one can't know everything about things, alone and unprotected…   (backing up in her excitement upsets lamp, etc. which goes over with a crash)

It is now a dimly lighted stage with only the fireplace and lights from outside.   After a few minutes more of this, with Gwendolyn talking all the while as she blunders about, Holmes scribbles a message for his page to deliver, and shortly two men in white coats come and take her away. Holmes then turns to the 7 per cent solution. During the whole of the lady's performance, Holmes is impassive. He just smokes and says nary a word.

Except for a few words from Billy, Gwendolyn has all the lines. It is reported that Ethel Barrymore memorized the part twenty minutes before the first performance of the piece. Irene Vanbrugh played it in London, with Master Charles Chaplin as the page. After its brief run, it was never revived.

Conan Doyle on Trial at Bow Street Court

Anonymous

*This is presented as a news article, sandwiching the report of the Holmes/Gillette court appearance between the reports of two other trials. It was published on February 19, 1902 in **Punch** as part of the hullabaloo about the return of Sherlock Holmes in the play by William Gillette. Its original title was "Authors at Bow Street"*

Some Sherlockians may think the pair are being charged for the wrong misdeed. Their crime, they suggest, is that Conan Doyle and Gillette allowed a scheming young so-called innocent, at least half his age, to engineer a half dazed and seemingly half-senile detective into a reluctant avowal of love.

****

ARTHUR CONAN DOYLE, 42, surgeon, and WILLIAM GILLETTE, 44, actor, two able-bodied men, were flung into the dock charged with the exhumation of SHERLOCK HOLMES for purposes of gain.

MR. JAMES WELCH, K.C., prosecuting for the Crown, said that not since the days of BURKE and HARE had so flagrant a case been heard of. Long after the death of MR. HOLMES, who had been in his day a detective of some skill, though not attached to Scotland Yard, (*sensation!*) the prisoners had exhumed him, and were charging, at the Lyceum Theatre, considerable sums to persons who wished to view the body. SIR GEORGE NEWNES, proprietor of the *Strand Magazine,* gave evidence of SHERLOCK HOLMES'S death.

DR. MORIARTY, called for the defense, stated, however, that SHERLOCK HOLMES was never really dead, but merely in a comatose condition. It was quite possible, he said, to fall off an Alp and still live, in fact he had done it himself.*(tremendous sensation!)*

Further evidence having been given by MR. FROGMANand The Hound of the Baskervilles, to the effect that SHERLOCK HOLMES was still vigorous, the Magistrates stopped the case,saying that if SHERLOCK HOLMES was not dead, he ought to be. They accordingly ordered DR. DOYLE to give him definitive and decent burial at the earliest possible opportunity.

MR. JAMESWELCH, having called the attention of the Bench to the fact that this exhumation had been ferociously commented on by the *Blutwurst* of Berlin, the *Libre Menteur* of Paris, and other Anglophobe organs, the Magistrates directed that DR. DOYLE should print and circulate his own cost translations of the proceedings in the Lithuanian, Suabian, Basque, Yiddish and Czech languages, with a special edition for the Ballybunion district of North Kerry.

Potluck Bones Dissects Musical Comedy

C. O'M

Parody takes its Sherlockian characters to interesting places. This one has Potluck Bones visiting a Victorian musical revue, where comedians do outlandish slapstick and when things begin to drag it's"Bring on the girls!" and out dance in perfect cadence the ladies of the chorus.(at least so said P. G. Wodehouse who wrote librettos for many a musical revue.)

*This piece appeared in **The Playgoer** (London) April, 1904 as"Why Musical Comedy Has No Plot."*

****

The epidemic of crime among the crowned heads of Europe having abated somewhat, My friend, Mr. Potluck Bones, the greatest detective in the world, was able to give a little of his precious time to the affairs of ordinary mortals. For some years Bones had refused to undertake a case for anyone under the rank of Grand Duke, but a rise in the price of tobacco had compelled him to alter his rules of business.

I am afraid that Potluck was getting cynical. Humanity, he declared, too good and too dull. Intellect counted for nothing, for Scotland Yard had developed an irritating habit of arresting the criminal while Potluck was making deductions, and clients only paid according to results.

My friend's great talents were in danger of being lost in the abyss of the commonplace when the celebrated case of **The Hi-ti Girl** came to the rescue. It was Potluck's first theatrical adventure, and therefore I have taken the liberty of transcribing the notes I made at the time.

We were seated at breakfast one spring morning, when our landlady, Mrs. Budson, entered and announced that a gentleman in a fur coat desired to see Potluck. As it was only four o'clock---Bones insisted on breakfasting at this hour---the visit was unexpected.

"Who can want to see you at this hour?" I couldn't help saying. "And a man in a fur coat too!"

"Oh, he's either a millionaire or a theatrical manager, one never knows. You remember my monograph on 'Coats and Crime' ? Show the visitor up, Mrs. Budson," continued Bones, as he put on a yellow dressing gown in order to appear like his photographs. "Where's my fiddle?"

Potluck had scarcely assumed his well known pose, when the door was violently thrown open, and a stout, fat-faced individual rushed in and sank in a half-fainting condition upon the floor, knocking the table over with him.

"Pick him up, said Potluck," lighting a pipe. "It's obvious the poor man is excited---it's too early for him to be drunk."

By this time our visitor had recovered, and Bones motioned him to a seat. The fellow seemed reluctant to obey, however, and I had a suspicion that he had overheard Potluck's last remark. The same idea must have struck my friend, for he casually picked up the poker and continued to toy with it until the stranger deposited himself upon the electric chair.

"Now, Mr. ---- I didn't quite catch your name," began Bones,

337

"I am Mr. Plantagenette Bailey of the Legall Theatre," he exclaimed, brandishing what looked like a menu card, but turned out to be his visiting card.

"Well, Mr. Bailey, what can I do for you?" said Bones blandly. "I presume you did not call to consult me about the weather, eh?"

"No, sir, my business concerns my profession. For twenty years I have kept the sacred lamp of musical comedy burning. It is in danger of going out, and I want you to prevent that. Will you assist me?"

"I should like more particulars, said Potluck, said Potluck, dropping in his chair and apparently going to sleep."

"Last Saturday week," continued Mr. Bailey, "I produced a new musical comedy, *The Hi-ti Girl*. It went strong, sir, very strong, but the critics say there is no plot to the piece. I maintain that there is, and I want you to prove my case."

I trembled for my friend's reputation, for I instinctively guessed that this would be too much for him. But I did not know that Bones was more than mortal. No case could be too difficult. It was true enough that fools rush in where angels fear to tread, but Bones got there before either the fools or the angels.

"You want me to discover the plot of a musical comedy?" exclaimed the great detective, stretching himself out and yawning. "I wasn't aware that musical comedies had plots."

"Those produced by me are remarkable for their plots, sir," replied the manager with dignity. "I pride myself on their complexity. It has been my endeavour to provide a plot that the audience cannot discover until the third act. What they think of the fourth doesn't matter."

338

"Than why have a fourth act?" I observed.

"My dear sir," he replied with a pitying smile, "how ignorant you are of theatrical matters. We must amuse the members of the audience while they are putting their coats on."

"With regard to this musical comedy of yours," interrupted Bones, "What is the principal feature of it---a dance or a song?"

"Well, there are plenty of both," Mr. Bailey answered. "But the greatest draw is Scooping the Scoop."

"What's that?" said Bones.

"The leading comedian, dressed in a rubber costume, jumps from the roof to the stage. His attire causes him to bound and rebound. I tell you, exclaimed the manager enthusiastically, "it's the surest draw in town. You see it is difficult to stop the man, and on three occasions we've had to puncture him with a pitch fork before he'd stop. The process lost us two fine comedians."

"Resigned, I suppose?" said Bones.

"No---buried. They were punctured at the wrong moment. It was the fault of our lancer. He happened to be a little unsteady with the pitchfork. A regrettable business, certainly, but we all run risks nowadays."

"The public loves a legitimate suicide," observed Potluck. The leading lady murders the music, while the principal comedian murders himself. Surely such a combination of horrors should fill the largest theatre in London."

(Bones spoke in Japanese---the fashionable tongue at the time, so

339

our visitor did not understand the drift of his remarks. There is nothing like tact.)

"Now, Mr. Bailey," said Bones genially and speaking in English, "Let us have particulars of the *motif* of this comedy of yours. A mere sketch will suffice."

"In the first place you must understand how the play is made. When we have decided upon the posters, we hold a meeting of the authors and composers. There are four of each. The authors try to remember all of the really funny jokes they have heard during their lives---the older the men, the better---while the composers attempt to combine the melody of the classical song with the catchiness of the comic song."

"I see," said Bones, "a sort of cross between '*The Lost Chord*' and '*When Father Laid the Carpet on the Stairs.*'"

"That's it," replied the manager. "I think you will be able to help me. Well, when we have the jokes and music ready, a librettist is called in to combine them. It is his duty to make a coherent story out of the material placed at his disposal. Our man is the well-known novelist, Nonden Scones, he took a double first at Oxford. I discovered him starving in Fleet Street, took an interest in the fellow, and---er---in short---made him. He is the best man in the game---now, thanks to my tuition."

"And yet some people decry the advantages of a university education," said Bones, turning to me. "Pray proceed, sir."

"The plot of The *Hi-ti Girl* is this. Four men are in love with the same woman. She discovers this and in order to be left free to marry the man she really loves, she persuades four friends of hers to impersonate her. They agree. In the second act the four imposters are married to the four men, each believing he is marrying Kitty Hi-fly, the Queen of the

Ballet. The fun is furious when the four men meet at their club and tell each other that they have married Kitty Hi-fly. There are all sorts of complications and surprises."

"I should think so," observed Bones dryly. "Is that all?"

"Yes, but it's enough."

"No doubt," said Bones rising. "Good morning, Mr. Bailey. I'll visit your theatre to-night and will let you know the result of my observations to-morrow morning."

"Good morning, sir," exclaimed the manager; "I'll keep a box for you and your friend. Good morning, sir."

"Well, what do you think of it?" said Potluck, as he carefully examined the footprints made by our visitor's dirty boots."

"Simple enough," I answered unthinkingly.

"Rubbish," cried Bones. "What appears simple to the average person is really difficult to the expert, whose erudition complicates matters."

"I can't see the good of examining his footprints," I said. "We are not tracking a murderer."

"Perhaps not, but I am wondering what Mrs. Budson will say when she sees this mess. We owe her for three weeks, you know," he added sorrowfully.

"Never mind, Potluck," I answered. "We must not ride in hansoms so often. You engaged half the cabmen in London last Saturday, you remember to follow that man you thought was a murderer, but who turned out to be a Covent Garden salesman taking a holiday."To my surprise I found Potluck had left the room. He is very sensitive, I may say here.

That night Bones and myself occupied a box at the Legall theatre. The great detective spent most of his time pointing out to me the various persons in the audience who had been in contact with him professionally. He seemed to know everybody who was anybody, as well as several nobodies. Not once did I notice his eyes turned in the direction of the stage, and I was about to call his attention to the play when he seized me by the throat and whispered excitedly,

"I've seen enough. Let's go home."

On our way back to Baker Street I endeavoured to draw Bones, but he was in one of his silent moods, and when like that he never speaks. Long association with Potluck had given me some of his wonderful talents. But why should I talk like this? I am a modest man.

"I tell you, Cotson," cried Potluck next morning, while we were awaiting the expected visitor, "You must give up writing books. Why not put me in a musical comedy? It's the best paying business on earth; and now that there is a slump in assassinations my services will not be much in demand."

"But who'll write the music?"

"I will, of course. Ay, and the words too. We'll get Leafette to do the scene painting and so keep the money in the family. What would you think of say, *The Anarchist Girl or Potluck to the Rescue,* eh?"

My reply was rendered inaudible by the noisy entry of Mr. Plantagenette Bailey, who seemed to be as excited as ever.

342

"Well, what news? he burst out with."

"Take a chair, Mr. Bailey," said Bones blandly, handing our visitor the only whole one in the room.

"Yes, yes; but I want to know if you were successful last night."

"Steady now, my friend," replied Potluck. "Have you got your cheque book with you?"

"Here it is," said the manager.

"That's the best thing I've seen for six months," cried Potluck, smiling. "You must know that I make an additional charge of two shillings a word. My American publishers insist on that."

"Very well," said Mr. Bailey, "but be as short as possible."

"Cotson, take down each word I say. Now, Mr. Bailey, the plot of *The Hi-ti Girl* has been gagged by your comedians. They've killed it by gagging, and if you want your plot to be recognizable you must get rid of your comedians."

"But the public insist upon gags. They are necessary if the piece is to be kept up to date, protested the manager."

"In that case, the public don't want a plot in musical comedy. If the critics say to the contrary, ignore them. The box office receipts are all you need concern yourself with. They are satisfactory, I understand."

"We're turning money away," answered the manager. "But I'm sorry we couldn't have a plot as well as the 'gags.' However, I suppose I can't have everything. Here's your cheque, Mr. Bones. If you should ever contemplate going on the stage I'll be glad to make you an offer.

Good morning, sir."

"The modern stage is essentially democratic," said Potluck, when our visitor had gone; "and democracy does not want high art. It prefers high kicking. The Ibsen school of dramatists write of Society with a capital S, forgetting that what the playgoer really wants is a musical comedy with a capital chorus. Mr. Tree's academy for teaching the young how to shout may help towards reviving interest in the drama, but it can only be a temporary revival, as the relatives of the students will soon get tired of going to see them act. Meanwhile, musical comedy flourishes, and a brisk trade is being done in barrel organs. Who can complain?"

Sherlock in Poem and Song

Various Composers

Very few poets wrote Sherlockian parody.

In June 1905 **The Metropolitan Magazine** *published a poemcalled"Sherlock Holmes." toasting the great detective in twenty stanzas. It was by Harry Graham (1874-1936) who also included it in his book,* **More Representative Men,** *published the same year.*

His most famous poetry was **Ruthless Rhymes,***(1899). (Billy, in one of his nice new sashes, Fell in the fire and was burnt to ashes; Now although the room grows chilly, I haven't the heart to poke poor Billy.)*

After extolling Sherlock for all the wonderful things he did, it ends, in the tradition of **Ruthless Rhymes***, with a swipe at poor old Watson:*

> **But though in grief our heads are bowed,**
> **And tears upon our cheeks are shining,**
> **We recognize that ev'ry cloud**
> **Conceals somewhere a silver lining;**
> **And hear with deep congratulation**
> **Of Watson's timely termination.**

****

Walt Mason (1862-1939), now largely forgotten, was once a popular newspaper poet. It was estimated that Mason's prose poems were read by 10 million every day, syndicated in over 200 newspapers. Both of his Sherlockian poems were reprinted in his **Uncle Walt.** *(1910) Sherlockian John Ruyle unearthed and re-published both.*

Mason's poems have a kind of whimsical attraction because they were set up as prose, with commas and semi-colons to separate the lines. The second and fourth lines rhymed.

Mason's day job was at the **Emporia** *(Kansas)* **Gazette,** *and its famous editor, William Allen White wrote the introduction to the collected poems. He called Mason "the Poet Laureate of the American Democracy." About the book of poems, he wrote, "we do not claim its medicinal properties will cure everything. But it is good for sore eyes; it cures the blues; it sweetens the temper, cleanses the head, and aids the digestion. In cases of heart trouble it has been known to unite torn ligaments and encourage larger families."*

His first Sherlockian poem, titled, "Sherlock Holmes," celebrates the return of Sherlock Holmes and begins:

The Great Detective had returned; he'd been some years away, and I supposed that he was dead, and sleeping 'neath the clay. Ah, ne'er shall I forget the joy it gave me thus to greet the king of all detectives in my rooms in Baker Street!

The second, "Sleuths of Fiction," has a different slant.

I'm weary now of Sherlock Holmes, and all the imitative crew; I'm tired of triumphs built upon a collar button, as a clew. The sleuth is always tall and thin, with nervous hands and hawk-like face; he scours the slums or moves around in marble halls, with equal grace; he always takes some kind of dope or plays the flute or violin, and when he's billed for active work he glues false whiskers on his chin. He always has a Watson near, a tiresome chump, who sits and broods, the

346

while the selling-plater sleuth reels off a string of platitudes. Detective yarns are all so stale! The plot is evermore the same; we always have the murdered man, with knives or bullets in his frame; the pantry window is unlocked; the safe's been opened with a file; suspicion shifts until it rests on every man within a mile; the local peelers blunder round, and ball things up in frightful shape, and then the Great Detective comes, with lens and rule and meas'ring tape; he crawls around upon the floor, examines all the water mains, and tastes the ashes in the stove, and sticks his nose into the drains, and then he says the problem's solved; forthwith he spends two weeks or more, in showing Watson and the world how easy 'tis to be a bore!

****

Music Hall performers, male or female, made the most of their songs by hamming it up with expressive and suggestive gestures as they performed before a raucous audience.

The first song of Sherlock Holmes, popular in the music halls, was from the revue **Under the Clock***, by Charles Brookfield and Seymour Hicks, Sherlock's first stage appearance. It featured Sherlock and Watson singing in duet,* **Sherlock, You Wonderful Man!**

Holmes:*I can unravel crime with the greatest of ease,*
Watson:*Sherlock, you wonderful man*
Holmes*: I can make two and two total up as I please,*
Watson:*Oh, he's a wonderful man!*
But if there's no evidence, what do you do?
    Not even a pip, or a thumb, or a shoe?
Holmes*: Is easy as A B C, make my own clue:*
Watson*: Well, THERE'S a wonderful man!*

The death of Holmes at Reichenbach Falls inspired a number of Music Hall songs about Sherlock Holmes, many skeptical of his passing.

One of the earliest, by Richard Morton, was performed in 1894 and was called **The Ghost of Sherlock Holmes,** *with this refrain.*

Sherlock! Sherlock! you can hear the people cry!
That's the ghost of Sherlock Holmes! as I gocreeping by!
Sinners shake and tremble where'er this bogie roams,
And people shout, He's found us out---"

IT'S THE GHOST OF SHERLOCK HOLMES!

Roger Johnson, an English Holmesian, has made an study of Victorian Music Hall. He singles out a Claude Ralston song, **Sherlock Holmes,** *as among the most popular. It appeared in the 1897 edition of* **The Scottish Students' Songbook** *and remained in later editions at least through 1951. A note thanks Ralston for allowing the song's inclusion, presumably without having to pay them copyright fees. Here is the last stanza.*

You say it is a pity that this splendid man should die,
I think the Swiss tale is a plant, I'll give my reason why.
There's a lady in the question, so he's gone and done a'guy
But he'll turn up again, will Sherlock Holmes.

Sherlocko the Monk and Hawkshaw

Gus Mager

It is astonishing that Sherlock Holmes appeared in a parody comic strip as early as November 18, 1893, a little over two years after the first short story. But the best of the Sherlockian comics was drawn by Gus Mager, as **Sherlocko the Monk**, *from 1910-12, with a gap 1923-1931, continued on through the 1950s, as* **Hawkshaw the Detective.***

Gus Mager (1878-1955), in his teens, sold cartoons to humor magazines, and at twenty-two was hired by the Hearst newspapers as a staff artist. He drew various comics throughout his career. Mager was also a serious painter in oils. In 1913, some of his paintings were displayed in the famous Armory show in New York. In 1923 the art critic William Murrell published a book of reproductions of forty-five Mager paintings and sketches, in his **Our Younger Artists** *series. Some Mager works are part of the collections of several museums including the Whitney Museum of Modern Art.*

Mager's Sherlocko was an elongated creature who lounges about in his dressing gown and occasionally is scratching away on a small fiddle. Watso is unusually short. Outside Sherlocko ambles along in the obligatory, but non-Conan Doyle, deerstalker and a long fur collar coat. He crawls around on hands and knees at the scene of the supposed crime looking for clues. He follows footprints, and analyzes other bits of evidence that he and Watso find lying about. And everywhere he smokes a briar pipe. Here is a sample:

[Watso listening to phone message]

CLIENT:*Quick Mr. Sherlocko---A suspicious looking man hasjust climbed over my garden fence.*

[Holmes and Watson at fence]

WATSO: *Here is where he crossed over into the next yard.*
SHERLOCKO: *Yes, and here are his footprints!*
DOG: *Gr-r-r! Bow-Wow!*

HOLMES[to client]*Your dog appears to be a vicious brute---Didn't he bark when the man passed so close?*
CLIENT: *No, He didn't and he's usually a good watch dog!*
SHERLOKO: *The dog must have known this visitor!*
WATSO:*These steps are easily followed.*

WATSO [tackling the intruder]*Surrender, you scoundrel!*
SHERLOCKO: *Hold, Watso! He will explain.Ah, Mr. Henpecko,--- Been outtoolate and trying toget intoyourhouse without disturbing your wife?*

HENPECKO:*Not so loud---Not so loud!--- You'll wake her up.*
WATSO: *I wouldn't be in your shoes.*

The Great Discoverer

Anonymous

Over the years, Arthur Conan Doyle took a lot of guff and chaffing because of Sherlock Holmes. But he was never known to complain about what so many others wrote in these Sherlockian parodies or pastiches.Here's one from **Punch,** *one of the most popular and widely circulated journals of the day, published anonymously August 22, 1906*

****

But for this distinguished detective, Sir A. Conan Doyle might never havebeen discovered. As it was, he was pottering about in comparative literary obscurity when the great detective, like a sleuth-hound, tracked him down, and revealed him to the admiration of the world. This was probably the greatest feat on the part of the renowned Sherlock Holmes.

A Closing Note

Before we put away this collection, we perhaps should pause and again tip our cloth hats with the ear flaps to that fine literary gentleman who was The Founder of Our Feast.

Sir Arthur Conan Doyle (1859-1930)

At 6:30 on the morning of July 7, 1930, Sir Arthur Conan Doyle died at his home---sitting up in a chair, as he asked to be, staring out at the Sussex countryside.

Also from MX Publishing

MX Publishing is the world's largest specialist Sherlock Holmes publisher, with over a hundred titles and fifty authors creating the latest in Sherlock Holmes fiction and non-fiction.

From traditional short stories and novels to travel guides and quiz books, MX Publishing cater for all Holmes fans.

The collection includes leading titles such as _Benedict Cumberbatch In Transition_ and _The Norwood Author_ which won the 2011 Howlett Award (Sherlock Holmes Book of the Year).

MX Publishing also has one of the largest communities of Holmes fans on Facebook with regular contributions from dozens of authors.

www.mxpublishing.com

Our bestselling books are our short story collections – of which we have several;

'Lost Stories of Sherlock Holmes', 'The Outstanding Mysteries of Sherlock Holmes', The Papers of Sherlock Holmes Volume 1 and 2, 'Untold Adventures of Sherlock Holmes' (and the sequel 'Studies in Legacy) and 'Sherlock Holmes in Pursuit', 'The Cotswold Werewolf and Other Stories of Sherlock Holmes' – and many more......

353

Links

MX Publishing are proud to support the Save Undershaw campaign – the campaign to save and restore Sir Arthur Conan Doyle's former home. Undershaw is where he brought Sherlock Holmes back to life, and should be preserved for future generations of Holmes fans.

Please show your support by 'liking' the Save Undershaw Facebook page:

www.facebook.com/saveundershaw

You can read more about Sir Arthur Conan Doyle and Undershaw in Alistair Duncan's book (share of royalties to the Undershaw Preservation Trust) – *An Entirely New Country* and in the amazing compilation *Sherlock's Home – The Empty House* (all royalties to the Trust).